You'll
Never
Know,
Dear

You'll Never Know, Dear

A NOVEL OF SUSPENSE

HALLIE EPHRON

wm

WILLIAM MORROW

An Imprint of HarperCollins*Publishers*

HarperCollins books may be purchased for educational, business, or sales promotional usc. For information, please e-mail the Special Markets Department at SPsales@harpercollins.com.

FIRST EDITION

Library of Congress Cataloging-in-Publication Data has been applied for.

ISBN 978-0-06-247361-5

17 18 19 20 21   LSC   10 9 8 7 6 5 4 3 2

For Franny and Jody

Sometimes a dream is your subconscious trying to sort out what happened when you were awake. Sometimes it's the universe trying to tell you something. And sometimes it's just a dream.

You'll
Never
Know,
Dear

Elisabeth Strenger peeled three boiled eggs under running water, dropped them into a chipped Blue Willow china bowl, and began to mash them with a fork. She took a quick puff on her cigarette, blew smoke out through the back window, and tapped ashes into the drain.

"Don't forget a titch of lemon." The fluty voice that sailed in from the front porch through the open living room windows belonged to Lis's mother, Sorrel Woodham. Everyone, including Lis, called her Miss Sorrel.

"*. . . A titch of lemon*," Lis sang back under her breath, directing her imitation at the dolls perched on a continuous row of shelves just below the kitchen's beamed ceiling. Miss Sorrel had begun placing dolls there back in the day when she had no trouble hopping up on a chair to do so. Now Lis did the hopping for both of them, along with any light and heavy lifting that needed doing around the house.

Miss Sorrel's dolls stared ahead, impassive, miffed perhaps that Lis never lavished them with more than perfunctory attention. At one end of the shelf were Victorian dolls with bisque heads, creamy complexions, glass eyes, Cupid's bow mouths, and stiff wigs. At the other end sat bald, celluloid baby dolls, placid and patient, their painted eyes forever open. Once a week Miss Sorrel supervised as Lis climbed from the chair to the table so she could give each doll a thorough dusting.

The kitchen dolls were not Miss Sorrel's best. Her Madame Alexander Alice in Wonderland with a hand-painted cloth face and yellow-yarn wig was tucked in beside a pair of rare Cherokee rag dolls in a pair of glass china cabinets in the dining room where the rest of her rarest and most valuable dolls resided. Also in a dining room cabinet was a shelf of porcelain dolls Lis's mother had made herself—Miss Sorrel dolls, as they were known to collectors. Their bodies were soft, and the legs and arms unglazed bisque porcelain. But their heads were why the Miss Sorrel dolls were considered art, albeit folk art: each face was a carefully sculpted and painted portrait of a real child. The Miss Sorrel dolls were as valued for their eerily realistic features as for their scarcity. The first ones had been portraits of Lis and her sister, Janey.

Though Miss Sorrel had long ago given up making Miss Sorrel dolls, she kept herself busy with "the projects": temporary residents, aged and injured dolls that had been brought to her to be repaired and refreshed. Those were carefully wrapped in acid-free paper and tucked into plastic bins, each doll catalogued and shelved in the workroom at the back of the house. There, Miss Sorrel worked with her longtime friend and next-door neighbor Evelyn Dumont to gently restore them. The women went through mounds of Q-tips cleaning them. Restringing legs and arms, reweaving and sometimes replacing wigs, resetting glass eyes, de-stinking plastic bodies, and doing whatever else was needed while preserving each doll's authenticity.

Binty, Miss Sorrel's aging Irish setter, wheezed hot doggie

breath on Lis's ankles. Miss Sorrel used to brush Binty and save the dog's once rich, lustrous strawberry-blond hair to make wigs for dolls.

Lis tossed Binty a crust of bread and turned her attention to chopping celery and green onion. Added them to the eggs along with mayonnaise, a shake of mustard, and yes, though she didn't need to be reminded, a squeeze of lemon. She mixed it all together, added salt and pepper, then scooped a dollop onto a finger and tasted before assembling sandwiches, cutting them in quarters, and stacking them on a plate along with a half-dozen strawberries she'd picked up at the Piggly Wiggly. Local berries wouldn't be in for another eight weeks or so.

Lis took off her reading glasses, anchored them to the top of her head, and carried the plate out onto the porch. It was an unusually warm January day, warm enough to sit out. A spectacular pair of camellia bushes bloomed in the front yard, one loaded with hot pink blossoms and the other white. The ground beneath the bushes was thick with periwinkle. In a matter of weeks, the air would be heavy with the sweet scent of wisteria that would hang from the sinewy vines that draped gracefully across the front of the porch, and by May mosquitoes could be so thick that sitting on the porch would be a nonstarter.

A police cruiser emblazoned with BONSECOURS POLICE in peacock-blue lettering across the side slowed as it approached the house. Lis stepped across to block her mother's view. The cruiser window rolled down and Deputy Police Chief Frank Ames waved.

It wasn't so much that Miss Sorrel didn't approve of Lis's seeing Frank, because she probably did, despite the fact that Frank was turning sixty and Lis was forty-six. He'd been a family friend since Lis was little, ever since he was a rookie on the police force.

It was more that Lis cherished what little privacy she had in what was still a small town, living as she was under the same roof as her mother with her mother's best friend, gossipy busybody Evelyn Dumont, right next door.

The cruiser continued past as Miss Sorrel rocked gently in the glider and sipped sweet tea from a glass dripping condensation. With her powdered face, spots of rouge on each cheek, and lipstick carefully painted on, Miss Sorrel was starting to look like one of the porcelain dolls she so prized. That, despite the un-doll-like creases that ran from the corners of her lips down either side of her chin, the crinkles that radiated from the corners of her eyes, and the skin that had started to lose its grip on her fine-boned skull.

Lis set the plate of sandwiches down on a metal TV table.

"Lovely," Miss Sorrel said. "Thank you, darling."

Darling. Never Elisabeth or Lis or Lissie. Safer not to risk Janey's name popping out.

Lis had been seven years old when her four-year-old sister Janey disappeared. One minute the two girls had been playing outside. *Now stay in the yard.* Lis supposedly watching Janey and resenting it. *Be a good girl and do what Lissie tells you.* Wondering why her brothers Davey or Sam or Michael never got saddled with babysitting. *How come you always get to be the mommy?* Bedding their doll babies in shoe boxes under their picnic-table house.

A black-and-white puppy with floppy ears had scampered through the yard. Lis took off after it into the patch of woods behind the house until she lost sight of the white tip of its tail down by the creek. There she waded into the shallow water, turning over rocks, looking for frogs and yellow-spotted salamanders. She remembered thinking: *Doll babies need pets.*

She'd tried to catch fish in her shoe but the water leaked out.

Butterflies flitted past her grasp. When she returned with her arms loaded with forget-me-nots and Spanish moss to line their shoe box doll cribs, Lis assumed Janey had gone into the house, taking her doll with her. That meant precious minutes ticked by without anyone raising the alarm.

Hope of finding out what happened to Janey had long ago faded, and yet still the shadow of her absence hung over the house, though the only physical reminders were photographs and Janey's unaltered bedroom, with a single electric Christmas candle perpetually switched on in its front window.

Miss Sorrel and Lis's father, Wayne Woodham, whom everyone called Woody, had taken great pains to assure Lis that Janey's disappearance was not her fault. But even then, Lis knew better. And if she had the power to lose Janey, then surely she had the power to bring her back. She used to stand in the upstairs hall with her hand on the doorknob to Janey's room, imagining that it was a displaced magic bedknob from *Bedknobs and Broomsticks*. They had a videotape of the movie, and Lis would play and replay the bit where Angela Lansbury's character casts a spell. Lis tried to repeat the syllables that sounded like gibberish: *hell born hen bane, a-go-night.*

She'd hold on to the doorknob. Imagine it getting warm and glowing pink, her sister's favorite color. Then she'd push open the door and there Janey would be, safe and sound, asleep in her bed.

Even now, the incantation flew through her head whenever she was about to go into the room that would always and forever be *Janey's room.*

Lis learned a hard lesson: look away for a moment and the thing you cherish most in this world could be . . . *would* be . . . snatched from you. The real beneficiary of this hard-won wisdom was Lis's daughter, Vanessa, whom Lis had smothered with vigilance. It had taken a supreme act of will for Lis to look away as Vanessa biked up and down the block, or walked three doors down to play with her best friend, or waited for the school bus without Lis glued to her side.

Now it took that same willpower for Lis not to think about what could happen to Vanessa living in that apartment in that not-great neighborhood outside of Providence, finishing a post-doc and working god-awful hours at that sleep lab. It helped a bit when Lis reminded herself that her daughter was poised on the cusp of the kind of career that Lis hadn't known she could dream about.

Lis tamped down the anxiety that flared whenever she thought about Vanessa. She'd texted her daughter earlier that morning, two hours ago. Two hours, that was about as long as it had taken for them to realize Janey was missing. It was all Lis could do to keep from texting Vanessa again. Poking at her until she got a response. Any response that signaled *safe, for now.*

Miss Sorrel tucked a wisp of her white hair into the long braid she'd coiled in a figure eight, anchored at the nape of her neck, then reached across for a sandwich, knocking over the stack. "Oh dear," she said, her hand fluttering over the plate. She'd been like that, jumpy, since yesterday. But that was to be expected. After all, yesterday was "Remembering Day," the anniversary of the day Janey disappeared almost forty years ago.

"Did you have a good night's sleep?" Lis asked, handing Miss Sorrel a sandwich. "Anything bothering you, dear?"

Miss Sorrel ignored the question and nibbled off a corner of the sandwich. Then another nibble and another, daintily licking her fingers when there was none left and reaching for another sandwich. Her appetite hadn't flagged in the slightest even as she shrank. Then she sighed heavily and settled back into the glider, briefly admiring the cameo ring she always wore. The ring was carved with the delicate figure of a slender woman wearing a semitransparent gown. It had been Lis's grandmother's, and it was one of the few things of her mother's that she hoped would one day be hers.

For a few moments Lis and Miss Sorrel sat in companionable silence, broken only by the clip-clop of horses' hooves. A horse-drawn wagon with tourists tucked in under carriage blankets moved slowly past. Miss Sorrel's nostrils flared. That overripe barnyard smell and the curious gazes of tourists and their cameras were the price one paid for living in Bonsecours's gracious historic district.

"Momma, should we go inside?" Lis said.

"Too late." Miss Sorrel fanned the air with an open hand. "My sensibilities have already been"—she paused for a moment as a white compact car pulled up in front of the house, its front fender dented and trunk lid held down with a bungee cord—"assaulted."

The car sat there for a few moments, its engine wheezing before it shut down. The woman who climbed out wore tight jeans, a V-neck flowered T-shirt, and sunglasses. The getup said eighteen but the face said closing on thirty. With a practiced gesture she tossed back long dark hair that hung past her shoulders, leaned on the open car door, and gazed across at the house. At Lis and Miss Sorrel watching her from the porch.

"She's early, dammit," Miss Sorrel said under her breath as she levered herself from the chair and waved. "Evelyn's not even here." Evelyn Dumont lived in the grand pink house next door on a big corner lot. The house had wide verandas in front on both floors, and narrow third-floor windows that seemed to peer

out from below the eaves. Evelyn and Miss Sorrel had been making and repairing dolls together since before Lis could remember. Girlhood friends who were both now widowed, as they'd
aged they'd grown more or less attached at the hip.

"Miss Richards? Hello there," Miss Sorrel warbled as she gestured to Lis to get rid of the sandwich platter. She adjusted the
scarf around her neck. "Come right on up."

The woman, who looked far too unfinished to be *Miss* anything, reached into the backseat. She pulled a paper shopping
bag and a Dunkin' Donuts coffee cup from her car, straightened,
and bumped the door closed with her hip. She tugged down her
top, which had ridden up, exposing a roll of flesh bunched over
low-riding jeans.

Miss Sorrel's typical clients were older women who arrived in
church clothes, their injured or simply aging dolls swaddled in
blankets or packed in boxes with tissue paper. Not this one. She
was swinging that bag, oblivious to the coffee that was dribbling
onto it from the cup as she climbed the steps to the porch. As
Miss Richards approached the steps, Lis could tell the moment
when her mother could actually see her because that's when her
expression soured from welcoming to *eau de manure*. And then,
because of her excellent manners, her mother turned up the corners of her mouth in a bright smile that didn't reach her eyes.

Lis knew what was coming next. She went inside and sponged
down the kitchen table. Then she lay down a yellow swaddle
blanket and a fresh pair of purple latex gloves for her mother to
wear when she examined the doll.

Miss Sorrel and Miss Richards came in, followed by Binty.
The low-ceilinged kitchen felt claustrophobic as it filled with Miss
Richards's cloyingly sweet perfume smell—gardenia squared.
The woman set the bag on the table and shoved away Binty, who

was trying to bury her nose in the woman's crotch. Was that a tattoo on the small of her back? Lis only got a quick peek, but it looked like Harley-Davidson eagle wings.

"Darling, would you get my logbook?" Miss Sorrel said.

Lis walked through the passageway to her mother's workroom. She flipped the light switch and banks of fluorescent lights that hung low over a pair of worktables tinked to life. On one table lay an aging hard plastic doll and a can of fixative, its chemical smell lingering in the air. From a drawer Lis pulled out the aging theme book in which doll repairs were carefully logged. She also picked up the digital camera. Every doll that came into the house was photographed and catalogued.

When Lis returned to the kitchen, Miss Sorrel had opened the woman's bag and was peering inside. Her face was so white that the spots of rouge on her cheeks stood out like a clown's face paint.

Lis set the theme book on the table and turned on the camera. Miss Sorrel looked across at her, startled. She cleared her throat. "Thank you, darling. I'll take care of it." She put out her hand and Lis gave her the camera. "Why don't you take Binty for a walk? She's been cooped up all morning."

In fact, Binty had been out most of the morning, and when Evelyn wasn't there to assist Miss Sorrel with a client, Lis usually stayed and took notes. But Lis took her cue. She grabbed a plastic bag in case Binty had more business to do and hooked her hand in Binty's collar.

"We'll be right outside. Give a holler if you need me," Lis said.

At the door she looked back. Miss Richards had taken off her sunglasses. The harsh light cast dark shadows around her eyes, and she seemed tense as Miss Sorrel pulled a baby doll from the bag and set it on the table. The curls in its wig were sparse.

Its porcelain face was heavily soiled, and one of its arms was missing. Its once-white hand-embroidered dress was matted and torn, and its glass eyes were cloudy.

Miss Sorrel normally turned down repair work on a doll that far gone. So why was she pulling on her gloves and turning the doll over and examining it so carefully, reverentially even?

Lis held open the door for Binty and followed the dog out onto the porch. The screen door slapped shut behind them. Binty hesitated at the top of the steps and whined. Lis picked the dog up and carried her down. Binty arched her neck and slurped Lis's nose, then stutter-stepped to the curb and lowered her behind, her back legs trembling.

Lis approached Miss Richards's car. She ran a finger along the fender, leaving a white streak in a coating that was the color of the toadstools that grew in the yard where an oak had been blown over by Hurricane Charley. Lucky for Miss Richards, car inspections were considered government overreach in South Carolina, because that car would never have passed muster in New Jersey. The license plate said it all: POJNK. Was it a vanity plate or just serendipitous irony?

Lis circled the car. There was a sticker on the back window. She lowered her glasses so she could see what it said. University of South Carolina. A student? Or maybe an employee.

Lis sat on one of the wide porch steps. She gazed back at the house she'd moved back into when she'd split with Brad. Vanessa had just turned four. Since then Lis had grown more tolerant of

her mother's quirks and limitations, her perfect hair and cali-
brated judgments.

Miss Sorrel had never been a particularly warm or physically
affectionate mother to Lis, but she'd made up for that with the
care and attention she'd lavished on Vanessa. Vanessa had been
desperately upset, bewildered at having to leave their nice split-
level suburban home in New Jersey and her friends. Lis hadn't
been able to see beyond her own anger at Brad. Child support
dried up barely a year after the divorce, so Lis had had no choice
but to come home. Tail between her legs, she'd crawled back to
Bonsecours. She'd told herself it was temporary.

Miss Sorrel had thrown herself into taking care of Vanessa.
Maybe it was because having Vanessa and Lis there helped her
feel less alone after Woody's death. Or maybe it was Miss Sorrel's second chance—Vanessa had been the same age as Janey
when she'd disappeared. With her fine fair hair and pale com-
plexion, Vanessa resembled Janey. Whatever the reason, Miss
Sorrel went to every one of Vanessa's dance recitals, school plays,
track meets, and softball games. Came with Lis to Augusta to
cheer Vanessa on as she pitched her team to a Dixie League
district championship.

She's no trouble at all, Miss Sorrel used to say of Vanessa, even
when Vanessa was a surly, hormone-riddled teen. *It's as if God
sent her to me.*

Of course God had nothing to do with the reason Lis had had
to move home. It was Brad who couldn't keep his pants zipped.
Lis still stung with humiliation remembering the phone call that
ended her marriage. She couldn't even recall why she'd called
Brad at work that day. The receptionist had answered. Brad was
on the phone. Did Lis want to wait? They'd gotten to chatting, as
they often did. Brad's job had him frequently tied up on the phone.

"You always sound so nice, Mrs. Strenger." Then there'd been a long pause. Later Lis wondered if the woman had stopped to consider what she was about to do, the thing that put a hairpin turn in Vanessa's life. "I can connect you now," she'd said with a little too much forced cheer, or so it seemed in retrospect. *Click.*

Then "Mmmmm, that sounds . . . interesting." A woman's soft, warm voice. "We'll have to try it that way." Lis had felt herself flush and she almost hung up, thinking there'd been a mistake.

But the chuckling she heard in response was oh so familiar. Then the voice she knew by heart said, "Think about it. Maybe sometime this weekend? I'll call you if I can escape."

"I miss you."

"I miss you, too, Honey Buns."

Honey Buns? Lis had stared openmouthed at the receiver. Honey Buns was Brad's pet name for Lis. Later she laughed about it—she'd always known the guy hadn't an original thought in his pea brain. But at the time, she'd found herself on her knees, doubled over and silently sobbing, the receiver on the floor beside her.

Weeks later she was in the kitchen of the house she and Brad had already put on the market, her hands coated in newsprint as she bubble-wrapped martini glasses that she'd much rather have been smashing into their faux fireplace, packing for the move into a smaller house that soon she wouldn't be able to afford.

She still couldn't believe she'd been so stupid. Never questioned the long runs Brad took. Never suspected something was up when he'd come home after an hour and a half looking flushed but barely winded and proclaiming himself too sweaty and stinky for her to get near him. Heading straight for the shower.

A week after that fatal phone call, she'd followed Brad when he went out for his run. Six blocks from the house, he ducked into a phone booth. Made a call. Came out and waited until a red Mustang pulled up.

He was so damned sure of himself, so focused on smoothing his hair and sucking in his gut as he waited, he didn't notice Lis standing out in the open, brazenly watching him from under a tree across the street. When the door of the Mustang had opened, Crystal Gayle's torchy voice pulsed from inside. After Brad got in and the car took off, Lis was stuck with "the sound of good-bye" in her head.

And that was the beginning of the end, or the beginning of a new beginning as Miss Sorrel tried to reassure her. But then, her mother had always been at best lukewarm about Brad. *All I want is for you to be happy.*

Well, Lis hadn't been particularly happy with Brad. But was she any happier without him? She glanced back at the house where she'd lived with her mother for the last twenty years. Lis was grateful for the home her mother had opened up to them, grateful for the job she'd been able to step into when Miss Sorrel gave up managing Woody's Charters. She was even more grateful that her mother never once rubbed her nose in her own neediness. It was only lately that she felt as if she couldn't breathe, as if her mother and this house with a hole in it that would never heal over were suction-cupped to her chest.

Binty hoisted herself and scratched at the ground. Gazed up at Lis with those soulful eyes and wagged her tail. A dog's life seemed a much more straightforward affair, Lis thought. She bent over, scratched Binty's chin, and nuzzled the dog's forehead.

Just then there was a cry from the house and Miss Richards burst out onto the porch, her long hair flying.

Miss Sorrel pressed up against the screen door. "Come back here, you . . . you . . . this very instant. Please"—her voice turned plaintive—"come back."

As Miss Richards blew past Lis, the woman tripped over her own feet and went sprawling. Binty came at her, snapping and snarling as she scrambled upright. Binty, who'd never so much as snapped at a squirrel. Lis grabbed the dog's collar and held her back.

Miss Sorrel came out and stood on the porch. She was holding the doll. "You have to tell me. Where did you get this?"

"I told you. I found it."

"Where? When? Please. You have to—" Miss Sorrel started down the stairs.

"Keep away." The woman backed away.

Within arm's reach now, Miss Sorrel held the doll out to her. Pleading. "Who gave it to you?"

"No one."

"Then who sent you here?" Miss Sorrel shoved the doll into the woman's chest.

"No one sent me!" The woman jerked the doll free from Miss Sorrel's hands. "Leave me alone." She raised the doll and threw it against a brick porch step. It landed face-first with a sickening crack.

The woman pushed past Miss Sorrel, ran for her car, got in, and slammed the door. Miss Sorrel went over and beat on the side window. "Where did you get it? Please. I have to know."

Tires squealed and smoke poured from the tailpipe as the car roared off, leaving behind the smell of burning rubber and spent fuel. Miss Sorrel just stood there staring down the street, trembling and breathing heavily, her mouth set in a grimace of fury and frustration.

Lis picked up the doll and sat on the front steps. She lifted its gown, the fabric brittle with age. The smell of mold and camphor rose from the doll's soft body as it stared with blank eyes up at the sky-blue porch ceiling. Its forehead now had a hole in the center, with cracks radiating out, but its one bisque arm and both legs were intact.

Miss Sorrel sank down on the step beside Lis. She reached across and turned over one of the doll's feet. Lis felt a frisson of recognition when she saw the mark impressed in the heel: a leaf, oval in shape, smooth edged with a vein running down the center. A sorrel leaf.

"It's one of yours," Lis said.

"Not just *one* of mine. Don't you recognize it?"

"I . . ." Lis fingered the stained christening gown. Was there something familiar about the doll? Its porcelain head was coated with greasy dirt, but Lis could see how subtly it was modeled and painted so that the flesh looked soft and plump, dimpled like a real child's. A narrow pink satin ribbon was tied in what was left of the fine hair in its fair wig.

Miss Sorrel took the doll from Lis and marched, shoulders first, up the steps with only slight hesitations to accommodate her weak knee. Lis followed her into the workroom where she laid the doll on the table and turned on the overhead light.

Miss Sorrel pulled from a drawer one of the soft cloth diapers she used for cleaning dolls. She dipped the diaper in water and a bit of Ivory soap and gently removed greasy dirt from the doll's face. Then she stood back.

The cracked head and milky eyes distorted the doll's face. Was this Janey's doll?

Lis went and got the framed picture taken of the family Christmas morning two years before Janey disappeared. The boys held their prized gifts: a dump truck for Davey, a radio for Sam, and a guitar for Michael. Standing beside five-year-old Lis was Janey, a sturdy toddler wearing a blanket sleeper. Lis compared the doll that Janey hugged to her chest to the doll Miss Richards had smashed against their front steps.

Blond curls. Half smile and dimple in her chin. And something you could barely see in the photograph—underneath the doll's unnerving, sightless eyes were the faintest of shadows. Lis's grandmother had had them. All the women in her family did, smudges under their eyes that grew darker with age and couldn't be washed away.

Still, Lis wasn't convinced that it was the same doll. But Miss Sorrel seemed to harbor no doubts. She cradled the doll and stroked its fair hair. "I always knew one day she'd come home."

3

Vanessa Strenger barely noticed the porcelain doll that sat on top of her bureau as she got ready to head into her night job. The doll had been her mother's, and it sat in whatever bedroom in whatever apartment Vanessa had lived since she'd left home for college, prying herself loose from her mother's protective grasp. She thought of the doll as her mother's avatar, a benign if suffocating spirit who watched over Vanessa, fueled by anxiety and the best of intentions.

Tonight, nine years and four moves since Vanessa had left home, if that simpering porcelain-faced doll's eyes had blinked open and she'd started bawling, Vanessa would not have noticed. She was that exhausted. She'd kept herself awake until late the night before and gotten up early that morning so she'd be thoroughly sleep-deprived by the time she arrived for her shift at the sleep study center. Sleep deprivation, in particular a lack of REM sleep, was a surefire way to induce vivid dreams, and vivid dreams were her bread and butter.

She tied the waist of her soft blue scrubs that doubled as comfy pajamas. Nuked a slice of frozen pizza and scarfed it down with a few swallows of tap water. Ran a brush through her long hair and fastened it back with a banana clip. More out of habit than vanity, she dabbed concealer under her eyes to mask the dark circles she had even when she wasn't wasted.

Ten minutes later she was in the car and on her way. She hummed to herself as she drove, determined to stay awake as she kept up with sparse I-95 traffic. She'd hooked up a camera sensor over her rearview mirror and rigged it to an alarm that would beep if her head bobbed or her eyelids closed for more than a blink or two. The alarm didn't go off, but only because she dug nail-shaped dents in her arm to keep herself awake. By the time she pulled into the parking lot behind the Melbourne Inn and parked under the lone streetlight, it was just shy of midnight.

The vast, nearly empty parking lot and the four-story brick building felt a lot more like your average anonymous motel off the interstate than it did a country inn. Vanessa scooped her cell phone off the passenger seat. No more messages from her mother. When Vanessa was little, her mother used to creep into her bedroom in the dead of night and poke her to make sure she was alive.

Vanessa dropped the phone into her purse and got out of the car. Mist had settled over a few forlorn piles of snow plowed into the far corners of a lot that had been optimistically cleared for crowds that were a memory only, now that a massive conference center had been built in the heart of downtown Providence.

Zipping her fleece vest, Vanessa crossed the parking lot. The soles of her clogs echoed on the macadam. She knew she was in no danger, but the empty darkness, clammy cold, and silence felt eerie. Her heart pounded as she ran the final fifty feet and up the back steps. She pressed the intercom button and waited for the security guard to buzz her in.

The door didn't unlock. Vanessa rang again. Still nothing. If the guard had fallen asleep again, she'd have to walk all the way around and bang on the front door. She pressed the button one more time, waved and grinned like an idiot at the security camera that pointed down at her from over the door. Finally, there was a buzz and the lock clicked open.

Vanessa's glasses fogged as she stepped inside. Beyond the small vestibule, the elevator stood open. It had been a year since University Sleep Study Institute had taken over the lower floor of the inn and still the landlord hadn't installed the promised engraved brass sign by the elevator. Instead, a hand-lettered card taped to the wall barely assured visitors that they'd come to the right place. Made the Institute feel like an outpost of Amateur Hour. Fortunately, dealing with the Institute's landlord or its image wasn't part of her job description.

Vanessa stepped in and pressed B. The elevator doors slid shut and the car descended. She leaned against the wall and rolled her head back. The vertebrae and tendons in her neck creaked. Her shoulders ached. She was beyond tired. *Survey data shows,* intoned the academician's voice in her head, *that the sleep-deprived are far more likely to experience vivid dreams.*

Far more likely? What did that mean, anyway? It was the kind of squishy analysis that dream researchers could have gotten away with once upon a time, back when dream research dwelled in the borderland between real and parascience and when the word *dream* in a research proposal more or less guaranteed rejection. Now dream research was hot and legit.

The elevator stopped, bounced, and the door started to slide open, then stopped, as if undecided. Vanessa wedged her hand in the opening and tried to nudge the door along, impatient. If she pressed too hard an alarm would go off, waking up patients who'd managed to get to sleep and ruining that night's data. She eased up and the door opened of its own accord.

Vanessa stepped into the hall. The cooler moist air smelled faintly of mildew. Beyond an artificial rubber tree growing out of fake sphagnum moss, doors lined the corridor. A housekeeping cart laden with towels and sundries stood at the far end.

The Institute's office, a suite next to the elevator, had a sliding window to the hall. PATIENTS CHECK IN HERE read a sign. Through the window, Vanessa could see Gary Corrigan, the sleep center's administrator, leaning back in a chair with his feet up on his desk. If that camera alarm in her car were watching him, it would be going off. He was out cold.

Vanessa rapped lightly on the glass. Gary scrambled upright and stared blankly in her direction. He stood and groped on the desk for his wire-rimmed glasses, put them on, and looked again. Gave a weary wave and let her in.

The office was furnished with two desks and chairs and some file cabinets. Oversized video monitors mounted on the wall were lit up, each with a bank of video feeds and readouts tracing brain waves, heartbeats, and eye movements. The air smelled of stale popcorn and burned coffee.

"Hey, Doc," Gary said, taking a step back. He looked at her, his head tilted. "You okay? You look—"

"Wiped. I know."

"You working or sleeping tonight?" he asked.

"Uh-huh," Vanessa nonanswered. She grabbed a blank intake form and started to fill it out. NAME. *Vanessa Strenger.* REFERRING PHYSICIAN. She skipped that field, because there was no way to code *self.* Besides, she wasn't that kind of doctor.

She skipped over the rest of the questions because she didn't have symptoms or a clinical issue to be addressed. Then signed her name at the bottom, giving her consent to be wired up, plugged in, and monitored for the next eight hours. She handed the form to Gary. "I'm so tired, I can barely see straight. Hoping to conk right out."

He rubbed his face and gave a weak smile. Under black stubble, his skin was as pasty as the underbelly of a flounder.

"You don't look too great yourself," she said. "Baby keeping you guys up?"

Gary straightened, tucked in his shirttail, and adjusted his belt below a growing paunch. He had a good excuse. He had a five-month-old colicky baby at home and he was working nights here, all while struggling to finish his dissertation. Meanwhile, his wife, Kathleen, a state cop, had exhausted her maternity leave and returned to work. Vanessa had filled in for Gary numerous times because Kathleen was tied up at work and he had to go home and take care of the baby. *I owe you big-time,* he'd say. And now he was turning a blind eye to how she was using the sleep lab.

He looked at her form. Frowned. *Any doctor who treats himself has a fool for a patient.* She knew how that went. But she wasn't treating herself. She was also using the lab's resources to develop a technique for directed dreaming, ammunition for a grant proposal that would support another year of research.

Vanessa avoided Gary's gaze as she dropped her purse and overnight bag on her desk and pulled a clipboard from its slot on the wall. "So what've we got?" She flipped through the intake sheets. Five patients were booked for sleep study that night, all of them signed in and bedded down. She'd make six.

Polysomnography testing had come a long way. Instead of patients having to spend the night pinned on their backs with the suction cups of a Holter monitor adhered to their chests and wires monitoring brain waves spackled to their scalps, they could sleep more or less normally with just a belt clipped around the chest and a finger guard measuring blood oxygen. An electrode at the outer edge of each eye tracked eye movement. A breath sensor hooked over the ears and taped beneath the nose like Hitler's mustache completed the picture. Wires from all the devices plugged into a small, cell-phone-like computer strapped to the patient's arm. If the patient turned over, everything turned over with him.

Still, it was amazing that anyone actually fell asleep with all that rigging. A glance at the video feeds and sine-wave readouts of tonight's guests showed that most of them already had.

In room 102, right next door, was George Cleveland. Age sixty-seven. Height five eleven, two hundred ten pounds. Truck driver. Insomnia could be a lethal problem in his line of work. The video feed showed him lying on his back, his eyes closed. His EEG tracings were jagged. Asleep, but not deeply asleep.

The woman in room 105 was fifty-three, five one, and a hundred seventy-five pounds. The video feed showed her lying on her back, too. Awake. She stirred. Adjusted the belt around her chest, itched at the adhesive under her nose, and flopped back down. Her intake sheet listed persistent shortness of breath, chest pains, and headaches. Typical symptoms of sleep apnea, along with dozens of other medical conditions, the most common of which her doctor would have ruled out before referring her to the Institute.

In 109, a male patient was bedded down apparently sound asleep, but the readouts were blank.

"Gary, the guy in 109? He's either dead—" Vanessa turned up the speaker for 109. Snoring. "—or unplugged."

"Aw, shit." Gary shrugged on a rumpled lab coat and left the room. Moments later, in the patient's video feed, the light from the hallway went on and Gary's backside filled the screen as he fiddled with the wires. The readouts came to life and waves began tracing across the screen, the deep regular spikes characteristic of deep sleep. Even Gary's presence hadn't jarred the man awake.

Vanessa glanced through the remaining records and checked out the patients. None of them were in REM sleep, the state that Vanessa studied. During REM, vivid dreams hovered so close to consciousness that dreamers could, theoretically at least, pluck their strings. Vanessa was getting close to mastering complete control.

Feeling a tremor of excitement, she unlocked one of the drawers of her desk and took out the small box that contained the prototype sleep mask she'd been testing.

Gary came back into the office. "Want me to hook you up?"

"No. I'm good. I can manage," Vanessa replied, as she always did.

Gary took a step closer. "What is that, anyway?"

"Something I've been trying out."

"Really? What?" He touched the box. "Is that what your research is about?"

Vanessa hesitated. She didn't want to share what she was up to. But hiding it would only make him more curious. She opened the box.

He looked in, then up at her. "So what's the big deal?"

"Big deal?"

"Well, you obviously haven't wanted me to see this."

"Here." She took the mask from the box and handed it to him. "It's something I'm trying out."

Gary turned the mask over. "Isn't this just like what we used all the time in the old days?"

This prototype looked like a same-old because she'd cannibalized one of their mothballed masks to create it. Embedded in the eye pads were wires and LEDs that not only monitored brain waves but also triggered a signal designed to induce semiconsciousness during REM sleep. She'd tried embedding the mask with a tiny flashing light, but that failed to catch her attention. She'd tried a sound but couldn't find one that didn't simply wake her up. Vibrations—two short and one long—were promising, the perfect balance, creating an entryway through which her conscious mind could seep into her dream and take control.

"You're right," she said. "Same old, same old with a few tweaks. I'm trying it out. As a favor. Someone asked me to see if it was comfortable and accurate and"—she was overexplaining—"well, you know."

He gave her a narrow look.

"Come on, give it back." She held out her hand. "I need to get some sleep before I pass out on my feet."

He held the mask under the desk light, turned it over. Rubbed his fingers over the eye pad. Turned it over again. Finally, he handed it back to her. "Sweet dreams."

Before climbing into the bed, Vanessa stuck a Post-it over the camera lens that fed images to the office computer. She also muted the sound feed. She wouldn't be able to fall asleep at all, no matter how tired she was, if she thought anyone was watching her or listening in. It was the same feeling she had whenever she went back to Grandma Sorrel's house and tried to fall asleep under the vacant gazes of the dolls perched on shelves in her bedroom, perfuming the air with decomposing plastic.

She put a pen and yellow highlighter and her dream diary, a bound book with half its lined pages filled, on the bedside table so all she'd need to do was reach for it when she woke up. Then she'd record her dream and flag the parts she'd been able to control.

The principle was simple. If you could control a dream, bend it to your will, then you could rob nightmares and the memories that sparked them of their power to terrorize you. It was more than an issue of interrupted sleep. People who suffered nightmares frequently were three times more likely to commit suicide, and that was regardless of whether they were clinically depressed or suffering from PTSD.

The technique had to be one that most people could master on their own, in their own homes, with the help of minimal equipment. Without a lucrative return from a new drug or high-tech gadget, private companies with deep pockets wouldn't be interested. But with PTSD endemic among veterans returning from war zones, the Veterans Health Administration was. Anything that held the promise of treating PTSD, especially a low-cost way of doing it, was in their sweet spot.

Vanessa had presented her prototype and some preliminary data to the research committee of an agency within the VA. They were encouraging but asked her to resubmit with a stronger literature review and more data to back up her proposal. More research. More data gathering. The deadline for resubmitting was weeks away, and she desperately needed that infusion of soft money or her postdoc at the college wouldn't be renewed for next fall's semester.

Her nightmare was that she'd have to crawl home, as her mother had done when she was about Vanessa's age, parachuting directly from a toxic marriage to a safe haven that was also a dead end. Twenty years later Lis Strenger was still living in the house where she'd grown up, managing the charter fishing business that Vanessa's grandfather had started. Vanessa would be damned if she'd let the same thing happen to her.

She got in bed and attached wires from the mask's eye pads to a modified smartphone she'd brought with her, then Velcroed a strap around her upper arm and tucked the phone into it. Once she had herself wired up, she turned up the audio and listened for the three distinct sets of sine waves that were continuously collected, each bleeping at a different pitch. Then she muted the feedback sounds, lay back, and closed her eyes. She was anxious about completing her research proposal. What if she didn't have enough research supporting her thesis to convince the committee? Or enough preliminary data? What if she didn't get it in on time? What if Gary ratted her out and she lost her access to the sleep center?

The mask felt heavy and hot. NOTE TO SELF: *need lighter weight, more breathable fabric.*

She adjusted the strap, turned over, and bunched the cool side of the pillow under her face. She could feel her heart beat. She should have skipped coffee that afternoon, but she'd needed it to keep from falling asleep.

She let her mind drift. Up came her bank statement and MasterCard bill. That glorious leather jacket she couldn't afford but had charged anyway. The stove in her apartment that smelled like it had a dead mouse in it. Make that a family of dead mice. And her mother who'd been after her to plan a visit to South Carolina.

Vanessa sat up. These were not thoughts that were going to put her to sleep. Forget grants. Forget dead rodents. Forget Mom. Bonsecours would still be there in the morning. Right now Vanessa needed to send herself somewhere peaceful, free of any guilt- or anxiety-driven narrative.

Closing her eyes and turning over onto her back, Vanessa took a few slow, deep breaths. Quiet. Blue sky. Water. Warm breezes. Luquillo Beach.

Vanessa had been to Puerto Rico twice, and both times spent an afternoon at the beach that was easy driving distance from San Juan. She imagined herself driving out of the city, through the suburbs with their pink and turquoise cinder-block houses with metal grilles across the windows, farther on through allées of palm trees and past stands selling icy, fresh green whole coconuts with the tops hacked off and a straw stuck in. She envisioned herself parking in the beach's massive lot and walking to sand so white and water so blue it felt more like a Disney island than a public beach. Along the curved edge of the shore, a few palm trees arched gracefully out over the water, their trunks nearly kissing the gentle waves.

In her mind's eye the beach was empty, which it probably never was in real life. She dropped her towel on the sand, took off her shift, and walked into the water. It felt silky, and she imagined herself floating in it, rocking gently, the water tepid against her body and the sun warming her face. She heard the rush of water, a toilet flushing somewhere in the inn. Caught a whiff of Pine-Sol. Her breathing slowed. She sank deeper into the warmth, a sure sign that she was drifting from consciousness into sleep. She imagined her body floating. She knew better than to try to sense the moment of letting go.

She was standing on the deserted beach, the air warm and still, a towel wrapped around her. The sun was low in the sky, the air cooling. She realized that she had to get back to the hotel. She had to be at the airport soon and she hadn't started to pack. She gathered up her sandals and hat and purse and shoved them into her woven Mexican beach tote. Realized she didn't have her watch. She rooted through the tote. Sifted through the sand. Knocked over the tote bag, causing everything inside to spill out.

Just then, a distant Klaxon sounded. Vanessa looked out toward the ocean but saw only sand, glistening wet sand almost to the horizon where a line of brilliant blue marked the boundary between the earth and darkening sky. As she watched, the band of blue grew wider. Closer, as if the horizon itself were closing in on her.

Tsunami. The word echoed the alarm that had to be telling her to leave the beach . . . *now.*

Terror gathered in Vanessa's chest like a cold fist. She had to get out of there. She tried to move, to run, but her feet felt rooted. The sand had turned to clay.

The alarm sounded again, muted now, barely audible. The air around her seemed to vibrate. The wave was coming for her.

The alarm continued, two short pulses and one long, repeated and repeated again. Louder now. More like a cow mooing or a very loud bee. . . . And in that instant Vanessa realized she was dreaming. That the sound was really a vibration, alerting her that she was in REM sleep.

If she *was* dreaming, then all she had to do to unstick her feet was will it to happen. She looked down at her dream feet. Pictured water pooling around them, and it did. She reached down and, cupping her hands, scooped up a handful of sand and water.

She laughed. Lifted one foot, took a step. Then lifted the other. A moment later she was racing out to meet the wave. Closer and closer, hearing the wet smack as her feet hit hard-packed sand.

She kept running until water lapped around her knees and the wave loomed overhead. She spread her arms and welcomed it. That's when she realized a lone figure had emerged from the wall of water.

Vanessa recognized the old woman in a flowered cotton bathrobe: Grandma Sorrel, her face as smooth and carefully painted as the faces of the porcelain dolls she'd once made, her long wet hair hanging loose around her face. She offered Vanessa the blanket-wrapped bundle that she was carrying.

Vanessa peeled back the blanket. A blast of mildew hit her. Inside the blanket was a baby, just its face visible, bright blue eyes wide open, a single blond curl spiraling over its forehead. *Her* forehead. Vanessa didn't know why, but she was sure that the baby was a girl.

As Vanessa backed away, she felt hollowed out, empty, and unspeakably sad. Why would she dream this? She didn't want a child. Really, she didn't. Please God, she couldn't be pregnant. The guy she'd met on Tinder? The one and only guy she'd met on Tinder? She couldn't even remember what he looked like.

" 'Nessa." Curiously, the whispery male voice seemed to come from the baby girl.

5

"Vanessa?" The voice that still felt as if it were coming from inside the dream continued, a bass note against the background buzzing vibration. "You need to take this."

No, I do not. Take her away. Take it away . . .

"It's a dream. You can control it." Vanessa wasn't sure if she'd spoken those words aloud or if that was her dream voice.

"You really need to take this call." Clearly a man's voice, its heavy presence felt as if it were pressing on her chest.

The vibration stopped, and for what was just a few moments but seemed like an eternity, Vanessa couldn't move, couldn't blink. Couldn't feel her arms or legs. Her only sensation was of that leaden weight pressing the air from her lungs.

At last she managed to open her eyes. Impenetrable dark surrounded her. Her heart galloped even as she realized why. The mask. All she had to do was take it off. But she couldn't move.

In the rational corner of her brain, she knew why that was, too. Sleep paralysis. She tried to relax into it. It would abate, she told herself, releasing its hold from her center out. Meanwhile, it was pretty cool. Sleep paralysis was notoriously difficult to study because you couldn't make it happen or predict when it would. Modern researchers didn't fully understand its physiology, though historians were convinced that the hallucinations it triggered had inspired the age-old myth of the succubus.

Finally, Vanessa was able to raise her hand and lift the mask from her eyes. In the dim light she could see Gary standing at the foot of the bed. He was holding something out to her. Her cell phone.

"I'm sorry," he said. "It's been ringing and ringing."

Vanessa took the phone. As if on cue, it chimed with a new voice mail. She expected the readout to say MOM, but it didn't. The number seemed vaguely familiar, and she recognized the area code, 843. That was Bonsecours. And it was the fifth call from that number. The first at 4:06 A.M., an hour ago. And there were four voice messages.

Vanessa flashed back to the dream, Grandma Sorrel emerging from a wall of advancing water and offering her a blanket-wrapped child. She knew a dream was just a dream, but still. Heart in her throat, she played the first message.

"I'm sorry to be callin' you like this in the middle of the night, out of the blue." A woman's voice, the southern accent even stronger than Grandma Sorrel's. "This is Evelyn. From next door to your grandma?"

Vanessa sat up. Of course she knew Evelyn Dumont, Grandma Sorrel's oldest friend. She'd never phoned Vanessa. Ever. It had to be bad news.

"There's been an accident. Your . . ." During the long pause, a siren wailed in the background. There were muffled sounds, like Evelyn was talking with her hand over the phone. "I'm sorry. Can't talk now. Call me back just as soon as you can."

If something had happened to Grandma Sorrel, why wasn't Vanessa's mother calling? Vanessa fumbled with the phone and called back.

"Hello?" Evelyn picked up right away.

"Evelyn? It's Vanessa. I just saw your messages. What's wrong? What happened?"

"Oh, thank goodness it's you." She sounded breathless, agitated. "Well, I'm not sure exactly what happened. For heaven's sake, it sounded like a bomb goin' off. Your momma and your grandma, they took them to the hospital." The words came out in a rush.

Bomb? Hospital? "Are they okay?"

"Got them out of the house just in time. That's what one of the medics said. Carbon monoxide."

"Carbon . . . Are they okay?" Vanessa felt as if she were floating, dimly aware that she'd already asked that. "What hospital?"

"Coastal Memorial. I called just now but they couldn't give me their status. They must still be in emergency." Vanessa remembered that Evelyn was a semiretired hospital nurse who'd worked at Coastal, the one and only big hospital in Bonsecours. "Don't worry about Binty. I've got her."

Binty? Vanessa had completely forgotten about the dog. "How bad is the house?"

"They've got it blocked off so I can't see around back."

Vanessa thanked Evelyn and said she'd ring her back once she'd figured out what she was going to do. Evelyn signed off with her usual, "Have a blessed day."

Vanessa called her mother's cell but there was no answer. Texted: ARE YOU OK? Stared at the phone, willing a text to pop up the way it usually did, like clockwork, ten seconds after she texted her mom. The question she knew she shouldn't even have to ask hung in front of her. *What should I do?* The obvious answer: catch the first flight to Savannah and drive to Bonsecours. Stay until . . . as long as they needed her. Possibly until it was too late to complete the research she needed to revise her grant proposal.

Maybe she'd have to forget about qualifying for this round of funding and hope that the university would find the resources to keep her on for another semester. Pray that in six months, the questions she sought to answer would still be hers to investigate.

Vanessa booked a late-morning flight to Savannah and called Evelyn to let her know when she'd be getting to the house. Then she called the hospital, only to be told that her mother was in "fair" condition and her grandmother "serious," and, no, they could not be reached by phone.

She packed, shoving underwear and jeans and T-shirts into her suitcase. Deliberately not packing a black dress. Evelyn's words—*Sounded like a bomb*—ran around and around her mind. Vanessa tried to imagine Bonsecours—bucolic historic Bonsecours with its bounty of pecan trees and magnolias, its live oaks festooned with Spanish moss—shaken awake by an explosion. Evelyn said it had come from the back of the house. That was where a pair of house-that-Jack-built additions had been tacked onto the main house: a kitchen and Grandma Sorrel's workroom. Vanessa had spent innumerable hours in the latter watching Grandma Sorrel and Evelyn Dumont bring damaged dolls back to life.

Vanessa picked up the one and only doll she had. Years ago her mother had slipped it into her suitcase, and Vanessa discovered it when she unpacked in her dorm room at Brown. It had been her mother's, the first portrait doll that Grandma Sorrel had made. A little girl doll, she wore a blue-and-white gingham dress and white hand-embroidered pinafore. If you took off her patent-leather Mary Janes and frilly socks, you'd find a tiny sorrel leaf embossed in the sole of her foot. The doll's lifelike face was a portrait of Lis, Vanessa's mother, and Vanessa hated the way the doll's gaze seemed to follow her as she moved about the room. Unsentimental to a fault, Vanessa never saved letters or photos or keepsakes of any kind, really, but she knew that Grandma Sorrel's spirit would haunt her to the end of her days if she didn't keep that doll. She tossed it on her bed and its brown paperweight-glass eyes clicked shut.

She hoped she wouldn't have to stay in Bonsecours for more than a week or so. In case there'd be time for her to work on her grant proposal, she threw into the suitcase her dream diary, the pack of three-by-five cards on which she'd been laying out the main points to add to her grant proposal, and a folder of research. She added her sleep mask, the miniature tablet computer she used to collect data, and her laptop.

All the while, she could feel the doll gazing at her from behind closed eyes, accusing her of willfully ignoring her grandmother's message. Dreams didn't *mean* anything, she reminded herself. Still, she couldn't shake the feeling that her grandmother was trying to tell her something.

Just before she left the house, she surrendered, wrapping the doll in a shirt and stuffing it into her bag. Having her mother's doll with her shouldn't have made her feel more anchored, but it did.

6

The women at the Providence airport departure gates had been wearing jackets and heavy sweaters in shades of gray and black. In Savannah, women were in short sleeves and bright colors, and the FlipFlop Stop was doing a brisk business. She checked her phone. No new messages. No news was good news, right?

The car Vanessa rented was a nondescript gray compact that fortunately had New Jersey plates and honked when she pressed the remote key or she'd never have picked it out in a crowd. She entered the hospital address into her phone's GPS, then started the car and found a country-and-western music station. As she drove from the airport, she cranked the volume, trying not to think about what she'd find when she got to the hospital.

We're not in Kansas anymore, she thought as she passed billboard after billboard on the interstate hawking fireworks ("Buy One Get One FREE!" "Get the best BANG for your buck!"). You could get arrested in Rhode Island for having a sparkler in the trunk of your car.

Her hands were aching from gripping the wheel when she stopped halfway for coffee and a donut and chased them with antacid tablets before continuing on. She exited the highway and continued across the vast Port Royal Sound. She'd forgotten how much more sky there seemed to be here, blue in all directions with turkey vultures teetering high overhead.

Live oaks, arching from the sides of the road, were the first indication that she was getting close. Their spreading branches dripped with the pale gray Spanish moss that hung indiscriminately from telephone wires and fences, too.

She turned at the sign for Coastal Memorial Hospital, found a parking spot, and hurried to the reception desk at the main entrance. "I'm here to see two patients, Sorrel Woodham and Elisabeth Strenger." The woman at the reception desk typed on her computer. Then typed again. She barely blinked, her look impassive as she handed Lis a VISITOR badge to fill out and said, "They're in Room 311. Elevator's around the corner."

Not dead. And apparently accepting visitors. Vanessa felt the tension in her shoulders ease. She ducked into the gift store off the lobby and picked up a package of breath mints, a tin of butterscotch candies, and a copy of *People* magazine. She sucked on a breath mint as she rode the elevator up. Stopped at the nurses' station for directions and then continued to the room.

The door was ajar with a heavy curtain across the entryway. Vanessa looked down at her jean leggings, loose sweater, and boots. She probably should have worn something more ladylike. Not that it mattered. She'd be grateful if her grandmother was up to registering disapproval and her mother wouldn't notice. Still, she unclipped her hair, shook it loose, ran her fingers through it, and clipped it back again as neatly as she could. Then she took a breath and stepped past the curtained opening.

The room had two beds. Her mother was in the one nearest the door, pale and still, a breathing mask over her face. The other bed was empty, the sheets pulled back. Vanessa felt panic rising in her throat. She wasn't ready to lose Grandma Sorrel. Not yet. Not like this.

Vanessa's mother stirred in the other bed. Vanessa swallowed and blinked back tears. The last thing her mother needed was to wake up and find Vanessa falling apart. Vanessa steadied herself and approached the bed.

Lis's eyes fluttered open. She held out her hand, and when Vanessa took it, she pulled her close. She held Vanessa's gaze for a few moments, then lifted her breathing mask. "You came." Lis winced and shuddered. "Ow. My head." Her voice was scratchy and raw.

"Of course I came. Evelyn called me."

"But what about your research? Your deadline?"

Vanessa waved a hand like it didn't matter. "I can work on it here, and if not, it will be there when I get back."

"But—"

Vanessa held a finger to her lips.

Thank you. Lis mouthed the words.

"How are you feeling?" Vanessa asked.

Lis half shrugged, half nodded. It would be like her to minimize her pain.

"Grandma?"

Lis put out a hand and tilted it side to side. Looked like *touch and go.*

Vanessa felt a wave of relief as her gaze traveled to the empty bed, then back to her mother's. "Where is she?"

"Oxygen chamber." Lis pointed toward the hall.

"You've got oxygen, too?" Vanessa asked, indicating the tank beside the bed.

Lis nodded and put the mask over her mouth.

Vanessa had a million questions, but it was clear that what

little strength her mother had was already sapped. She planted a kiss on her mother's forehead and then went out to the nurses' station.

A nurse in green scrubs was seated behind a semicircular counter, tapping into a computer. She raised her eyebrows at Vanessa while she continued to type.

Vanessa said, "My grandmother. Sorrel Woodham? I was hoping I could see her."

"She's your grandma?" the nurse said with a tired smile. She typed something into her computer. Waited. "She's receiving treatment. She'll be in there for two more hours."

"Two hours? Can't I at least *see* her now?" Vanessa bit down on the words and her vision blurred. "Please. I've just come from the airport."

A hesitation and the nurse's expression softened. "A few minutes, but that's all." She came around from behind the desk. The rubber soles of her shoes squeaked as she led Vanessa down the hall.

The nurse stopped in front of a double doorway and waved her badge over an electronic lock. The door clicked and she pushed it open. The room beyond was spacious, antiseptic white and stainless steel, with about eight beds, all of them occupied. Machines hummed and clanked and wheezed. Vanessa followed the nurse to the far corner where Grandma Sorrel lay encased in a transparent pneumatic tube that looked like Snow White's coffin. A monitor next to it was tracing out acid-green waves in a slow, steady pattern.

Vanessa rested her hands on the clear casing. Grandma Sorrel looked small and fragile. She seemed to be staring off into the middle distance, maybe at the interior of the tank. The skin was stretched taut across her skull and there were red blotches on her cheeks. Her eyebrows were singed and both hands were heavily bandaged, and if she could have seen her own hair, she'd have pitched a fit. Whatever had happened, Grandma Sorrel had gotten it worse than Lis.

The nurse came up beside her. "This is a hyperbaric chamber. It's the most efficient way to administer pure oxygen to someone like your gram. And it's doing her a world of good. Her color is better and she's less confused." She flipped a switch on the chamber's control panel and picked up what looked like a telephone receiver. "Mrs. Woodham?"

"Miss Sorrel," Vanessa said. "That's what everyone calls her."

"Miss Sorrel?" The nurse tapped lightly on the roof of the tank.

Grandma Sorrel's eyes focused past the transparent shell.

"There's someone here to see you," the nurse said. She handed Vanessa the receiver and pulled over a plastic chair. "I'll come back in a few minutes."

Vanessa sat in the chair and pulled it closer. "Grandma?"

Grandma Sorrel blinked. She reached with a bandaged hand and winced when it hit the inside of the chamber.

"You can hear me?" Vanessa asked.

Grandma Sorrel nodded. Her mouth formed a kiss.

"I just flew in. I needed to see you and Mom before I went to the house."

Grandma Sorrel blinked and said something, but the voice coming through the handset was faint.

"I didn't catch that," Vanessa said.

Grandma Sorrel raised her voice to a scratchy whisper. "She came back."

"She?"

"Ask Evelyn." Grandma Sorrel lifted her shoulders from the

stretcher. "It. It's—" The tendons in her neck strained with effort as she moved her mouth closer to the speaker. "Have to find her."

"Don't worry," Vanessa said. "We'll find her. I promise." Easy to promise since she had no idea what her grandmother was talking about.

Grandma Sorrel waved a clawed hand. "And the girl. The other one. The other one."

"The other girl?" Vanessa put her mouth close to the receiver and said, "Grandma, who?"

"Not *who*," Grandma Sorrel said. She strained to lift her head. The monitor alongside the hyperbaric chamber started to beep.

Vanessa leaned closer, but before she could speak she felt a hand on her shoulder. The nurse had returned. "Sorry." The nurse took the handset from Vanessa and hung it back up. "She needs her rest. And from the look of it, honey, so do you."

"I don't want her to be alone when she wakes up."

"She won't be." The nurse gestured around the room. Vanessa had to admit it was full of people.

"If anything changes, will someone let me know right away?"

"Leave your number and I promise we'll call you."

"Are you sure she's—" Vanessa started. But Grandma Sorrel had closed her eyes and the lines of tension in her face and neck were already erasing themselves. Vanessa didn't need to see brain waves to know she'd fallen asleep.

"I'll be back," Vanessa whispered.

On her way to Lis's room, Vanessa detoured to a restroom. After she'd washed her hands and splashed water on her face, she held on to the sink, nearly doubled over. The nurse was right. She was completely wiped out, exhausted, jangly nerved and running on fumes.

She was also terrified. Grandma Sorrel had always been the ballast in their lives. The force that had anchored Vanessa and her mother when their world fell apart. The person who made everything seem normal. The one who told it like it was. Like when Vanessa got engaged to her college boyfriend and Grandma Sorrel had told her she'd buy Vanessa a bridal gown if that's what this was about, but she'd be damned if she'd sit still and watch Vanessa throw herself away on a man who was pressuring her to become a nurse so she could pay for his medical degree. Furthermore, Grandma Sorrel pointed out, why in heaven's name would you want to spend your life with a man who chewed with his mouth open? Once that had been pointed out to her, Vanessa could no longer ignore it. That mouth-open chewing tanked the relationship.

She took down her hair and clipped it back again. She dabbed on a little lipstick. Then she went to her mother's room to say good-bye, but Lis was sleeping, too, the oxygen mask hanging on the tank by the bed.

Vanessa lowered the shade to darken the room. Sitting on the windowsill was a vase bursting with orange and yellow chrysanthemums, white daisies, and sunflowers. The accompanying card was signed *Cap'n Jack*. Vanessa smiled. Cap'n Jack was the legendary fishing guide who'd run Woody's Charters with Grandma Sorrel after Woody died. When Vanessa was a little girl, still wounded and confused by her father's vanishing act, Cap'n Jack was a steady presence in her life. Like a favorite uncle, he always had a piece of candy in his pocket and all the time in the world to listen to her.

She found a piece of paper and wrote her mother a note saying she'd be back the next morning and left it propped on her mother's tray table with the butterscotch candies and magazine.

She'd have to wait until then to ask her mother what Grandma Sorrel had been trying to tell her. Who came back, and why was Grandma Sorrel so anxious about it?

When Vanessa got back in the rental car, her own haunted eyes stared back at her from the rearview mirror. The shadows under her eyes were even darker than usual. She started the car, pulled out of the lot, and headed for the house where she'd grown up.

Traffic slowed as the road rounded the bend in the river. Vanessa rolled down the car window and the odor of the broad tidal flat along the Bonsecours River flowed in, thick with the pungent, slick, gooey pluff mud that was exposed by a receding tide.

Vanessa inhaled, loosened her grip on the wheel, and let herself be transported back. As a kid she'd had more than one pair of sneakers sucked off her feet when she'd ventured out onto the mud, despite the cautionary tales of foolish sailors who'd gotten their boats stuck, stepped out onto what looked like a mudflat, sunk in it up to their hips, and drowned when the river's famous nine-foot tide came in. Or that was the story Grandma Sorrel used to tell Vanessa, anyway.

Ten minutes later Vanessa pulled up and parked in front of Grandma Sorrel's house. Wisteria vines hung bare across the front of the modest white clapboard house. Its façade—a deep front porch spanning the front and three peaked roof gables framing the only second-floor windows—appeared unscathed by the explosion. The only sign of damage visible from the street was yellow tape stretched across the front porch, a board nailed across the front door, and the broken pane of leaded glass in the front window.

Vanessa climbed the steps. Glass crunched underfoot as she ducked under the tape. The porch swing creaked. On the table sat a nearly empty glass with some pale brown liquid in it, the remains of sweet tea, judging by the flies that were on the rim. Peering into the dark entry hall, she caught a whiff of smoke and could just make out the oriental-patterned runner on the stairs.

She headed back down the porch stairs and walked up the driveway. The house was much deeper than it was wide, and the acrid smell grew stronger as the back of the house came into view. The windows of Grandma Sorrel's workroom were boarded over and a large propane tank in the back was toppled onto its side. Clearly this was where the explosion had occurred.

Vanessa was bending over to pick up a shard of broken glass when a man's voice startled her. "Ma'am?" She straightened and turned around. A police officer stood in the driveway, the brim of his cap shading his face.

Ma'am? Was she getting that old or was it old-fashioned southern courtesy?

"I'm . . . my grandmother . . . I just . . ." She stammered, feeling like she was in junior high, caught in the girls' bathroom without a hall pass.

"Vanessa?" The officer tipped back his cap with the heel of his hand and squinted at her.

"Vanessa!" Evelyn Dumont appeared behind him with Grandma Sorrel's dog, Binty, in tow. Small and plump, Evelyn had on a white ruffled blouse and voluminous flowered skirt. Once a brunette with hair down to her waist, she was now platinum blond, her hair teased into a tight bouffant. With her shiny apple cheeks, she'd always reminded Vanessa of a Kewpie doll in a granny gown. *Miss Evelyn won a baby contest and never got over it,* Grandma Sorrel used to say when her best friend was out of earshot.

"Guessing you don't remember me," the officer said, touching his cap brim. "Frank Ames."

"Officer Frank. Of course I remember you. You drank Budweiser." Vanessa remembered the six-packs her mother kept in the refrigerator for when Office Frank would come over. He and Lis would sit out on the porch talking, late into the night. Vanessa had always felt safe in his presence. His eyes exuded a calm watchfulness.

"Deputy chief of police, now," Evelyn said.

"Still Officer Frank to you," he said with a crinkly smile. "Haven't heard that in quite some time. Your momma used to call me that, too. And there's still nothin' like an ice-cold Bud on a hot summer night." He took a step back and gazed at the house. "Sorry this is what you have to come home to."

" 'Nessa, honey," Evelyn said, coming over and hugging Vanessa to her soft bosom. She smelled of jasmine, and her tight blond curls felt stiff against Vanessa's face. When she pulled back, she brushed away some powder that had gotten transferred to Vanessa's dark top. Like Grandma Sorrel, Evelyn never went anywhere without perfect hair and full makeup.

Vanessa bent down to pet Binty and accept wet kisses. Poor thing, you could see her shoulder bones through her thinning coat.

Evelyn said, "Lucky thing Frank was on duty last night. Got here just in time."

"It was the kiln," he said, shaking his head. "Set real high's what caused the explosion. On top of that, it wasn't venting properly. And on top of that, no batteries in the carbon monoxide detector. Another hour and they'd have been goners."

"You've been to the hospital?" Evelyn asked Vanessa.

"I've just come from there."

"Goodness me, but you made good time. How are they? You talked to them?"

"Both. The nurse said they're both getting better."

"The good Lord willing," Evelyn said, crossing herself. "I made sure they got a room together. Even though I'm just part-time now, I still have some clout."

"When I was there, they were treating Grandma Sorrel in the ICU. I told Mom that I'd come back and get things ready for when they come home." Vanessa looked again at the boarded-up windows. The capsized fuel tank. She didn't want to think about how fragile Grandma Sorrel had seemed, like a piece of porcelain in a glass case.

Evelyn said, "I knew it would take a while for you to figure out what's what, so I went ahead and made some calls. The glass people are coming tomorrow to fix the windows and an electrician will be by to deal with the power situation. Someone's coming to handle the propane, too. Then we'll see what all else needs doing."

Tears pricked at Vanessa's eyes as she thought about everything that needed to be done. "Thank you. I don't know what we'd do without you, Evelyn."

Officer Frank said, "I'm sure Lis and Miss Sorrel will be relieved to hear that things are under control. Damaged property and boarded-up windows are always a temptation. Wouldn't want street people thinking they can move in."

Vanessa took in the pristine stately homes across the street and on either side. "Is that a problem?"

"You'd be surprised." He paused. Gave her a long look. "Or maybe not."

Vanessa felt her face flush. Did her long straight hair, jeans, and over-the-knee boots say *city girl*, and worse, *Yankee*? Then she realized Officer Frank had probably heard from her mother about the "very dangerous" part of Providence where Vanessa was living. The one time Lis had visited she hadn't been able to see beyond the nearby warehouses and factory buildings that the city hadn't yet figured out how to transform.

Evelyn stepped up to Officer Frank. Her forehead came up to his chin. "Thanks for stopping to check on us. I know Lis would be most appreciative, you keeping a watchful eye." She let her hand float gently down until she was touching his arm.

Office Frank took a step back. "You staying here at the house?" he asked Vanessa.

"I was planning to."

"Be careful, you hear? Your grandma's been using that kiln for decades and all of a sudden it blows up on her?" He shook his head. "Arson investigator didn't find anything suspicious. Just turned up too high. But still, it doesn't sit right." He gave her a business card. "You call me right away if anything else feels off."

Like what? Vanessa tried to take the card but he held on.

"Promise me you'll call. Any time." When she nodded, he let go of the card and strode off to his car.

"You have a blessed day," Evelyn called after him.

"Workin' on it," he called back.

After Officer Frank had driven off, Evelyn said to Vanessa, "Don't know if you know, but he's sweet on your momma. Has been for a very long time. She thinks folks don't know, but we just don't let on. Nice for Lis, don't you think? Especially at her age?"

Bless her heart, that was Evelyn's version of a compliment. "Nice that he was watching over them," Vanessa said.

"Doing his job and we do appreciate it, don't we?" Evelyn

winked. Then her face turned somber. "You talked to your grandma? I imagine she's relieved you're here."

If she'd been relieved, that hadn't been evident. "She was upset. She tried to tell me something. Something about, 'she came back.'"

"She came back?" When Evelyn blinked, a little mascara smudged into her eyelid. "Did you ask her what she meant by that?"

Well, of course I asked her. Vanessa swallowed what Evelyn would rightly have taken as sass. "I tried to, but there wasn't time. The nurse shooed me out." She pictured her grandmother struggling to communicate, the strained tendons in her neck and wrist. "She also said something about a girl. That she had to find the other one."

"The other what?"

Vanessa spread her hands. "I thought she meant the other girl. She said you'd know."

"Hmm." Evelyn folded her arms and wrinkled her brow. "Keep in mind, she's not herself."

Vanessa could still see Grandma Sorrel's face with that familiar stubborn expression. Maybe she'd been a little confused and anxious, but she'd been herself.

"Mercy. Maybe it was about that doll." Evelyn's gaze shifted to the house.

"What doll?"

Evelyn's look darkened. "We'd better go inside. I'll show you."

7

Vanessa found the house key Grandma Sorrel kept under a green-and-blue Majolica garden seat by her herb garden while Evelyn closed Binty into a chain-link enclosure behind the house. When Vanessa opened the door to the kitchen, a powerful stench drove her back. It wasn't just smoke; there was a layer over it like burnt rubber.

Holding her breath, Vanessa stepped into the dark entryway that Grandma Sorrel called her mudroom. Once upon a time, she had imagined this dark, closetlike room that connected the house to Miss Sorrel's workroom as her portal to Narnia. Now she wondered if the coats that hung on hooks on the opposite wall would ever be wearable again.

Vanessa held her hand over her mouth as she made her way into the kitchen. A layer of soot had settled on every surface. The linoleum floor was streaked with footprints. The walls were stained a yellowish brown near the ceiling. A broom and dustpan leaned against the wall alongside a collapsed black plastic garbage bag. She reached over the sink and opened the window. A chilly breeze wafted in. Everything in the room, especially the dolls lined up on the shelf that ran all around the room, would need to be washed and aired out in the sun.

Evelyn briskly moved past Vanessa and began filling the sink with soapy water.

"Thanks for being here," Vanessa said. "I don't know what I'd do." She had to admit that Evelyn was practical, capable, and efficient, a source of emotional ballast when she wasn't trying to boss you around.

"*Pfff.* You'd have figured it out. Now you just set yourself down, 'Nessa dear. First I need to show you something so you'll understand." Evelyn opened a drawer and pulled out a file folder bulging with what looked like newspaper clippings. She set it on the table and opened it. The clipping on top was a fresh, crisp classified ad. Circled in red marker were the words: *LOST DOLL $5K CASH REWARD.*

The text ran above a photograph of a porcelain doll. The phone number listed was Grandma Sorrel's. The ad had run in the Charleston *Post and Courier* two days ago.

Vanessa shuffled through the pile of clippings. There had to be at least fifty classified ads, each of them offering a reward for the same pictured doll. They'd run in Columbia's daily, *The State,* the *Atlanta Journal Constitution,* the Charleston *Post and Courier,* and more. The earliest one was dated 1988. Back then the reward had been $100.

Vanessa gave Evelyn a questioning look.

"Your grandmother had to do something," Evelyn said. "She used to say you could hide a plug in a socket and the police would be asking you where to look. And we knew for sure that once Buck was gone, no one on the force would make finding Janey a priority." Buck had been Evelyn's husband, the longtime chief of police. Vanessa's grandfather's best friend. Vanessa had seen pictures in the family photo album of Woody and Buck casting off lines together from the flybridge of one of Woody's Charters's boats.

Evelyn added, "So she started posting that advertisement. Once a year. Every year. On the anniversary of Janey's disappearance."

Every year? "How did I not know about this?"

"She didn't want you to know. It was upsetting each time, posting that ad and then waiting."

"Did anyone respond?"

"For that reward? Lord a mercy, every year a passel of 'em would turn up on her doorstep with some pitiful doll, hoping to pass it off as Janey's." Evelyn leaned her back against the sink. "But Miss Sorrel knows her doll babies, and she always said when Janey's doll came back, she'd know her. *When* she comes back. Not *if.*" Evelyn clamped her lips shut and her eyes misted.

Vanessa looked through the ads again. All of them were published on January 23, Remembering Day. On that day, every year, Grandma Sorrel closed herself up in Janey's bedroom and emerged hours later looking pale and drawn. For supper she'd cook Janey's favorites—crispy fried chicken and banana pudding laced with chunks of graham cracker—and set a place at the table for Janey. Vanessa had hated Remembering Day.

"Yesterday," Evelyn said, "the doll came back."

"Janey's doll?" Vanessa said. She shivered. She could hear Grandma Sorrel's hoarse voice and see her anxious face through the clear shell of the hyperbaric chamber—*She came back.*

Evelyn paused. "That's what your grandmother thought. I'll show you." She snagged the most recent classified ad from the folder and gestured to Vanessa to follow her into the dining room.

The background of the dining room's cabbage-rose wallpaper had turned gray. Grandma Sorrel's silver tea service sat, dulled by a layer of soot, on a stately Chippendale sideboard. As always, dolls were everywhere. Small dolls were tucked between Grandma Sorrel's cherished Blue Willow china on shelves hanging from the wall. Larger dolls nestled in cradle-like baskets on the floor or hung from the walls and ceiling like ripening hams. They'd all need to be cleaned.

Evelyn headed to the fireplace. She drew her finger through a thin coating of soot on the top of the fireplace mantel and frowned. On the mantel sat a battered porcelain doll with a cracked face, one arm, and milky eyes. Evelyn held up beside it the classified ad with its grainy black-and-white photograph of Janey's doll. "What do you think?"

Vanessa looked back and forth between the photograph and the doll. The doll in Janey's arms was the right size. It had on a similar long white dress and what was left of its blond hair was tied with a thin ribbon. But the resolution was nowhere near sharp enough to see whether the doll in the picture had a dimple like the one on the mantel, and the wig on the real doll was too threadbare to make a comparison.

"What do *you* think?" Vanessa said.

Evelyn took the doll, cradling it in her arms like a real baby. She touched the embroidery on its dress. "It's my cross-stitching." She turned up the bottom of the doll's bare foot. "And there's the sorrel leaf." Lightly she traced one of the cracks that radiated from the doll's forehead. She fingered the bits of blond hair and the thin pink satin ribbon. The doll's cloudy eyeballs gave it a haunted look. "Poor baby," Evelyn said, pressing the doll against her shoulder and rubbing its back.

Vanessa half expected the doll to burp. "Can it be repaired?" she asked.

"She"—Evelyn said, setting the doll gently on the mantel— "can be. Somewhat. The eyes can probably be cleared. The dress cleaned, hair added. But the face. Porcelain." Evelyn tsked. "It can be patched, but I'm afraid it will never be perfect." She picked up the framed Christmas photograph and wiped it with a dish towel, then set it back on the mantel beside the doll. There in front of the tree stood her mother's three older brothers, uncles whom Vanessa had rarely met. Beside them were Lis and Janey. Whenever Vanessa thought of Janey, this was the image that came to mind, the fair-haired two-year-old standing in her pajamas with her thumb in her mouth and a brand-new baby doll in her arms.

"It could be Janey's," Evelyn said. "I can tell by the mark on the foot that it's an early Miss Sorrel doll. But you know, we made a lot of dolls, back in the day. Of course I *want* it to be the one. Your grandmother, bless her, reckons it is. And once she sets her mind." Evelyn tilted her head and peered closely at the doll. "But I'm not sure. Janey's doll was only the second portrait doll your grandmother made, but it was somethin' else. Expressive. Exquisitely painted. This was once a nice doll." Evelyn made a sour face. "But something about the head. It seems somehow . . . unfinished."

Vanessa couldn't see past the age and damage. "Who brought it?" she asked.

"A woman about your age, your grandma said. I didn't meet her, but I gather she was"—Evelyn's nose wrinkled—"rude and nasty. Sashayed in and then left in a huff when Miss Sorrel asked her where she got the doll. Sorrel was beside herself, but what could she do? She couldn't force the woman to tell her."

Of course Grandma Sorrel would have been distraught. She still was. Vanessa could hear her rasping voice coming through the handset of the hyperbaric chamber. *Have to find her.*

Evelyn squeezed Vanessa's arm and then headed to the

kitchen. Vanessa barely registered her calling out from the other room, something about taking down the curtains and washing them. She was thinking about the dream she'd had in the sleep lab last night.

It had just been a dream. Still, how weird was it to get woken up from a dream about Grandma Sorrel with a call telling her that she and her mother had been hurt? Vanessa knew it was human to search for meaning where there was none, but she suddenly wanted more than anything to go back into that dream, unwrap that bundle, and get a good look at what Grandma Sorrel had been trying to give her. Had it been a baby, or a doll molded in the image of a little lost girl?

Vanessa picked up the doll, intending to clean it and shelve it in a china cabinet where her grandmother kept her own collection of Miss Sorrel dolls along with the other dolls she cherished most. Protected. Behind glass.

That's when she noticed that the door to one of those china cabinets was ajar. It was only as she pressed it shut that she realized. Every one of its shelves had been emptied.

The battered Miss Sorrel doll fell from Vanessa's grasp. "Evelyn," she called out. "Evelyn!"

"What on earth?" Evelyn appeared in the doorway.

Vanessa pointed to the empty china cabinet. "Did you move Grandma's dolls?"

Evelyn did a double take. "Oh . . . my . . . heavens. Of course I didn't." She shook her head as her gaze traveled from shelf to shelf and on to another glass-fronted china cabinet on the adjacent wall. Its shelves were also empty. "Her Jumeau Bébé. Her Madame Alexanders. All the German bisques."

"And all her Miss Sorrel dolls," Vanessa added.

Evelyn shot her a panicked look. "Maybe they're in the workroom? Maybe she was working on them when . . ."

Vanessa raced through the kitchen. She groped for the light switch in the dark passageway to the workroom. But when she flipped it on, nothing happened.

"Here." Evelyn came up behind her and handed her a flashlight.

Vanessa switched the beam on. She could hear Evelyn's shallow breathing close behind her as they moved through the passage into the workroom. With its windows boarded over, the workroom was nearly pitch-black. Vanessa took shallow breaths. She could feel the scorched scent clinging to her as she ran the flashlight beam quickly from wall to wall.

Parts of the spacious room seemed untouched. Hand-labeled plastic bins, now coated with soot, were still intact on shelves where Miss Sorrel stored dolls that were being repaired. None of the missing dolls were on the worktables or underneath, or in a pair of gray metal file cabinets that stood undamaged in a corner.

In a far corner, plaster had been blown away and lath was hanging from the ceiling. The kiln's door was hanging by a single hinge. Vanessa ran the flashlight beam across the floor. Behind the kiln lay a length of battered steel tubing. "What's that?"

"May I?" Evelyn took the flashlight from Vanessa and shined the beam over the top of the kiln, then back on the tubing. "The flue pipe."

Officer Frank had said that the kiln wasn't venting properly. But it wasn't like Grandma Sorrel not to check the vent. Setting the kiln too high was a rookie mistake, not one she'd make. Vanessa flashed the beam across the ceiling until she found the once-white, round plastic casing of the smoke alarm. A little door in it hung open to reveal the empty battery compartment. Grandma Sorrel would never have failed to replace batteries in the carbon monoxide detector, either.

As if reading Vanessa's thoughts, Evelyn said, "You haven't seen your grandma in a while, have you?"

That stung because it was true. Vanessa hadn't even come home for Christmas. All she knew about Grandma Sorrel's state of mind was what she'd gathered from weekly phone calls.

Evelyn handed the flashlight back to Vanessa. If the missing dolls were in the workroom, they weren't in plain sight. A horrifying thought occurred to Vanessa. Had the kiln, once used to fire porcelain dolls, been used to cremate her grandmother's most treasured? Was that why the temperature had been turned up so high? Could you even fit so many dolls inside? How long would it take, and how much evidence would be left behind?

She shifted the flashlight beam to the interior of the kiln. Gingerly she reached in and touched the tile lining. It was still warm, but barely. She pulled out a shelf and dumped a mound of blackened chunks and ashes on the floor. Crouched and picked out a few of the larger pieces of what looked like porcelain. Possibly a doll's arm. A foot. She turned one of the pieces over. On the bottom she could just make out the impression of a sorrel leaf. "Grandma Sorrel still uses the kiln?" she asked Evelyn.

"Occasionally. These days we get most of the spare parts we need off the interweb. That's your grandmother's department. But yes, sometimes she needs to use the kiln, and bisque can shatter during firing. Once one piece shatters, it can set off a chain reaction. Who knows how long that was in there."

"But she cleans out the kiln after she uses it, doesn't she?" That was a chore Vanessa used to help with. Miss Sorrel had impressed upon her the danger of an unclean kiln. Anything overlooked could explode when the kiln heated up again, damaging whatever was in there being fired.

Vanessa flashed the light inside the kiln again. Her eye caught on a semitransparent blob of glass fused to a piece of base metal. She reached in and pulled it out. Vanessa knew what it was, or what it had been. Eyes. And eyes didn't get fired; they were set into a doll after the head was fired, so these melted glass eyes had to have come from a finished doll.

Still, the amount of detritus in the kiln didn't begin to suggest it had been used for cremating thirty or forty dolls. One or two seemed more likely.

"Do you think maybe Grandma Sorrel took her best dolls upstairs?" Vanessa said. She knew she was grasping at straws, but she gave Evelyn the flashlight and crossed back through the passageway to the main house and up the stairs. She looked in her mother's bedroom, then Grandma Sorrel's bedroom, then the big bedroom her uncles had shared, and finally the tiny one she'd slept in growing up. She checked in every drawer and closet, in every shelf and crawl space, and under every bed.

There were dolls and doll parts everywhere. Rag dolls. Plastic dolls. Rubber dolls. Dolls with faces made of wizened apples and others with bodies made of corn husks. But none of them were the dolls that had been so special that they'd earned a spot in one of the china cabinets.

Vanessa stood in the upstairs hallway outside the closed door to Janey's room, the one room left to check. Grandma Sorrel was the only person who ever went in there. Vanessa had to force herself to open the door and step past the threshold. She'd always been haunted by the idea that the woman who would have been her aunt might rise from her grave and try to return home. She'd imagine a spectral figure knocking on the inside of the bedroom door in the middle of the night, desperate to get out of that room; or rising up out of the drain while Vanessa was in the tub; or emerging like a finished porcelain doll from Grandma Sorrel's kiln.

But there was no ghost in Janey's room. Nor was there any sign of the missing dolls. The only thing on the pink quilted bedspread was a plump brown kangaroo who'd pitched over onto his nose. Vanessa checked the closet, which was filled with little girls' dresses. A pair of plastic bins on the closet floor were filled with dolls, but they were Janey's dolls. Toys, as opposed to collectibles. Vanessa reached for an oversize boy doll wearing red overalls, its wide-eyed manic expression like a ventriloquist's dummy. Its wiry red hair smelled of dust. Janey might have been the last person to touch it before it got piled in the bin. Vanessa dropped the doll back into the box.

She took a final look around the room with its always-on light in the window. Righted the kangaroo so it could survey its surroundings.

Vanessa went back downstairs. In the dining room she picked up the damaged doll that might have been Janey's from the floor where she'd dropped it. She smoothed its pinafore and set it in the otherwise empty china cabinet.

Robbed. That was the only explanation. They'd been robbed by burglars who bypassed a silver tea service and tray that were sitting in plain sight on the dining room table. By burglars who'd known just which dolls were worth taking and where to find them.

9

"Did you find them?" Evelyn asked, looking up from the kitchen table where she was writing when Vanessa returned. She had a dark streak of soot across her forehead. She took one glance at Vanessa and added, "I didn't think so. I'm making a list to take to the police." Evelyn rotated the piece of paper so Vanessa could see. *Ideal composition Shirley Temple. Baby Dionne Quint.* The list went on for twenty entries. So far. "There should be photographs of all these filed in the workroom. Miss Sorrel has always been meticulous about record keeping. At least she'll be able to collect on her homeowners."

"Seems weird that the dolls are all that got taken," Vanessa said.

"The most valuable ones," Evelyn corrected.

"A robber knows which ones are valuable?"

"Anyone even remotely connected to the world of dolls would know about your grandmother's collection. She was president of UFDC, for heaven's sake." Vanessa must have looked puzzled because Evelyn added, "United Federation of Doll Clubs. We went to the convention together every year. Gave workshops. She used to write a column for *Doll News* and she often wrote about her own dolls. Posted pictures. You don't need to be a genius to guess that she'd keep her best under glass and on display."

Suddenly Vanessa felt dizzy and chilled. She sank down in a kitchen chair and closed her eyes.

"Are you all right?" Evelyn asked.

"It's . . . I . . . Actually, I'm not feeling all that great."

Evelyn pressed the inside of her wrist to Vanessa's forehead, waited a few moments, then wrapped her hand around Vanessa's wrist, taking her pulse. She lifted Vanessa's chin and looked into her eyes. "Honey, when did you last have something to eat?"

Vanessa tried to remember. A donut and a pair of antacid tablets on her way from the airport.

Evelyn was already at the refrigerator. She poured a glass of orange juice, placed it in front of Vanessa, and started a piece of bread in the toaster. "I'll take the list and pictures to the police later today so they can follow up expeditiously."

As Vanessa drank her juice, she wondered if *expeditiously* involved an assist from Officer Frank, or if Evelyn's pedigree as the former police chief's wife gave her entrée enough.

"But as soon as she's strong enough to take the bad news," Evelyn went on, "we should run my list by Miss Sorrel. She'll know if I missed any." She took the empty juice glass to the sink. "And no more work for you around here until you're steady on your feet again. I'm sure it's just low blood sugar. I'll clean out the kiln and make a start putting things in order out back."

The toast popped up and Evelyn slapped it on a plate. She took a jar of peanut butter and some grape jelly from a cabinet, slathered some on the toast, and slid it in front of Vanessa. Grape jelly had always been Vanessa's favorite.

"You eat that and then go upstairs and go to sleep." Without missing a beat, Evelyn pulled a chair over to the sink, climbed up on it, and reached for the curtains. "I'll just take these down and run them through the washer and see if the living room curtains need a wash, too, and . . ."

As Evelyn went on, enumerating the cleanup chores, Vanessa let her voice flow over her. Evelyn loved having to take charge. But Vanessa's hand shook as she lifted the toast to her mouth and took a bite, chewed, and tried to swallow. For the moment at least, she enjoyed the sensation of being taken care of.

It took only a few minutes and the rest of the toast for Vanessa's head to clear. She helped Evelyn carry a load of curtains next door to wash. On the way back, she stopped at her car to get her suitcase and took it up to her bedroom. Under the rapt gaze of two shelves of dolls, she put the suitcase at the foot of her bed, opened it, and pulled out her mother's Miss Sorrel doll. This was the very first Miss Sorrel doll ever made. It was a portrait of her mother at five or six years old, its dress embroidered by Evelyn, its wig made of Vanessa's mother's dark hair.

Evelyn left, and Vanessa spent the next several hours scrubbing kitchen walls and counters. Then she vacuumed the entire house, only taking time out to eat a tuna casserole she found in the freezer. It was barely ten o'clock that night when she fell into bed, beyond exhausted. There was still a huge amount of cleaning to be done, but at least she and Evelyn had gotten a start.

Normally she felt cozy and safe, alone in the house and tucked into bed in this room that had once been called the "sewing room." But tonight she felt spooked. The walls of the room felt as if they were closing in around her, and Vanessa was startled by the occasional creak or thump that normally she'd have written off as the house timbers and its cranky heating system coming to terms with one another. *The dolls are having a party,* Grandma Sorrel used to say.

As tired as Vanessa was, she couldn't seem to close her eyes and calm her mind. She could feel her mother's Miss Sorrel doll staring at her from the bureau. She got out of bed and picked up the doll. Cradling it, she looked out onto the dark empty street. A scraping sound close by sent her heart into overdrive. The windowpane rattled and there was the sound again. It was the twisted, bare wisteria branches, rubbing against the sill.

She crept out into the hall. The doors to her mother's and grandmother's empty bedrooms were open. Light seeped from under the closed door of Janey's room. Continuing downstairs, she made a circuit of the house, checking that every window was latched and all the doors locked. She turned on the front porch light and, for good measure, turned on the light in the dining room. She opened the china cabinet and set Lis's doll on the shelf beside the damaged doll. At least there'd be two Miss Sorrel dolls to greet Grandma Sorrel when she came home.

Vanessa crouched so she was at eye level with the dolls. What had Grandma Sorrel been doing in her workroom in the middle of the night? Why had Vanessa's mother been downstairs, too? Why would either of them have turned on the kiln? And what did any of that have to do with the robbery and the return of this mangled doll that might or might not have been Janey's?

Well? She waited, but neither doll had answers for her. She stood and pressed the cabinet doors shut.

10

The beeping of alarms and clattering of carts in the hospital hallway interrupted Lis's sleep. On top of that, she couldn't stop thinking about the doll that woman had brought them. Its cracked face and cloudy eyes haunted her. Miss Sorrel had recognized it immediately, certain that it was Janey's doll.

Janey's doll. Janey's doll. Janey's doll. After all these years, it was the first thread of evidence that Janey hadn't simply gone up in smoke.

When Lis woke the next morning, it felt as if she'd been chewed up and spit out. Her head ached, and the thought of breakfast made her gag. There was a tin of candy and a magazine on her tray table along with a note from Vanessa saying she'd be back that morning.

She didn't remember Vanessa leaving, but she dimly remembered waking up to find Frank asleep in the chair beside her bed. She wondered if his visit had been a dream. Then she noticed a vase filled with pink roses and baby's breath that had appeared overnight on the windowsill alongside the flowers from Cap'n Jack.

She smiled. There was no card, but she knew the roses were

from Frank. He always gave her pink roses, ever since the first single pink rose he brought when he took her out on their first real date. Never mind that they'd been necking on her porch for months or that he'd picked the rose from Evelyn's garden. In the years since, on the rare occasion when he gave her flowers (sentiment wasn't his strong suit; dependability was), they were always pink roses.

Lis pressed a button to raise the hospital bed and struggled to lift her head. Gray light seeped in between the slats of the window blinds. The other bed in the room was empty. Her mother must have been taken again for special treatment.

Lis sat up and dangled her legs over the edge of the bed. The room started to spin, and her heart galloped in her chest. She unhooked the oxygen mask from the tank beside the bed and inhaled, then lowered her head between her knees and breathed deeply.

This time when she sat up, the world stayed anchored. She got to her feet and managed to reach the bathroom. When she came out, a nurse was waiting for her. Young and fresh faced, like she'd just started her shift. Lis was used to the routine. Pulse. Blood pressure.

"My mother?" Lis asked. "Where is she?"

The nurse slipped a thermometer into Lis's mouth. "Your mother is in intensive care," she said.

Lis held the thermometer. "What?"

"She's stable right now."

Stable? What did that mean? But before Lis could ask, the nurse took the thermometer and read it. Tucked it into her cart. As she tapped on a computer tablet, she said, "The doctor will fill you in. Let me get you some fresh water." She picked up the orange plastic pitcher from Lis's bedside table and disappeared into the bathroom. When she came back out, she put the pitcher on the table. "Try to rest. The doctor will be here any minute."

Dismissed. The cart clattered as the nurse pushed it out of the room. Lis lay back and closed her eyes. What wasn't the nurse telling her? They wouldn't have moved her mother to intensive care unless she'd suffered a setback. Was it serious? Life-threatening?

Lis saw herself sitting at her kitchen table reading the morning paper, Binty at her feet, the chair across from her empty. She'd be able to read the bridge column first, do the crossword puzzle, decide which TV show to watch. She could go back to buying whole milk. Stop dusting the dolls.

But she wasn't ready to lose her mother, and not this way. Miss Sorrel would have found it too abrupt and unseemly.

The nurse's "any minute" stretched to twenty and Lis was struggling to put on her bathrobe and fighting back another wave of nausea, determined to find out for herself how Miss Sorrel was doing, when there was a polite tap at the door and Dr. Allison came in with Vanessa trailing behind. Dr. Allison had been their family doctor forever. With his silver hair and trademark red bow tie, he had a calming presence.

"How is she? Where is she?" Lis said.

Dr. Allison pulled a chair up to the side of the bed and took Lis's hand between his. Vanessa stood at his side looking pale and worried. "Last night your mother suffered a mild heart attack. We're monitoring her in intensive care."

"Heart attack?" Lis repeated. Miss Sorrel had pain in her joints from arthritis and occasionally an upset stomach. Her heart had never been a problem.

"As I say, it was mild. It's not an uncommon complication

after carbon monoxide poisoning." As the doctor spoke, he took Lis's pulse. "It looks like she was exposed to it longer than you were. Maybe she was closer to the source? And, of course, she's older and more vulnerable. We expect her to make a full recovery. With a little luck, she may even be home in a few days.

"You, however," he said, shining a light into one eye and then the other, "are recovering nicely." He listened to her chest, then stood back and appraised her. "How are you feeling?"

Lis caught Vanessa's anxious look. "Better," she said.

Lousy was closer to the mark, but she didn't want to alarm Vanessa. Besides, she had to get home and figure out how to track down the woman who'd brought them the doll. Could it be Janey's? Lis had given up long ago on finding her sister, but Miss Sorrel hadn't, not even for a moment.

"Better," Dr. Allison repeated, giving her an amused look. "Nauseated?"

She nodded.

"Short of breath?"

She inhaled and coughed.

"All to be expected. You just need time to convalesce. But there's nothing that we can do for you here that you can't do for yourself at home." He glanced at Vanessa. "With a little help."

Was her daughter ready to step in for however long it took for Lis to feel like she could do for herself? How many more days would it be before Miss Sorrel was able to come home? And what if Lis didn't recover as quickly as the doctor seemed to expect? Evelyn would always be right next door, of course, but what if Evelyn had her own health crisis, or . . . Lis tried to take a deep breath but her chest hurt.

One of Miss Sorrel's favorite sayings came back to her: *Don't worry about the mule, just load the wagon.*

"Can I see my mother now?" Lis asked.

Dr. Allison nodded. "Get dressed and get your things together. Then Vanessa can wheel you over. In the meanwhile, we'll put together the paperwork so you can go home."

11

"You just try getting out of that wheelchair before I get back to collect you and I'll shoot you myself," Vanessa said before she planted a kiss on Lis's head and left her in the hospital's loading zone, a bag with her belongings piled in her lap. Even outside Lis could feel the hospital's odors—Clorox and plastic and sweat—clinging to her as she waited obediently for Vanessa to return with the car.

Doctor Allison had said Miss Sorrel would make a full recovery, but seeing her mother lying in the ICU, pale and unresponsive (sedated, according to the nurse on duty) on a ventilator with tubes snaking through her nose, had done little to reassure Lis. At least the monitor beside the bed beeped steadily and traced out a reassuringly consistent pattern. She'd hated leaving her mother to wake up with no familiar face beside the bed, so it had been a blessing when Evelyn showed up and took her place.

A man holding flowers and balloons rushed past her into the hospital. A siren screamed nearby and moments later fell silent. That must have been an ambulance arriving to the emergency entrance around the corner. Was that where they'd wheeled her and her mother in . . . could it have been just two days ago? Lis searched her memory, but all she remembered was how dizzy and weak she felt when she woke up in the ER, so light-headed that just lifting her head made her start to black out. She'd been shocked when the doctor told her she was suffering from carbon monoxide poisoning. Even more shocked to find out that she and her mother would have died if the kiln hadn't blown up and brought a fire rescue truck.

She remembered the night before. How Evelyn had come over and examined the doll that the woman driving that old junk car had brought them. How she and Miss Sorrel had stayed up late examining the doll. Arguing. Their voices carried up to Lis's bedroom. Lis hadn't been surprised to hear Miss Sorrel puttering about in her own bedroom late that night. Or later still when she woke up and heard her going downstairs. It wasn't until Lis got up to go to the bathroom and saw her mother's bedroom door open that she thought she'd better check.

Lis had gone downstairs. The house was quiet. Dead silence. She'd gone into the kitchen. The lights were on but Miss Sorrel wasn't there. The light in the passageway to the workroom was on, too. Then . . . next thing she remembered, she was waking up in the ER, feeling like she had a cinder block on her head, and there was Vanessa sitting at her bedside looking like an angel who hadn't had a wink of sleep in days.

A car horn tooted and Vanessa pulled up. She helped Lis into the car. Lis gritted her teeth as Vanessa buckled her in the same way Lis had done for Vanessa when she was three years old. The "new car" smell in the rental car was nauseating, and Lis nearly lost it waiting for Vanessa to start the engine so she could roll down the window.

"You okay, Mom?" Vanessa said, sliding Lis a sideways glance.

Lis winced and nodded, though she felt anything but okay. She wasn't about to turn around and go back.

As they drove along the river's edge, the smell of low tide nearly did her in again. It was one of those smells you got used to when you lived with it, and Lord knew she'd lived with it most of her life. But somehow the stay in the hospital had reset her scent detector. She sat rigid, her arm gripping the door, trying not to gag, grateful that Vanessa didn't pepper her with questions on the ride home.

As soon as they pulled up in front of the house, Lis noticed the broken window alongside the front door. Their rescuers must have had to break in, though she wasn't sure why. The door hadn't been locked. *Never have, not fixing to start doing it now,* was Miss Sorrel's position on that subject.

Vanessa turned off the engine. "Before we go in," she said, turning to face Lis, "I need to tell you something."

Please, not Binty, Lis thought.

"It's about the dolls," Vanessa said. "Someone broke in and stole them."

Lis stared at the front door. At the broken window. Not a fire-fighter, but a burglar had done that? Assumed the door would be locked because that was what people did.

"All of them?" Lis said, even though that was ridiculous. Someone would have had to back a U-Haul up to the house and it would have taken most of the night to load them all.

Vanessa swallowed. "They took all the dolls from the china cabinets in the dining room."

Lis's stomach dropped. It occurred to her that before going to bed, Miss Sorrel might have put Janey's doll in a coveted spot in one of those cabinets. Could it have gotten scooped up by burglars who'd only known enough to target the dolls that were on display behind glass? The other dolls were rare and valuable, for sure. But Janey's doll, which was of no value to anyone but Miss Sorrel, was irreplaceable and priceless for the promise it held.

Determined to find out for herself, Lis opened the car door, got out, and started up the walk, reluctantly taking the arm Vanessa offered her as she climbed the front steps. She noticed the charred smell the moment she stepped onto the front porch. Through the front door. Through the living room and into the dining room.

Lis went limp with relief when she found the doll Miss Richards had brought them sitting on a shelf in one of the china cabinets. Thank God. Beside the damaged doll sat another Miss Sorrel doll, this one in good condition. Lis recognized her own Miss Sorrel doll. She pulled it from the shelf.

"Whatever made you bring this home?" she asked Vanessa.

"Don't laugh. Grandma Sorrel came to me in a dream."

Lis laughed. Knowing how Vanessa dismissed anything that smacked of parapsychology, this seemed highly unlikely.

"Really," Vanessa said. "I just didn't know why. Now I get it."

"Well, I'm glad you packed it. It will make all this"—Lis gestured to the empty shelves—"a tiny bit less painful."

Lis closed her eyes. She could see Alice in Wonderland. Judy Garland. The baby Dionne Quints. The Cherokee rag dolls. And more, different forms from different decades and centuries even, each of them one of the very best examples of its kind. And, of course, Miss Sorrel's collection of dolls she'd crafted herself.

Vanessa said, "How are we going to tell her? She'll be devastated."

"We'll just tell her. She's a lot stronger than she looks." Lis's gaze traveled through the doorway into the kitchen. She was relieved that the high shelves were still packed with dolls.

"Evelyn doesn't think any of the other dolls were taken," Vanessa said.

"There's that at least," Lis said.

"She told me about the other doll." She gestured toward the broken doll, now sitting alone on its shelf. "And the ads Grandma's been posting."

"That's the first doll anyone's brought us that's remotely—" A lump formed in Lis's throat and her vision blurred. "Your grandmother always insisted that somehow she'd know if Janey was dead."

Lis had given up long ago on finding Janey, though from time to time she'd see a fellow customer at the BI-LO or a pedestrian walking a dog along the river walk, feel a tremor of recognition and wonder—could that be her lost sister?

Vanessa waited a moment before she asked, "Do you think this is Janey's doll?"

Lis sighed. "Your grandma's the expert, and she thinks it is. She was sure of it."

Vanessa didn't say anything. Lis realized she was giving her an odd look. "What?"

"Evelyn says she thought at first that it was Janey's doll," Vanessa said. "Now she's not sure. She—"

Lis cut her off. "Whose instincts do you trust on this? Your grandmother's or Evelyn's?"

Vanessa paused for a moment. "Honestly? I'd have to say Evelyn's. Grandma Sorrel desperately wants it to be Janey's doll. Whose do you trust?"

"Your grandmother's. Absolutely." Lis pulled the damaged doll from the shelf. She didn't need her glasses to see that the doll was in even worse shape than she remembered. Its wig was threadbare and the soiled pink hair ribbon had fallen down around its neck. The spiderweb of cracks starting in the doll's forehead now extended across the nose to split its upper lip. "And Evelyn's. For sure."

"They can't both be right."

"No," Lis said. She put both dolls back in the cabinet and pressed the doors shut. "Which means we need to find the woman who brought the doll. Before Grandma Sorrel comes home, we need to find out whatever we can about how she got that doll." Lis narrowed her eyes. Thirtyish. Long dark hair. "She had a tattoo. Right here." Lis touched the small of her back. "Harley wings."

"You saw her tattoo?"

"Don't give me that look. Her shirt rode up when she bent over."

"So we'll just ride around town and ask anyone about my age with long hair to bend over and lift her top," Vanessa said with a wink. "A name would help."

"Miss Richards."

Vanessa rolled her eyes. "First name?"

"She didn't say . . ." Then it occurred to Lis that the woman had called for directions and Miss Sorrel had called her back. "I don't know her first name, but her number should still be in the phone."

It should have been easy. Vanessa left her mother, wrapped up in a crocheted afghan and napping on the couch, and picked up the kitchen phone. When she pressed caller ID, the first number that came up had a local area code. That was probably it. She pressed redial and waited. The call connected, but after six rings the line went dead. Miss Richards wasn't answering. Apparently she wasn't taking messages, either. Vanessa tried calling the number from her cell phone, thinking maybe Miss Richards was screening her calls. Still no answer.

Vanessa got her grandmother's laptop from the pantry. Grandma Sorrel had never been old school about business matters. Hers had been one of the very first small businesses to set up a storefront on Etsy.

It took a few minutes for the computer to wake up and connect to Wi-Fi. Vanessa pulled up a reverse phone lookup and typed in the number from caller ID.

We did not find a match came back.

Vanessa typed "Richards" and "Bonsecours" in the White Pages website search bar. Back came sixty matches. When she widened the search to the entire state, back came more than two thousand matches. And it wasn't inconceivable that Miss Richards, despite her local area code, had driven there from Georgia where there were five thousand more.

"Why don't you run the plate?" Lis's voice over her shoulder startled Vanessa. She turned around. Her mother's face was creased with sleep.

"You got her license plate?"

"She was driving a junker. That's why I noticed the plate. P-O-J-N-K." Lis pulled up a chair next to Vanessa as she brought up South Carolina's DMV website. But "running the plate" was not the slam dunk they made it seem on TV. Vanessa found the car registration database but couldn't get past the opening screens. No, she was not police or an insurer or a tow company or an officer of the court, and hard as she tried she could find no sign-in for *nosy citizen*. Something called the Driver's Privacy Protection Act—apparently an analog to health care's HIPAA—barred the curious public from snooping through their fellow citizens' data. She supposed she should be grateful for that, but right now it was damned inconvenient.

"Can't you hack into it?" Lis said.

Vanessa laughed. "Not even in my dreams."

Just then there was a tap at the kitchen window. Vanessa looked up to see Evelyn standing outside and peering in at them.

Vanessa waved at her and a moment later Evelyn was backing into the kitchen carrying a napkin-covered basket. Smelled like freshly baked corn bread. Binty followed Evelyn in. Vanessa crouched to pet Binty and accept kisses all over her face.

"What are you two up to?" Evelyn asked as she prepared three plates, loading them with ham and coleslaw and corn bread from the basket.

"We're trying to track down that woman who brought over

the doll," Lis said. "Find out how she got it. Before Miss Sorrel gets home and we have to tell her about the robbery."

Evelyn looked down her nose at the computer. Vanessa gave Binty one last pat and sat down. DEPARTMENT OF MOTOR VEHICLES was emblazoned across the top of the computer screen. "You're using that to find her?" Evelyn asked.

"Trying to," Vanessa said.

"You know, you can't just run a license plate." Evelyn's steely gaze passed from Lis to Vanessa to the computer. "Only some-one in law enforcement can do that."

"A police official?" Vanessa said, glancing over at her mother. "I wonder where we could find one of those."

"A police officer won't help you break the law," Evelyn said.

Lis sighed. "You're probably right. Frank's a pretty straight arrow. But if we can't look up the plate, we can at least look for the car. I'll recognize it. And it had a USC parking sticker."

"What you're talking about," Evelyn said, "is stalking." She folded her arms across her bosom. "Chasing after a complete stranger who answered a want ad because she thought she was going to cash in with a doll she picked up in some garbage heap." Evelyn's gaze traveled from Lis to Vanessa. "It's not your call. Let Miss Sorrel be the one who decides what to do next."

"But—" Vanessa started to protest, but Lis shushed her.

Lis said, "Evelyn, I appreciate your concern, but we're not going to wait. Miss Sorrel thought it was Janey's doll."

"Sorrel thought?" With a clatter, Evelyn put the plates on the kitchen table. "When I talked to her, she wasn't sure at all."

"Well, when I talked to her—" Lis started.

Evelyn put up a hand. "Before you go haring off on some wild-goose chase, at least find out if it's Janey's doll. Run a DNA test."

"On the doll?" Vanessa said.

"On the wig," Evelyn said.

"Evelyn, you're brilliant," Lis said. Spots of pink appeared on Evelyn's pale cheeks. "Of course. Miss Sorrel made all her dolls' wigs out of real hair. So if that's Janey's doll, that's Janey's hair. Hair has DNA."

If you can't go over, go under, around, or through. That had always been Grandma Sorrel's advice to Vanessa whenever she was discouraged. If they couldn't look up the address in the DMV database, and Officer Frank wasn't about to bend the rules, there might still be another way to track down Miss Richards.

Vanessa excused herself to go wash her hands before eating, something of which she knew Evelyn would approve. She turned on the water in the bathroom and took out her cell phone. It was after six and Gary's shift started at eight. He'd be at home having dinner.

Gary's wife, Kathleen, answered. Vanessa could hear the baby crying in the background. "Kathleen, I need a huge favor. Can you run a South Carolina license plate for me?" Before Kathleen could tell her no, she added, "I know you're not supposed to, and I wouldn't ask if it wasn't important. I need to track down someone who might know what happened to my mother's sister who disappeared forty years ago. She'd just turned four." Vanessa paused, hoping Kathleen would think about what rules she'd be willing to bend if her own little girl disappeared. "If you can't, you can't. I completely understand."

"Have you asked the local—" Kathleen started.

"I can't get them to take it seriously." Vanessa felt a small pang of guilt, since this was a bald-faced lie.

"I really shouldn't." There was a long pause before Kathleen added, "But I'll see what I can do."

When Vanessa got back to the kitchen, Lis was at the table eating and Evelyn was sitting across from her, expounding. "Nursing. *Psssh.* It's not like the old days." This was a rant Vanessa had heard before. "We wore starched white uniform dresses, white hose, and a cap. Clickety-clack, up and down the hallways in white clinic shoes, not sneakers." Evelyn picked a piece of corn bread from her plate and nibbled on it. "Now they show up to work in pink and purple pajamas. Wear their caps only on Halloween, and even then they don't know how to pin them to keep them from falling off their heads."

Vanessa settled at the table to enjoy her dinner.

After Evelyn left, Vanessa dried the dishes that her mother was washing. "Why's she so dead set against us looking for the woman who brought the doll?"

"Because she'd rather stir butter than eat it," Lis said.

"Seriously?"

Lis turned off the water, wrung out the dishcloth, turned and leaned her back against the sink. "Giving her the benefit of the doubt? She and your grandma have been so close for so many years. She's seen what's happened every time there's a flicker of hope. The crushing disappointment after. She doesn't want to see her hurt again."

"Suppose I can find out where that woman lives. What do you think Grandma would want us to do?"

"Reckon she'd . . ." Lis balled up the dishcloth and threw it into the sink. "Doesn't what I want matter? Ever?"

That took Vanessa aback. Lis usually left making choices to

Grandma Sorrel and Vanessa herself. But Lis had been Janey's sister. She'd been the one saddled with responsibility for watching her.

"Fair enough," Vanessa said. "What do you want?"

"I want to find that bitch and make her tell us where she got that doll." *Bitch?* Vanessa had never, ever heard her mother use that word. "And then I want to find out where those people got it. And then—" Lis hiccupped. "I want to find out what happened to Janey."

Vanessa tried to put her arms around her but Lis pushed her away.

"USC," Lis said, brushing away tears with the back of her hand. "The heck with waiting for an address. Let's start there."

The next morning, Lis woke up to find that Vanessa was already up and had hot oatmeal waiting for her. She'd printed out a map of the local USC campus and highlighted all the parking areas.

Before they left, Vanessa called the hospital to check on Miss Sorrel. She was out of intensive care and in a private room, and Evelyn was already there in the room with her. "We'll come over at around one to spell you," Lis told Evelyn.

Evelyn said that would be fine, adding, "You won't be out there looking for that—"

Lis interrupted with, "See you soon, and thanks again for the delicious supper." She hung up quickly. She would have hated to have had to lie.

While Vanessa dealt with the contractor who came to measure new windows for the workroom, Lis washed and blow-dried her hair, penciled her eyebrows, brushed on some blush, and applied concealer under her eyes. Looking normal would take her a few steps closer to feeling normal.

Before she came downstairs, she checked her e-mail. She hadn't checked it since Monday, and it had been four days since she'd checked messages for Woody's Charters. Cap'n Jack had called to offer his help and to reassure her that he had everything under control. Fortunately, January was not their busy time of year, and Cap'n Jack had been doing his job far longer than she'd been doing hers. He'd been the first employee Woody and Miss Sorrel had hired. He knew his way, better than anyone, around every nearby waterway. After Woody died of a heart attack in his fifties, Cap'n Jack took over managing the back office, too, until Miss Sorrel was strong enough to step back in. Lis had been in college, and Woody's death had rocked both her and Miss Sorrel's worlds.

"You look rested," Vanessa told Lis when she came back downstairs.

Still, Lis's hand shook a little as she poured herself some coffee. "Amazing what a good night's sleep will do. It helps, knowing you're here."

Vanessa planted a loud wet kiss on Lis's face. "Hey, you were there for me when I had the measles and mumps and mono."

The drive to the compact local outpost of the sprawling university took fifteen minutes in what passed for rush-hour traffic in Bonsecours. Just after the street took a hard right at the river, a sign marked the start of the USC satellite campus. A hodge-podge of modern brick, cinder block, and historic buildings was set back from the street across from a neighborhood of modest, decades-old houses. Lis had driven past many times but had never actually been on USC's grounds.

Vanessa pulled into the first driveway. Friday morning classes must have been in session because the parking lot was full. Slowly they wove their way through the dirt-packed lot, looking for the car.

"Dirty white sedan with its trunk held down with a bungee cord," Lis reminded Vanessa.

But no cars with jerry-rigged trunks were parked in the first lot. Or in the lots that surrounded the adjacent complex of institutionally bland buildings. Vanessa drove through a narrow alley between buildings and back out onto the street. There was just one more parking entrance, but instead of pulling into it Vanessa pulled over to the curb. "Oh sh— . . . sugar."

Lis turned to see the blue lights of a police car stopped close behind them. What was that all about? Vanessa hadn't run a red light. Hadn't been speeding. If anything she'd been driving too slow.

Vanessa reached into the backseat for her purse and pulled out her wallet. Reached across Lis into the glove box for the rental company's plastic pouch of documents.

A tap on the window. Vanessa rolled it down and handed out her license.

"Vanessa?" Frank Ames said, bending over and looking across at Lis. He tapped his cap. "Elisabeth."

"Hey, Frank," Lis said. "What'd we do?"

"It's your rear tires." He handed Vanessa back her driver's license.

Lis and Vanessa both got out and walked around to see. Sure enough, both rear tires were nearly flat. Passersby slowed to gawk.

"It's a rental car," Vanessa said.

"Those tires will just about get you to the gas station. There's one a little ways up the road." Frank turned to Lis, giving her a concerned look. "How's your momma doing this morning? Everything okay? I'm sure she'll come through this in one piece, sharp as new."

Lis had been fine until that moment, but something about that sympathy-laden look of his unraveled her. Her eyes filled with tears. "Better. She's out of intensive care. But I'm not looking forward to telling her about the burglary."

"Evelyn brought me a list of dolls that were taken," Frank said. "And photographs. That's much more than we usually have when there's a burglary."

Evelyn was amazing. She must have gone to the police early that morning before she went to the hospital.

Frank went on. "We've issued a crime alert to antique stores and pawnshops and police departments. If anyone tries to move them locally, we'll know."

Lis tried to say *I hope so,* but the words stuck in her throat. Frank pulled her into a bear hug. He was a full head taller than she, and she burrowed into his chest, inhaling the smell of coffee and pencil shavings. When a passing car tooted, Frank let her go. Lis brushed away a tear and tried to ignore the stare that Vanessa was giving her.

"I thought you were on desk duty this week," Lis said. "What are you doing working this side of town?"

He straightened his tie. "I was fixin' to ask you ladies the same question. You thinking about goin' back to school?"

Lis and Vanessa exchanged a look. Lis could hear Evelyn's smug voice, *A police officer won't help you break the law.* She broke into a cold sweat, even though they weren't doing anything illegal.

"We're on our way to visit Miss Sorrel," Vanessa said, filling the momentary silence. Not a lie exactly.

"Hospital's in the other direction," Frank said. "And I know you've been driving in and out of the parking lots here because I've been watching you."

"You followed us?" Vanessa said.

"Of course he didn't follow us." Lis paused, looking at Frank for confirmation.

"I did wonder what you were up to," Frank said. "Why didn't you tell me about the doll?"

Lis knew he was referring to the doll Miss Richards had brought them. Evelyn must have told Frank about that, too. "Miss Sorrel ran her ad, as usual," Lis explained. "We get one or two dolls, every year." She folded her arms and stared down at Frank's always shiny boots. "It was the same. As usual."

"Only not as usual," Frank said. "Because this time your mother thought it was Janey's doll."

"How do you know that?" Lis said, though she knew that had to have come from the same source.

"I want the crime lab to examine it. If it's the one, this is the first piece of tangible evidence we've ever had." Frank frowned. "Who brought it? Who is she? *Where* is she? And how did she—"

"That's why we're here," Lis said. "Her car had a USC parking sticker on it. So we thought—"

"Whoa." Frank's frown deepened. "So you two thought you'd play detective and drive around the campus looking for her car?"

"I'll recognize the car. And I wrote down her plate number."

"I'm impressed." Frank took off his hat and scratched his head. He watched as a few cars meandered past. He took out a spiral notebook and a pen and handed it to Lis. "Write it down for me, would you please?"

Lis wrote down the number and handed the notebook back to him. From inside the car Vanessa's phone chirped. "Are you going to bring her in?" Lis asked.

"You bring in the doll," he said. "I'll follow up on this." He closed the notebook. "You need to let the police do their job,

Elisabeth. I want to find out where that doll's been all these years as much as you do."

As much as Lis did? That was easy for him to say. Yes, he'd helped with the search from day one, but he'd never actually met Janey. Hadn't grown up feeling her absence every minute. Hadn't been afraid to look in a closet or under a bed, terrified of finding her body or the bogeyman who'd come back to grab the other sister, the one that maybe he'd meant to take the first time around. Hadn't had to endure the curious, often hostile stares Lis had received from strangers who thought they knew better than the police and were convinced that Janey hadn't been taken. That she'd been killed by someone in the family and then tossed off one of Woody's sportfishing boats.

"Maybe it's time you grew a backbone," Vanessa said as she started the car and pulled into traffic, heading for the gas station. "He can be awfully patronizing."

"Frank?" Lis said, though she knew that was what Vanessa meant.

Vanessa lowered her voice to a gravelly imitation of Frank's. "You ladies do need yo-wa protectin'."

Lis smiled.

"You like that about him," Vanessa said.

"I find it amusing that you find it so annoying. And yes, I do like it. Because that's not what all men do."

Lis knew Vanessa caught her meaning. Vanessa's father's number one priority had been himself.

"Are you thinking about marrying him?"

"And you're always telling *me* not to ask personal questions."

"Don't change the subject."

"Maybe. If he ever gets around to asking me. And I'll appreci-ate it if you don't go putting your oar in. Bad enough I have Miss Sorrel's and Evelyn's two cents to deal with."

"They want you to get married?"

Lis thought about that for a moment. "Actually, sometimes I think Evelyn wants him for herself."

That made Vanessa laugh.

Lis's friendship with Frank had grown, simmering and cool-ing by turns over the years. He'd been a rookie cop when she was seven and Janey disappeared. While Evelyn's husband, Chief of Police Buck Dumont, tall and barrel-chested with a swagger that proclaimed himself *in charge,* had come to the house many times, asking her questions, the person she remembered most was newly minted police "Officer Frank."

Miss Sorrel had hovered nearby as he asked Lis gently prob-ing questions. What did Janey like to do? Was there anywhere special she liked to hide? What had she been wearing? Had she been crying? Did she have any bruises or Band-Aids? Was she often afraid? Were there any grown-ups who'd taken a spe-cial interest in her?

Officer Frank kept coming by long after the house had been searched attic to cellar, after crews of police officers and volun-teers carrying long walking sticks combed the woods behind the house and scoured the river and its many nearby inlets for any sign of Janey or the denim overalls and pink-and-purple-striped top she'd been wearing when she disappeared. Frank had al-ways had a smile for Lis and a lollipop tucked in his pocket, and he gave her a tin DEPUTY badge that she still kept in her jewelry box.

After Officer Frank ran out of questions and Janey's trail had gone cold, he'd swing by and talk to Miss Sorrel and Woody, the three of them keeping their voices hushed so Lis couldn't hear. Eventually those visits dropped off until at last the ripples of Janey's absence were felt only in their house. In the empty bedroom. In the chair at the dining room table where no one sat. In the photographs that her parents stopped taking.

Some time after Lis moved back home after her divorce, Frank started coming around again. Deputy chief of police, though everyone knew Chief Buck Dumont had been grooming him to be his successor. But when Buck died, Frank hadn't stepped up to apply for the position. If you asked him, and Lis did, he'd say he just didn't have the stomach for all the bullshit you had to deal with when you rose to the top of that particular fiefdom. He'd rather just keep his head down, do his job, and one day retire and collect his pension, now just a few years away.

Frank may not have been a world beater, but he was solid and sweet and dependable, everything that Brad was not. And, as he often told her, he'd never given up on finding Janey.

"Here we are," Vanessa said, interrupting Lis's thoughts. She'd pulled into a gas station and parked at the pump. Then she leaned across and showed Lis a message that had come in on her cell. It read:

MAGGIE RICHARDS 25 PALMETTO COURT BONSECOURS SC.

"You found Miss Richards?" Lis said. Vanessa nodded. "How?"

"Don't ask," Vanessa said.

Lis watched as Vanessa pasted the address into her map app and brought up a location about fifteen or twenty minutes west of them. Lis checked her watch. They had plenty of time to deal with the tires, drive over to check out Maggie Richards, and still be at the hospital before Evelyn was expecting them.

Vanessa got out and went around to the back of the car. Lis got out and joined her. Both rear tires were nearly flat.

A man in coveralls came over to them. "Can I help you ladies?"

"The tires," Vanessa said. "I'm not sure if they need to be repaired or what."

He dropped down to have a look. "New tires," he said, "by the look of them."

"It's a rental," Vanessa said.

Lis watched as he had Vanessa roll the car a few feet up and back as he crouched alongside and inspected one tire, then the other. He got back to his feet, wiped his hands with a cloth, and stuffed it into his back pocket.

"Don't see any obvious reason why they'd go flat. Better air 'em up, then keep an eye on them. Prob'ly someone let the air out is all."

"How can you tell that?" Vanessa asked.

"Both tires? No obvious puncture? Hard to figure otherwise."

Both tires. Lis thought about that a few minutes later as she screwed the cap back on the valve of the second tire she'd finished filling. Was it a random gotcha, a burp in the universe? Or was it someone expressing an opinion? The car did have New Jersey plates and this was South Carolina.

Lis got back in the car and Vanessa started it up. A few minutes later they were on the highway heading to the address at which Maggie Richards's car was registered.

"Mom," Vanessa said, "can I ask you something?"

Lis looked across as Vanessa shot her a sideways glance.

"You never talk about Janey, but you once told me that things weren't the same after she disappeared."

"Did I say that?"

"Not in so many words, but yes."

"Janey." Lis sighed and looked out the window. Usually she left the room whenever her sister's name came up. Riding in the car, she was trapped. "Before. After. Yeah, things changed. The obvious, of course, like police watching the house and people always looking at me. After all I was *the sister*. But beyond that, your grandma changed. Before, we used to pile into her lap in the big rocking chair and she'd sing, *You are my sunshine*." Lis began to hum the tune. "After, she stopped singing. Stopped rocking. It felt like she closed up, tight as an oyster. Daddy would go to hug her and she'd just stand there with arms stiff at her sides.

"She didn't get mad. She didn't cry. She didn't . . . anything but what absolutely had to be done. Kept us clean and fed, the house neat as a pin. Barely noticed when the boys used her good sheets to dress up as Sand People and turned her flower bed into a Tatooine battlefield. She even closed down to Evelyn for a while. But Evelyn was persistent. Wouldn't take no. She'd stop by every few days. An angel food cake. A banana bread. A casserole. Your grandma would take it and then talk to her through the screen door. Drove Evelyn nuts.

"I think their friendship survived because of the dolls. They kept making them. I realize now how hard it was for my mother. She was doing what she needed to do to get through the day. But she was more like a scarecrow than a person.

"So, to answer your question, yes, things changed. *She* changed. Then she changed again when you came along, didn't she?" Lis reached across and squeezed Vanessa's arm. "She thawed. Got her heart back."

Vanessa said, "You know, it's an amazing thing. The resilience of the human psyche. How pain can be tamped down and hidden for a lifetime. Grandma Sorrel couldn't bear the possibility of losing you, too."

That simple truth was one that Lis hadn't understood herself until she'd had Vanessa.

14

Palmetto Court turned out to be a mobile home park off bucolic-sounding Meadowlake Drive. Vanessa could smell the "lake," a swampy affair across the street from a gas station and liquor store. A few scraggly palmettos, their trunks surrounded by whitewashed stones, flanked the entrance to the park.

Vanessa turned into the narrow lane that ran between rows of single-wides set on concrete slabs. She hit the first speed bump too fast and slowed to the posted speed limit, fifteen miles an hour, as she drove past lots that barely accommodated a mobile home and a driveway. One front yard was planted with a pair of trees, pruned into perfect rounds with plaster bunny rabbits frolicking at their bases. Next door, a red Ford pickup with a bashed-in tailgate sat on tireless rims in a barren yard alongside a nearly windowless mobile home with a massive TV satellite dish hanging off the back. Through the front window you could see a torn shade pulled over a collapsed venetian blind.

Near the end of the second block, number 25 sat on a tidy barren lot. Vanessa parked in front. The home was basic, not much more than a flatbed shipping container with windows and a door punched in.

"This place is creepy," Lis said, giving a shudder. "We could easily have ended up living somewhere like this if it hadn't been for your grandmother."

"Looks as if our Miss Richards isn't home," Vanessa said. No car in the driveway. Curtains drawn. "Shall we go see?"

"Not we. You. If she's home, she'll recognize me, and I'm not sure she'd even open the door. Your grandma and I didn't part with her on the coziest of terms. Binty near tore her to pieces."

"Binty?"

"Surprised me, too."

Vanessa opened the car door. The street felt sad, not dangerous. Still, Vanessa had to push herself to get out of the car, and once out she felt extremely exposed. "Mom, get in the driver's seat, would you?" she said to Lis. "And keep the engine running."

Lis came around and took Vanessa's place at the wheel, cell phone at the ready.

Pebbles crunched under Vanessa's feet as she walked up the driveway and across a footpath to wooden steps that led to a side entrance. Alongside the door was a vigorous geranium, a splash of red against the dingy putty-colored siding. She climbed the steps. The window by the front door was open, and from inside she could hear voices. Laughter. Applause. Music. A TV was going.

At the door, Vanessa hesitated. Her neck prickled as a car drove slowly by and parked in front of the trailer two doors down. A man in a baseball cap, hoodie, and dark glasses got out, stared at her for a few moments, and went inside. Vanessa glanced back at her rental car. Lis, sitting at the wheel, motioned for her to ring the bell.

Vanessa never opened the door to someone she didn't know.

She took a deep breath and pushed the doorbell. Then she forced an innocuous smile.

The TV sound continued. She didn't hear footsteps. She knocked and waited some more. When no one came, she leaned past the railing so she could look in through the narrow opening between the curtains in the window. She caught a whiff of cigarette smoke, but all she could make out was a dark empty kitchen.

She knocked again. There was a pile of about a half-dozen brightly painted stones surrounding the potted geranium. She picked one up. Turned out they weren't stones but mounds of glazed pottery, each one just big enough to fit in the palm of your hand. The background was painted burnt umber. Over that, in gold, was a round, cherubic smiling face surrounded by curls and a pair of wings. The image reminded her of angels she'd seen in cemeteries incised into very old stones that marked the graves of children. *Memento mori.* But those angels had skulls, not faces, floating between their wings. Still, even with this simple sweet face, the image of these angels felt tinged with loss.

Vanessa remembered her mother's description of the tattoo she'd glimpsed on the small of the woman's back. Had it been Harley eagle wings or this: a sweet-faced cherub?

She was about to knock again when she heard a hollow tinny blast that took her a moment to place as a car horn. Vanessa turned away from the door to see a car roll up behind hers. Dinged, dirty, belching exhaust, the off-white car parked behind hers. Vanessa couldn't see, but she guessed that its trunk was held down with a bungee cord. A woman about her age got out.

"Get away from there!" The woman charged at Vanessa, shaking her fist, her long hair streaming behind her. Had to be Miss Richards.

Vanessa came down the steps. The woman stopped just a few feet away, breathing hard, her face red. "They promised me no one would come to the house." What Vanessa had taken to be rage and anger at first, up close looked more like fear or anxiety. "Go away. I told them—"

"I'm sorry!" Vanessa put her hands up. "I'm sorry. I didn't mean to intrude. It's just that—"

"What don't you people get about *leave us alone?*" The woman pulled herself up. She tugged down her dark blazer and smoothed her skirt. "I told them we don't need your damned help."

We? Did she have family living in that trailer with her? "I don't know who you think I am. My mother and I just came to ask a few questions about the doll."

"The doll?" The woman went still. She turned to look at Vanessa's car where Lis sat at the wheel. "You're not from Social Services?"

Vanessa shook her head.

"Then you really have no business here. Who the hell are you?"

"My name is Vanessa Strenger. I'm Sorrel Woodham's granddaughter." Vanessa paused to see if the name meant anything to her. It didn't seem to. "My mother is Elisabeth Woodham Strenger." She pointed to the car. "We came to ask you about the doll you brought to our house a few days ago."

The woman took a step back, her gaze wary. "What doll?"

"Are you telling me you didn't answer an ad in the paper and bring a doll over to my grandmother's house two days ago?"

Lis stepped out of the car and slammed the door. "Remember me?" She started walking toward them.

"We're not trying to hurt you or get in your face," Vanessa said. "But that doll you brought over to my grandmother's house? You didn't stay long enough to collect the reward."

Maggie Richards folded her arms. She wasn't buying it. Vanessa wished they'd stopped at the bank on the way over so she could flash some hundred-dollar bills in Maggie's face to show good faith.

"It's yours," Vanessa said. "I promise. Five thousand dollars. Just as soon as you tell us where you found the doll."

"The ad didn't say that."

"The doll belonged to my sister, Janey," Lis said. "She disappeared forty years ago, when she was four years old. That doll disappeared with her. So you can understand why we're willing to pay so much to find out where you got it."

The woman chewed on her bottom lip. "I just answered the ad. It didn't say anything about a little girl. And I gave you and that old lady the damned doll."

"That old lady is my mother," Lis said. "Every year she places that ad even though everyone tells her it's futile. For forty years she's never given up hope. And now you turn up with her doll. You can understand why we're desperate for you to tell us how you got it."

"Found it." Maggie Richards gave an uneasy look over Vanessa's shoulder toward the door to the home. Then back at Lis. "I don't know where it came from and she doesn't either." She folded her arms across her chest.

Lis said, "There's someone in the house? Was it her doll?" Vanessa could hear the hope and desperation in her mother's voice.

"She won't talk to you. She doesn't trust strangers. You go near her and so help me, I'll call the police." Maggie Richards narrowed her eyes at Lis. "Besides, I don't believe you. If it's so important, why didn't your mother come here herself?"

"Because she's in the hospital," Lis shot back. "The night after you came to us with the doll, our house was robbed and we had a gas leak. She's being treated for carbon monoxide poisoning and a heart attack."

Maggie blinked. "I'm real sorry about your mother," she said, her tone softening. "And I'm real sorry about your sister, too. I saw the ad in the paper. It looked like an old doll my mother had from when she was a kid. Even when we were living on the street, she hung on to it. We kept it in the trunk when we were living in the car." It was quite the hard luck story. Something about it felt rehearsed. Vanessa resisted the urge to mime playing a tiny violin. "Then we got a rent subsidy so we could move into this." Maggie gestured toward the mobile home. "And my mother left the doll in the car, like she forgot about it. So I thought, well, if there was a reward, we could sure use the money. But the last thing she needs"—her voice rose, revving again with outrage— "is for you people to come here and harass—"

The door to the mobile home swung open. In the doorway stood an older woman, her dark hair short and curled tight around her head, her cheeks sallow. She wore tight jeans and a hot-pink tube top that made her look even more skeletal than she was. "Maggie?" the woman said in a hoarse voice. She coughed. Puffed on a cigarette. "I thought you said they wouldn't come sniffin' around."

"It's okay, Momma. They're not from Social Services. And they're leaving." Maggie Richards turned to Vanessa and Lis. "Right now."

15

"I'm Lissie," Lis said to the woman standing outside the door of the trailer. "Lissie" was the name Janey used to call her. She looked for a flicker of recognition in the woman's expression as her brow creased.

Could this be Janey? The woman, whose hand shook as she took another drag from a cigarette she held between stubby fingers, was about the right age. But nothing else about her stirred in Lis a memory of her sister. Her hair wasn't fair and fine, it was dark and short and permed into a tight frizz around her head. Yes, there were shadows under her eyes, but this woman radiated raw nerves. She probably didn't get enough sleep. Her eyes were light, but were they that spooky blue that Lis remembered, so pale that the color seemed to leach into the white surrounding her irises? Lis wasn't close enough to tell.

The woman dropped the cigarette on the top step, mashed it out, and kicked it into the dirt with the toe of a sneaker spattered with gold paint. Her eyes narrowed. "Not from Social Services?"

"They're not," Maggie said.

"From the church?" The woman looked down at Lis with

contempt. "Take your preaching somewhere else. We're not interested."

"They're not from the church, either, Momma. And they're leaving." Maggie turned to Vanessa. "Please go now. She doesn't know you. She doesn't know anyone and she doesn't want to know anyone."

The woman's gaze shifted and she stared off down the street. With her head turned toward the sun, the shadows under her eyes disappeared and her eyes telegraphed growing agitation. Lis followed her gaze to a police cruiser that was rolling slowly toward them.

"Police?" She spat out the word. "What the hell do they want with us now? Did you call them?" she said to Lis.

"Momma," Maggie said. Then louder, "Mom!" The woman looked across at her. "Don't freak out. I'm sure it's got nothing to do with us."

"Then why is he stopping here?"

"He's not."

But the cruiser pulled up and parked right behind Vanessa's rental car. BONSECOURS POLICE. Frank Ames got out and stood there, hanging on the open car door. He tipped his cap back with the heel of his hand and squinted across at Lis and Vanessa. "What in Sam Hill are you two doing here?" he said. "I thought I told you to back off and let me . . ."

I thought I . . . Lis blocked out the rest of his words, suddenly furious. That was the tone of voice Brad used to take with her, instructing her on what she could and couldn't do, what she should have made for dinner after something else was already cooked, what opinion she should have held instead of the patently stupid one she'd just expressed.

"So this is the car?" Frank said with a granite scowl. Lis could almost hear the gears shift in his head as he moved closer to Maggie's car, stooped to look at the license plate, and inspected the battered rear. Then he crossed the lawn to where Maggie stood. "Are you Maggie Richards? I'm Deputy Chief Frank Ames, Bonsecours Police. Is that your car?"

Maggie barely glanced at the ID he showed her, her anxious attention tethered to her mother.

When she didn't answer, Frank said, "Ma'am?"

Maggie stuck her chin out. "Yes, *sir.* Yes, it is."

"Broken taillight. Detached bumper. Condition it's in, that car is a menace."

Maggie looked from Lis to Frank and back again. "He's a friend of yours? Thanks a lot."

Frank said, "Then there's the matter of some overnight parking tickets you never bothered to pay. A few dozen, in fact."

Maggie faced Frank. "We were living in the car. All right? And I had to park somewhere, didn't I? They don't bother to tell you where you can and can't park overnight. It's like some closely held secret, like where they hide the public toilets. And if we'd had the money to pay the tickets we wouldn't have been sleepin' in the car."

Frank barely blinked. "Expired registration, too."

Maggie swallowed hard. "Please," she said. "I just started a new job, and as soon as I've saved up some money, I promise I'll—"

"That's enough. Clear off!" That came from Maggie's mother. She must have gone back into the house because now she was standing on the top step holding a gun. The double-barreled, break-action shotgun looked a lot like one Lis's father loaded with shells filled with rock salt to keep squirrels and rabbits from plundering their kitchen garden. Old-fashioned but effective.

"I don't care who you are," she said, jerking the butt upright so the barrel clicked shut. "You got no business marching in here and threatening us. We waited for years to get this place with no help from your kind. My daughter paid for that car with money she saved. Don't think I don't know what you're up to."

"Mom, it's okay. Please," Maggie said. "I can pay the parking tickets and register the car. You're just making things worse. Put that old thing away. I don't mind answering his questions."

"Well, I mind. I don't want any policemen here. Git." Her mother waved the gun. "Clear. Out. All a you all. This is private property and you got no business here."

"Ma'am," Frank said, making a placating gesture, "I know you don't want to shoot anyone. So please, put the gun down." He paused. "If you don't, I'm going to have to call for backup. Then I'll have to have you arrested and your daughter's car towed away. Or you can put down the gun and we can have a nice, calm—"

Slowly, deliberately Frank reached into his pocket. At the same time, there was a click. Maggie's mother had pulled back the hammer and cocked the gun.

Frank said, "Put. The gun. Down."

"I know that song and dance," Maggie's mother said. "Then you round us up and get us thrown out of here. I know what you're up to. Hiding behind that badge. You sent those women to soften us up?"

"Mom, they just want to know about that old doll of yours," Maggie said.

Her mother went still. "Doll?"

"The doll of yours that was in the trunk of our car? I answered an ad. They wanted to buy it for five thousand dollars."

"Five thousand dollars?" Maggie's mother laughed. "They must think we just fell off the turnip truck."

"Really," Lis said. "All we want to know is where you got the doll. There really is a five-thousand-dollar reward, and it's yours if—"

"If what?" The gun wavered. "Who really sent you?" She swung the gun around and aimed at Lis.

In the instant before Lis dropped to the ground, something flew past her. Maggie's mother's head jerked back and she went down like she'd been kicked by a mule, banging her chin on a railing on the way down. The gun fell into the grass.

Frank was up the steps in two leaps with Maggie right behind. The woman was out cold. Blood flowed from her mouth where it looked like she'd bitten her lip. More blood coursed across her forehead and pooled on the floor. Lis had to look away.

Frank checked the woman's pulse, then dashed over to the cruiser and pulled a first aid kit from the front seat. He raced back. Punched in a number on his phone. Cradling his phone between his face and his shoulder, he opened the first aid kit. Found latex gloves, which he snapped on. Then got out a packet and opened it with his teeth, pulling out a gauze pad that he pressed to Maggie's mother's face.

"I need an ambulance," he said. "Twenty-five Palmetto Court. Female. Knocked unconscious by a rock a minute ago. Pulse one ten. Bleeding from the forehead and lower lip." He turned to Maggie. "What's your mother's name?"

"Jenny," Maggie said. "Jenny Richards."

Frank repeated that information for the dispatcher. Moments later he pocketed the phone. "They're on their way. They said not to move her until they get here."

16

Frank stayed hunkered down beside Jenny Richards on the steps of the trailer waiting for the ambulance. Maggie stood motionless at the foot of the steps, as if in shock. All the shouting, followed by a siren, had brought neighbors out onto their lawns.

Lis crept over to Maggie. "I'm so sorry this is happening. We had no idea the police would come, or that he'd threaten you and your mother like that."

"When you're homeless, that's what they do. They make you feel like shit," Maggie said as she watched the ambulance pull to a halt behind the police cruiser. The siren went mute and the passenger-side door burst open.

Lis and Maggie backed away as an EMT, a burly guy with a close-cropped beard, burst from the ambulance, dashed up the trailer steps, and crouched by Jenny's side. He wore dark blue trousers and a shirt with an official shield-shaped patch on his shoulder. He took her pulse and shined a penlight in each of her eyes.

"And we've been homeless off and on my whole life," Maggie added under her breath. "You can't blame us for not trusting police."

The EMT conferred with Frank, and Frank came over to

Maggie. "They need to know if your mother has health insurance," Frank said.

"She has Medicaid. I'll get the card," Maggie said and ran inside.

"This is your fault," Lis said to Frank.

"I told you to let me follow up."

"I might have if you'd told me you were going to track her down and come right over here."

"I'd have told you that if you'd told me you were coming here. You could have gotten yourself killed." There he went again, like she was the little woman who didn't have sense enough to come in out of the rain.

"*You* could have gotten us killed. Stomping in like a storm trooper. Threatening them."

Maggie came back out with her mother's health insurance card. The EMT took it and keyed the information into a tablet.

"May I see?" Frank said.

Grudgingly, Maggie nodded. Frank took the card and copied information into his notebook before handing it back to Maggie. Casually Frank flipped his notebook around so Lis could read. JENNY RICHARDS DOB SEPTEMBER 9, 1972.

He pointed to the year. Nineteen seventy-two was a year after Lis was born. Two years before Janey had been born.

The EMTs were loading Jenny on a stretcher. In a minute she'd be gone. Alone, one-on-one, that was the only shot Lis had of getting Jenny to tell her where she'd gotten Janey's doll.

"You'd better pack her a bag," Lis said to Maggie. "Whatever you think she'll need if they have to keep her overnight. Glasses. Medication. A toothbrush."

Maggie ran into the house and Lis went over to the ambulance driver. "Where are you taking her?"

"Coastal Memorial."

"Coastal Memorial," Lis relayed to Vanessa. "Meet me there." She climbed into the back of the ambulance with Jenny Richards.

"Hey!" The driver came around and motioned for her to get out. "No passengers back there."

"I need to be here if she wakes up." Lis scootched back on the cushioned bench. "She's phobic, afraid of men in uniforms, and she's got PTSD. You'll have your hands full if she comes to and freaks out when all she sees is your friend here." She indicated the burly bearded EMT who was about to climb in.

"It's against regulations. No one rides in back except—"

Lis slid farther in and took Jenny's hand. "You're not going to stand around arguing with me, are you? She needs to get to the hospital."

"Ma'am, you have to get out. Now."

"If she were four years old, you'd let a relative ride in back with her, wouldn't you?"

"She's not four," he said, but Lis could feel him wavering, probably weighing how much trouble it would be to climb in and wedge her out of there versus how much trouble he'd be in if he didn't.

Frank came over and pulled him aside. Lis watched as they talked, the driver pointing in her direction and getting more exasperated by the moment. Frank shaking his head. Looking at his watch. Gesturing with open hands, like what could he do.

The driver trudged back alone, avoiding eye contact with Lis. The bearded EMT got in the back with her, closed the doors, and showed Lis how to buckle herself in. She waited until the ambulance was on its way, the siren blaring, before she indulged in a fist pump.

17

Vanessa had been stunned to see Lis climb brazenly into the back of the ambulance. Even more so that no one extracted her. The ambulance kicked up a cloud of dust as it screamed out of the trailer park.

"Heads up," Officer Frank said, tossing Vanessa an angel paperweight he picked up from the ground near the steps to the trailer. She caught it. "Lucky shot?"

"Girls' fast-pitch softball. Three-season state champs."

"Thanks. I owe you."

Vanessa dropped the angel paperweight into her pocket. "No, you don't. I had to do something. I was afraid you were going to make her shoot someone."

"She wasn't about to do that." Officer Frank picked up the shotgun from the grass. He broke it open. "Not loaded." He turned and eyed the mobile home. "Soon as I get back to the office, I'll run a background check on both of them and see what I can find out. Promise me you'll bring me the doll. There could be some forensic evidence, even now, that will help us tell if it was Janey's doll."

"I will."

"Today."

Vanessa gave him a little salute.

"I know Miss Sorrel thinks that doll is Janey's," Officer Frank went on, "but she hasn't seen it in forty years. Wishful thinking can cloud judgment. It's like eyewitness testimony; these days we take it with a grain of salt and corroborate with hard evidence."

He was right. More than anything Vanessa wanted her mother and grandmother to find some kind of resolution to the mystery of Janey's disappearance, but that didn't warrant jumping to conclusions. Still, if—big *if*—the doll turned out to be Janey's, it might lead them to finding her bones.

Maggie backed out the front door of the mobile home. She set down a canvas bag, locked the door, turned around, and blinked toward the empty spot on the street where the ambulance had been parked. "They're gone?" She glared at Vanessa. "She's alone?"

"Not alone. My mother went with her."

"*Your* mother? I'm her daughter. She needs me." Maggie hurried over to her car. She opened the front passenger door and was about to toss her bag in when Officer Frank stopped her.

"Sorry," he said. "I can't let you drive that. Not until it's properly registered."

"But—"

"Let me drive you," Vanessa said. "It's the least I can do. And I'll drive you back here later, too."

Maggie held her bag to her chest and squinted at Vanessa. "Why are you doing this? Any of this? Chasing me down. Making my mother go crazy. And now, acting like my new best friend?"

"I feel responsible. If my grandmother hadn't posted that ad, if we hadn't shown up here out of the blue—"

"If *he* hadn't shown up," Maggie said. "Nothing freaks my mother out more than an officer in uniform."

Vanessa popped open the trunk of her car. Maggie hung there, uncertain. Vanessa gently pried the canvas bag from her arms, set it in the trunk, and pressed the lid shut. Opened the passenger door of the rental car.

Maggie's gaze traveled from Vanessa, to Officer Frank, and then down the street where the ambulance had driven off. Finally she closed her own car door and got in Vanessa's car.

Vanessa slid into the driver's seat and started the car. "You want the windows open?"

Maggie sat stiff in the passenger seat. She shook her head.

Vanessa drove slowly out of the mobile home park and onto Meadowlake Drive. When they were stopped at a red light, Vanessa said, "So you're a student?"

"That cop tell you that?"

The light turned green and Vanessa accelerated. "Parking sticker on your car. I'm a student, too."

Maggie slid Vanessa an appraising look. "I'm finishing my degree. Probably *was* finishing it, now that I have this to deal with." She gazed out the window as they passed a sign in front of a Baptist church: IN THE DARK? COME IN. "And I thought things were finally turning around for us. We really could have used that reward." She shook her head. "Shoulda known. Sounded too good to be true. Now it's all gone to shit."

"It hasn't," Vanessa said. "*That cop* is going to run some tests. If the doll turns out to be Janey's, you'll get the reward." And if not? Vanessa had to stop herself from offering to help Maggie and her mother if the doll turned out not to be Janey's. She was wary of getting too involved with such hyperbolic personalities. Besides, even if the doll turned out to be Janey's, these women might be scam artists. "Why did you run off after you brought over the doll?"

"You wouldn't understand." Maggie folded her arms across her chest.

Right, Vanessa thought. *Assume the worst and shut down.* "You have no clue what I would or wouldn't understand."

Maggie stared out the window for a long time. "I freaked out. I don't know how my mother got the doll, and it's entirely possible that it was stolen, and that's all we needed. Felony charges. You'd stir things up, the cops would show up, and Mom would go ballistic . . . just like she did. And we'd be back to square one. Which is exactly where we are."

"You said you and your mom have been in and out of homeless shelters?"

"You wouldn't know anything about what that's like, would you?" Maggie said with a bitter laugh.

Vanessa didn't take the bait, though she knew full well that she and Lis could easily have found themselves homeless if Grandma Sorrel hadn't come to the rescue when they'd hit bottom. "But you're not in a homeless shelter now."

"I have no illusions about where we're living." Maggie gave a tiny smile. "It's a trailer. Not even an apartment. But it beats a shelter. We qualified for a rent subsidy. Finally. I'm starting a job, or I was. I still can't afford to get my car fixed or pay off my parking tickets, but we've got a place to live and health insurance, and Mom really is much more stable now that she's taking something. No more nightmares, thank God for that." Maggie bit her thumbnail. "As you can see, she is still traumatized. But she'd never have shot anyone."

"Not deliberately, I'm sure," Vanessa said. Still, Jenny's waving around that gun had been scary as hell. "Has she always been like that?"

"Hair-trigger temper? Paranoid? On the edge of a nervous breakdown? Superprotective and private is what it boils down to. But you would be too if you'd been through what she has."

"Where did she grow up?" Vanessa held her breath as she waited for an answer.

"Somewhere near Charleston."

Feeling as if she were taking a tiny step out onto thin ice, Vanessa asked, "Do you know if she was adopted?"

"Adopted?" Maggie seemed surprised. "No. Though she never talks about her childhood. Just that her parents were religious and strict. She ran away from home when she was fifteen. Lived on the streets, did drugs, made money the only way she could." Maggie kneaded her hands together. "Even she doesn't know who my father is, and frankly I don't care. Because after she had me, she changed. Stopped doing drugs. Worked wherever she could find a job. Made sure we had somewhere to sleep, even if it was a tent or a homeless shelter. Most important thing, she used to say, was to keep me in school. It was a promise she made to me and to herself."

"You make her sound pretty heroic."

"Too good to be true, is that what you're saying?" Maggie said.

Vanessa felt herself flush. Was she that transparent?

"She is," Maggie went on. "And now I'm trying to pay her back, best I can. Anyway, all's I know about that doll is that she kept it. When we were living in the car, the doll was in the trunk. When she didn't bring it into the trailer, I didn't say anything because I was relieved that she wouldn't drag that dirty old thing into our nice clean house. So when I saw your ad, I thought it would be okay to bring it to you. Holy cow, five thousand dollars." She whistled. "We all know how well that went."

Vanessa hesitated before asking one more prying question. "You never met your grandparents?"

"Are you kidding? My mother is still afraid that they'll show up on our doorstep. Come after me. She swears that if she had to go back to that place, she'd kill herself. That's what I grew up being afraid of. That she would."

18

Lis had to hang on to a strap as the ambulance accelerated up the main road, but her attention was focused on the woman lying unconscious on the stretcher next to her. In the harsh light in the ambulance, Jenny Richards's face seemed deathly pale against the fresh bandaging the EMT was applying to the gash in her head. The blood-soaked gauze pad that Frank had pressed to the wound had been discarded in a waste receptacle mounted to the ambulance wall.

The EMT raised one of Jenny's eyelids and flashed a light into her eye. Then he did the same to the other eye. Up close, Lis could see that Jenny's eyes were blue. A very pale blue.

This could be Janey.

Lis snaked her hand under the blanket, found Jenny's hand, and held it. Just as Miss Sorrel had lived in a bubble, believing that Jenny couldn't be dead, Lis had never let herself seriously consider that Janey could be alive. The Janey Lis had imagined for so long was wearing a pale blue nightgown, angel wings sprouting from her back, and a golden halo overhead, a far cry from this. If Jenny Richards was Janey, did she even remember that she'd once lived in a cozy white house near the water? That wisteria bloomed outside her window? That she'd had a sister and three brothers? Did she have any idea that her older sister had left her vulnerable to being scooped up? How had she ended up so clearly traumatized, and how much of her past was buried in her subconscious?

And the doll. Had she held on to that doll all these years because it was the one tenuous link she had to a past she could barely remember, or one that she was trying to forget? Those were all questions Lis couldn't answer. Maybe Vanessa, with her fancy Ph.D. and psychology experience, would have a theory.

A simple DNA test would answer the big question: Was Jenny Janey?

The ambulance stopped and the back doors opened. Attendants pulled Jenny's stretcher out and the bearded attendant who'd ridden inside followed. Just before Lis crawled out, she pulled a latex glove from a box dispenser, put it on, grabbed the blood-soaked gauze from the trash, and peeled the glove off inside out around the gauze. Just like the plastic bags she used to pick up Binty's poops, the glove became a makeshift pouch to protect the blood sample.

She was no expert, but she was pretty sure that fresh blood made a more suitable sample for DNA testing than a few strands of hair that had been cut twenty years ago.

Nothing about the emergency receiving area looked remotely familiar to Lis, though she and Miss Sorrel most certainly had been wheeled through there after they'd been pulled unconscious from the house. All she remembered was waking up alone. Feeling so sick that she could barely lift her head and not knowing where she was or what had happened to her. Lis was determined that when Jenny woke up, someone would be there to tell her what hit her.

Lis tried to trail behind as Jenny's stretcher was pushed through double doors and into the treatment area, but a woman wearing scrubs and a name tag stopped her. "Sorry, you need to wait out here."

"But she needs someone to stay with her," Lis said. "She'll freak out."

"She needs to be assessed and treated. If she needs you, we'll come get you. Promise. Please take a seat." The woman pulled the door closed.

Lis turned and took in the waiting area. Metal chairs with orange plastic seats were lined up under the windows along two walls. About a half-dozen people were waiting, several staring like zombies at a television monitor where thick red liquid was pouring into a glass. Lis's stomach turned over before she realized it was a commercial for V8 juice. Then *Wheel of Fortune* resumed.

Lis sat down where she couldn't see the screen, but the snare drums, trumpet sounds, and Pat Sajak's voice were impossible to ignore. Ten minutes later, *Wheel* was over and Dr. Oz was going on about the virtues of bean burgers. Reduce blood sugar! Burn off fat! Lis wouldn't have been surprised if next he claimed bean burgers were a cure for impotence and an antiaging elixir. She wished she had earplugs.

Just then, Vanessa and Maggie rushed in. "Where is she?" Maggie said. "Is she all right? Did she ask for me?"

"She was still unconscious when they wheeled her in," Lis said.

"I need to be with her," Maggie said.

"Good luck with that," Lis said. "I tried. They said they'd be out to tell us once she's been assessed."

"Oh, God," Maggie said. "She's going to flip out when she comes to and she's surrounded by strangers. Isn't there any way I can get in there?" She gave Lis a long, pleading look. "Don't you know anyone who can pull strings?"

Of course Lis did. Why hadn't it occurred to her earlier? Evelyn had worked at the hospital for years. According to her, she'd practically run the place. She'd still be with Miss Sorrel, waiting for Lis and Vanessa to take over.

Lis didn't want to get Maggie's hopes up. She excused herself to go to the ladies' room and, instead, made her way to her mother's room.

Another favor from Evelyn. Lis groaned as she rode up in the elevator. She'd long ago recognized how Evelyn wielded her generosity as a form of control. For every jelly donut or slice of pecan pie or basket of fried chicken that she brought over, Lis had to endure a smothering hug, always laden with reminders that Evelyn was Lis's godmother and her mother's best friend. But strings attached or not, Evelyn could elbow her way around rules like nobody's business.

She found Evelyn standing in the hallway outside Miss Sorrel's room. When she saw Lis, she pointedly looked at her watch, as if Lis didn't realize that it was well past the time when she'd promised to be there.

"I'm sorry we got delayed," Lis said, "but I have a good excuse." Quickly she told Evelyn about the flat tires, then about going to find the woman who'd brought them Janey's doll. "She lives with her mother. In a trailer."

Evelyn sniffed. "Of course she does."

Ignoring that, Lis continued, "Frank followed us to the trailer. Turns out the mother's terrified of police. She brought out a gun and Vanessa hit her with a rock and knocked her out. And now she's in the ER. Alone. And I know you can get them to bend the rules so her daughter can go in and sit with her."

Evelyn considered that for a moment. "I probably could. But I'm not sure why I would."

Evelyn was going to make her grovel. Lis lowered her eyes and gritted her teeth. "Of course you were right. We shouldn't have gone looking for her. But it seemed worth the risk. If she'll tell us where she got the doll, then we're one step closer than we've ever been to finding out what happened to Janey."

Evelyn narrowed her eyes, then drew herself up. "You leave it to me, Lissie. Stay here with your mother and I'll see what I can do."

19

A half hour after they'd arrived at the hospital, Vanessa and Maggie were still waiting for someone to update them on Jenny Richards's condition and Lis was nowhere to be found. Vanessa had tried texting her mother and was about to go searching for her when Evelyn marched through the double doors wearing a starched white nurse's uniform, a cap pinned to her hair, and a stethoscope wrapped around her neck. She barely glanced in Vanessa's direction as she sailed past, not checking in with anyone as she swiped her badge through a reader and pushed her way through double doors and into the treatment area.

"That's our friend," Vanessa said. "My mother probably got her to come down. If anyone can get a rule bent around here, she can."

Maggie folded her arms tight across her chest and paced back and forth in front of the doors through which Evelyn had disappeared. She strained to see through the small panes of glass.

After a few minutes, Evelyn reappeared. Maggie rushed up to her. "How is she?"

"You must be the daughter," Evelyn said, stone-faced. She glanced at Vanessa, then turned to Maggie and pursed her lips. "You'd best tell me the truth. What's your mother on?"

"On?" Maggie said.

"There's obviously something more going on than a head bump and a split lip. What is your mother taking?"

"I . . . I don't know." Maggie looked stricken. "Something for anxiety." She opened the canvas bag she'd packed with her mother's things, rummaged around, and came up with a zippered cosmetic bag.

Evelyn took it from her and dumped the contents out into the seat of a chair. At first glance, it looked to Vanessa like the typical innocuous assortment that anyone would grab on the way out of the house for an overnight. Aspirin and Advil. Calcium chews and eyedrops. Toothbrush and toothpaste. A couple of vials of pills.

Evelyn singled out an amber vial. Opened it and shook some white, lozenge-shaped pills into her palm. "How long's she been taking these?"

"I have no idea. I've never seen them before."

"This," Evelyn said, picking up one of the pills and pulling a face, "is Endocet. A painkiller."

"Painkiller?" Maggie thought a moment. "Her doctor must have prescribed that after the car accident. About a month ago. Mom wrenched her neck. Like I said, all I know about is Ativan. She's been taking that for a few months. It's supposed to make her less anxious."

"Well, this is not Ativan," Evelyn said, "and no one would prescribe it for anxiety. You've heard of the painkiller oxycodone? Endocet is one of the brand names for that narcotic, with the same active ingredient. It's highly addictive. When they brought your mother in, her blood levels were through the roof. And from the looks of it"—she held up the vial—"she didn't get it from a pharmacist."

"What's that supposed to mean?" Maggie said.

"There's no label. No script."

"I don't believe it. Where else would she get a prescription drug? She rarely leaves the house and never alone. Plus she hates drugs. Even convincing her to take Ativan was hard. She used to be—" Maggie stopped herself.

"I know." Evelyn gave a smug smile. "A drug addict. So she'd know how to get drugs."

"She'd know, but she wouldn't. She hasn't been down that road, not for years. Why would she start using now? I'm telling you, I've never, ever seen her take a single one of those pills."

"Right, because she was taking them when no one was looking because she knew what they were. She's been taking a lot. Much more than is safe." Evelyn put the pills back in the container, snapped it shut, and dropped it into her pocket. "Maybe it started innocently. Her doctor prescribed a painkiller and before she knew it she needed more and more to get the same relief. And if she has a history of drug usage, well, she's more prone to overmedicating herself. And she has the contacts she needs to get more."

"No way. This is crazy," Maggie said.

"Endocet has a short half-life," Evelyn said, "and I'm afraid she's already in withdrawal. If she goes cold turkey . . ." Evelyn raised her eyebrows and shook her head.

"What?" Maggie asked.

"Days of vomiting. Cramps. Night sweats. Acute anxiety. Depression. Insomnia. Paranoia and delusional thinking. She'll feel as if she's going to jump out of her skin. You can't just take her home. She shouldn't be left alone."

Maggie dropped onto a bench and put her head in her hands. "It just keeps getting worse, doesn't it? When am I going to catch a break?"

"I'm afraid this isn't about you, dear," Evelyn said.

Evelyn could be so damned officious and tone-deaf. Vanessa wanted to slap her.

Evelyn said, "It's almost impossible to go through withdrawal without a relapse. Not without medical intervention. Fortunately, the hospital has a detoxification unit and they have a bed free. I checked." *Of course you did,* Vanessa thought. "They'll keep her under general anesthesia through the most painful part, then bring her back sedated, and keep her here through the next critical days until she's back up on her pins."

Maggie looked so deflated and bleak, Vanessa sat down and put her arm around her. "I've worked with people who've been through terrible traumas. From everything you've told me, it sounds like your mother is tough and resilient. And if Evelyn says they know what they're doing here, you can believe that they do."

"Oh, they know what they're doing," Evelyn said. "But I won't sugarcoat it. It will be rough. It takes days to recover, and though there will be nurses on the unit, these days they're stretched thin. I'd recommend strongly that you hire someone to monitor her care round the clock."

"A private nurse? Around the clock?" Maggie was ashen. "But we can't even afford . . ." She stared off into the middle distance, her jaw clenched. "I'll do it. I'll call and tell them I can't start the job. I'll take a leave of absence from school if I need to. Get my car fixed and registered."

Vanessa couldn't shake the thought that none of this would be happening if she hadn't leaned on Gary's wife to look up Maggie's address. Officer Frank would have treaded much more softly approaching Jenny if he hadn't felt he needed to show Lis and Vanessa that he was in charge. "You'll do no such thing," she said. "I'm staying for at least another week anyway." Another week away from the lab wouldn't be the end of the world, and, besides, she could always work on her grant proposal here.

"You?" Evelyn said. "Vanessa, Elisabeth is barely out of the hospital herself, and neither of you know a thing about withdrawal or psychiatric nursing care. What if she vomits while she's under anesthesia? Or has a seizure? Or codes in her sleep? Or has hallucinations? Or tries to hurt herself? Someone should be there with her the minute she comes out of anesthesia. Sakes alive, would either of you have even the slightest notion what to do? It's not as if you're going to have time to google it."

She smoothed her uniform. "You need somebody a lot more qualified, a private duty nurse who knows her way around this hospital and knows what kind of support a recovery like this requires."

Somebody a lot more qualified. Evelyn had to realize that she was setting herself up, or was she too fixated on being a know-it-all? "You're absolutely right. It has to be someone with the training and experience," Vanessa said, laying it on thick. "Someone we trust. Too bad we can't get you, Evelyn. You'd know exactly what to do."

Evelyn smiled. "It's been ages since I was a duty nurse, but staff will be there to help. As I say, it's been awhile though . . ." For a few moments she seemed to be thinking. She had that way of settling herself that reminded Vanessa of a plump hen, preening and ruffling her feathers. "I might consider doing it. Yes, I might be able to help. After all, Buck and I were Janey's godparents."

"We don't know if she's our Janey," Vanessa said quickly.

"She's not your Janey," Maggie said.

"No, she's probably not," Evelyn said. "But Miss Sorrel thinks she could be. I'd be doing this for her."

"My mother's not a drug addict," Maggie said.

"Blood levels don't lie," Evelyn shot back.

Maggie shifted uncomfortably. "I have no way to pay you."

"Maggie, honey," Evelyn said, just as sweet as pie, "you'll re-pay me by finishing your course work, starting your new job, and getting your car repaired and registered so's you can drive your momma home when she's clean."

"We've always taken care of ourselves," Maggie said, her jaw set.

"It's no sin," Evelyn said, "to accept a little help. And a bless-ing to be able to give it."

20

"I don't mean to judge, but you know drug addicts are compulsive liars," Evelyn said to Vanessa as they walked to the parking lot. The sun was low in the sky, making some of the hospital windows look as if they were on fire.

Vanessa was heading home to pick up the doll and take it to Frank at the police station. She'd checked in with Lis, who'd assured her that the nurses said they didn't need one of them, never mind both of them, watching Grandma Sorrel overnight. She was improving steadily and would surely be released in a few days. Evelyn was on her way home to get what she needed to spend the night at the hospital in the drug treatment unit taking care of Jenny Richards.

Evelyn went on, "She's probably been in all kinds of trouble. Wouldn't surprise me if they both have. And along comes Miss Sorrel with meal ticket written all over her." She waved her keys and clicked to unlock her car doors. "I don't want your grandmother to get her hopes up, only come to find out that woman's not who she says she is."

"Grandma Sorrel's already got her hopes up." And *that woman* was not saying she was anything. It was her daughter who'd brought over the doll and she wasn't saying her mother was Janey, either. Vanessa agreed with all of them; she didn't think Jenny was Janey, even if the doll turned out to be Janey's doll. But she couldn't pass up an opportunity to bug Evelyn. "You have to admit, Jenny Richards is about the right age."

Evelyn nailed Vanessa with a skeptical gaze. "About the right age." She opened her car door and heaved herself into the driver's seat, slammed the door, and lowered the window. "My niece Amelia's about the right age. You could go to the Piggly Wiggly and find a half-dozen women in the dairy section who are about the right age."

There was no arguing with that. "Well, right now I'm taking the doll over to the police and they'll tell us if it could be Janey's doll."

"Well." Evelyn harrumphed and started her car. "It's about time."

The winter sun had set and the streetlights had come on by the time Vanessa got to the police station with the doll Maggie Richards had brought them wrapped in a baby blanket and stuffed into a shopping bag. She parked on the street and walked around to the front of the annex to Bonsecours's recently renovated municipal complex.

A pair of uncomfortable-looking wrought-iron benches flanked a black stone monument in front of the wide steps that led to the police department. The lettering on the monument came to life in the gleam of passing headlights: BONSECOURS FALLEN OFFICERS' MEMORIAL. Below that, a laurel wreath was etched into the stone and beneath that, names of fallen officers. The name that topped the list was familiar:

Chief of Police
ROBERT "BUCK" DUMONT
EOW FEBRUARY 23, 1988

Buck Dumont had been Evelyn's husband and Vanessa's grandfather Woody's best friend. He'd been chief of police for a decade or so before drowning in a fishing accident in the Bonsecours River. That had been before Vanessa was born.

Vanessa climbed the steps, continued past the two-story columns that flanked the portico, and entered the building. Inside it was spare, institutional white with vinyl floors. Vanessa waited at the window that separated the public from clerks at work on the other side. An older woman with blond streaks in her dark hair looked up from one of the desks, glanced at the wall clock—it was ten minutes to five—and came over to Vanessa, her expression bored but polite. A name badge pinned to her white starched shirt read MATTIE DAY.

"I'm here to see Officer . . . I mean, Deputy Chief Ames," Vanessa said. Ms. Day slid a clipboard over. A sign-in sheet. Vanessa wrote down her name.

When Ms. Day took the clipboard back, her face lit up. "Vanessa Strenger? You must be Miss Sorrel's granddaughter." She turned around and called to another woman working in the inner office at a desk. "Vera, look who's here! It's Miss Sorrel's grandbaby." Was that a smirk that Vanessa saw passing between them? Bonsecours really was a small town.

Ms. Day turned back to Vanessa. "Working in Rhode Island, are you?"

"Goodness, aren't y'all well informed?" Vanessa smiled.

"A psychologist I heard. Not married."

Vanessa smiled again and gave a bobblehead nod.

"Or not married *yet*, that's what we like to say. So sorry to hear about the accident. And the robbery on top of it. Shocking. Bonsecours is turning into New Orleans. How are they? You send our best, you hear?" Ms. Day delivered all this without taking a breath.

"They're . . . fine. Thank you for asking." There was no point going into chapter and verse. "I'll let them know you asked."

"You just hang on, then, and I'll tell the deputy chief you're here."

While she waited, Vanessa examined the array of annual police force photographs that hung on a wall. In each, the officers were lined up in rows. In a photo dated 1987, Vanessa recognized Buck Dumont. Standing dead center with a bit more space around him than the other officers, he was also taller and broader with a bushier mustache than anyone. All he needed was a pointy helmet to pass for a Viking. Nineteen eighty-seven, that would have been the year before he died.

The door to the inner area opened, and Officer Frank came out. His gaze fell to the bag Vanessa was holding and he ushered her inside.

"Fax came for you," another clerk said, intercepting them. She handed him a sheet of paper.

Officer Frank stopped, looked at the fax. Looked across at Vanessa and then back at the fax. Vanessa tried to read his expression. He didn't seem taken aback or surprised. More like grim satisfaction.

He folded the paper over quickly, but not before Vanessa caught the block letters across the top: CERTIFICATE OF DEATH. "Vanessa," he said. "Come on back."

Vanessa followed Officer Frank down a corridor and into an office. Despite Frank's name on a plaque outside, the office was so aggressively impersonal that it felt as if he'd just moved in. The broad top of the steel desk was cleared of papers. A massive map of Bonsecours hung on the wall behind it. A corkboard filled the adjacent wall and was hung thick with a half-dozen *Wanted* posters. Next to them were pictures of Miss Sorrel's stolen dolls.

Officer Frank must have followed her gaze because he said, "None of the dolls have turned up so far. We're monitoring eBay—" He slid the fax sheet under his desk blotter.

"eBay?"

"And Craigslist. The Internet's become the preferred venue for fencing stolen goods. Especially stolen goods with a narrow appeal." He tilted his head and appraised the photographs. "I'm still not altogether satisfied that we know what we're dealing with. A burglar who steals dolls and leaves behind so many easy-to-carry valuables? Then, for good measure, explodes a ceramics kiln? Feels like a gumbo with too many ingredients." Officer Frank opened the drawer of a file cabinet and pulled out a folder. From it he slipped a copy of the classified ad Grandma Sorrel had been running for the last thirty years. He smoothed it on the desk. "Let's see what you brought me."

Vanessa took the doll from the bag and laid it on the desk alongside the picture. She couldn't read Frank's expression as he gazed down at it. He opened his top desk drawer, took out a magnifying glass, and examined the stamp on the foot. The disfigured face. He lifted the dress, exposing the doll's soft body, its once-white linen covering nearly brown with dirt and age.

Finally, he turned his attention to the doll's hair, or what was left of it. He took a scissors from his drawer and snipped a few inches from a bundle of strands.

"Can you test the DNA?" Vanessa asked.

"Unfortunately, a hair shaft doesn't have the material we

need for DNA testing," he said as he took a matchbook from a desk drawer. "But it's pretty simple to test whether it's real hair or synthetic." He struck a match and touched it to the hair. The flame flared as the hair caught and then quickly went out, leaving a nasty scorched smell in the air and dark ash on the desk. "Most synthetic hair melts." He poked at the ashes with his finger. "This didn't."

Vanessa's stomach turned over. Not that she was surprised. The hair on any Miss Sorrel doll was harvested from the head of the little girl portrayed. "So it's human hair?"

"Maybe. I want someone to take a closer look."

He snipped some more hair, a single strand this time, and dropped it into an envelope. Vanessa followed him back to the reception area and up a flight of stairs to a second-floor office. The sign on the door said FORENSICS LAB.

At the hospital, Lis had taken up the post beside Miss Sorrel's bed. Her mother slept, but she seemed anything but peaceful. Her eyes twitched behind closed lids. Her chest rose and fell rapidly. A glance at the monitor by the bed confirmed—her heart rate was climbing.

Lis pulled her chair closer. "Mummy," Lis whispered. She hadn't called her mother that in years.

Miss Sorrel muttered in her sleep and turned her head one way, then the other. When Lis touched her arm, her mother's shoulders seemed to lift off the mattress and her eyes flew open, focused unseeing on the middle distance. She put her hand to her chest and lay there, breathing heavily with her mouth open.

"Shhh," Lis said, taking her hand. "Relax."

Miss Sorrel looked around the room, panic in her eyes.

"You're in the hospital, remember?" Lis said. "Were you dreaming about Janey?"

Miss Sorrel batted away the thought with the back of her hand.

"What then?"

"The doll. I couldn't find it." She struggled to sit up. "But she's back. She came back. Didn't she?" She collapsed against the pillows.

"Janey's doll?"

"Is it hers?" Miss Sorrel gave Lis an anxious, searching look.

"We don't know," Lis admitted.

"Find. Out."

"We're trying to. Vanessa's taken the doll to the police. They'll examine—"

"The police . . . *pfff.*" The lines at the corner of Miss Sorrel's eyes deepened as she took a deep breath and held it. Exhaled. "They've never . . ." She squeezed Lis's hand so hard it hurt. Then her face crumpled and she started to weep. Lis felt as if the chair had dropped out from under her. She'd rarely seen her mother lose her composure, never mind cry.

Lis's vision went blurry and her chest cramped. She waited until her mother released her grip on her and closed herself into the bathroom on the pretext of filling the water pitcher.

She caught her own reflection in the mirror. She looked half dead, haunted and haggard, sad and beaten down. The circles under her eyes had circles. No surprise there. Her mother wasn't bouncing back the way Lis had expected her to, and Lis still felt rocky, verging on nausea most of the time. Her life wasn't about to return to boring and mundane any time soon. On top of that, she was smarting from the way Vanessa had implied—no, *accused*—Lis of rolling over and letting herself be bossed around by other people. Evelyn (*You leave it to me, Lissie*) and Frank (*You need to let the police do their job, Elisabeth*) manipulated her like a puppet. At least Vanessa had gumption. She didn't let anyone tell her what she could and couldn't do. It was only because Vanessa wouldn't take no that they'd found Jenny Richards.

Lis patted her pocket where she'd stuffed the bloody gauze pad wrapped in the Latex glove and returned to Miss Sorrel's bedside. When her mother dropped back to sleep, Lis used her phone to look up a local DNA testing services lab and called them. She was put on hold to the strains of "Für Elise." Finally a woman picked up. "Laurel Bay Testing Services. How can I help you?"

"Do you analyze blood for DNA to see if two people are related?"

"A paternity test?" the woman asked.

"No. Sisters."

"A siblingship test. Of course. We need a DNA sample from both individuals and a maternal sample as well." She went on to say that expedited test results came back in three business days. Payment in advance. Lis could bring in the samples any time, weekdays until six, Saturday until five. "Unless, of course, you need a legal DNA test."

"Excuse me?" Would the other test results she got be *il*legal?

"If you need to present the results in court for something like child support or to claim an inheritance, then you also need to have written consent from the donors and a documented chain of custody. Best if they come in and we take the samples on-site, then there's no question."

"It's a private family matter," Lis said.

"Of course. At Laurel Bay, we understand that. DNA testing is always a private matter, and you can rest assured we will exercise the utmost discretion with your test results. We have counselors on-site . . ."

Lis tuned out. Sounded like a canned speech, upselling add-on services. But she appreciated the sentiment. Privacy mattered to her, too, and for Jenny it was paramount.

"How much does it cost?" Lis asked when the woman took a breath.

It wasn't cheap. Expedited results for a siblingship test were

$550. All Lis had to do was fill out the forms and drop off the samples. She had Jenny's blood, she could help herself to a hair from Miss Sorrel's hairbrush, as long as it had the hair follicle. The lab would swab her cheek at no extra cost when she got there. "Just takes a few seconds," the woman on the phone assured her. They were open until six.

"Just one more question. How certain are the results?"

"If you provide usable DNA samples, results will be conclusive."

A chill went down Lis's spine as she hung up. How many things in life could you say that about?

22

"I didn't know Bonsecours had its own forensics lab," Vanessa said as Officer Frank held open the door marked FORENSICS on the second floor of the police station.

"We've got our own lab and a small in-house staff," Frank said. "We don't have the resources to analyze DNA, though. We send that to the state lab in Columbia for testing. Of course we'll send over Jenny Richards's sample to see if it matches Janey's."

"You have Janey's DNA? But she disappeared so long ago."

"I told you, we never gave up. About thirty years ago, when the state started DNA testing, Miss Sorrel gave us a sample. I think it might have been Janey's toothbrush. Then ten years ago NamUs, the national missing persons database, opened. We sent them Janey's DNA to see if it matched any unidentified persons they had. They'll analyze Jenny's DNA. Sadly, that's not going to happen overnight. State lab's backlogged months. In the meanwhile, we do what we can here."

Vanessa entered the roomy lab. Officer Frank was right that the in-house team was small. The forensics lab had much more space than equipment and just two white-coated technicians who barely looked up from their work. Fluorescent lights buzzed overhead. Walls were lined with shelves loaded with beakers, racks of test tubes, and labeled bottles. One of the technicians, in a white lab coat and blue rubber gloves, stood at an orange countertop. He (or she?) had on an industrial-strength breathing mask and was peering into a plastic bag. Officer Frank put out his arm to keep Vanessa back. "Jean?" he said. "You got a minute?"

Vanessa held her breath as the technician glanced across at them, nodded, and sealed the baggie. She removed her mask, set it on the counter, and put the baggie into a small refrigerator. Peeled off her gloves and tossed them in the trash.

Vanessa inhaled. It turned out that the room had no smell other than cleaning fluid and bleach.

"Jean, this is Vanessa Strenger. Vanessa, may I introduce Dr. Hunter, our resident forensics specialist."

"What can I do for you?" Dr. Hunter's eyes widened as she looked at Vanessa, perhaps realizing that Vanessa was related to Lis who was dating Frank. Or maybe Vanessa was being paranoid.

"Can you take a look at this for us?" Officer Frank opened the envelope and showed her the doll's hair. "Unofficially, what've we got."

Dr. Hunter walked over to the counter on which sat a large microscope, easily twice as big as the ones Vanessa had used in her college chem lab. She pulled down a box of glass slides, fixed a slide with what looked like a drop of glue, and set the hair onto it. Set the slide onto the bed of the microscope, turned on the light, switched lenses, and looked through the eyepiece. She lingered for a moment before looking up. "What do you want to know?"

"Is it human?"

"No." She looked again through the eyepiece. "Definitely not human." She adjusted a knob. "I'd say most likely it's dog."

"You can tell just by looking?" Vanessa asked.

Still looking through the eyepiece, Dr. Hunter said, "I can't tell you what breed, and it could be a wolf, but we don't have a lot of those around here so I'm guessing not. But it's definitely not human. I'll show you." She removed the slide, broke off a single strand of her own hair, and glued it onto the slide alongside the hair that was already there. Put the slide back into the microscope and looked, again adjusting the focus, then stepped away. "See for yourself."

Vanessa looked through the eyepiece. Even she could see right away that structurally, the two hairs looked nothing alike.

Dr. Hunter said, "Dog hair has a continuous medulla in the center. In the microscope, it presents as a solid line."

Medulla. That must have been what looked like a strand of licorice, plainly visible, running all the way through the middle of one of the hairs. The other hair was more of a solid mottled brown with a few dark flecks.

Dr. Hunter turned off the microscope light and removed the slide. "We could run a bunch more fancy tests, but it's only going to confirm. That hair's not human."

Officer Frank turned to Vanessa, his look somber. "I'm so sorry. I know it's a huge disappointment."

But Vanessa wasn't disappointed. Something about Jenny's story had struck her as a little too pat, and the last thing Grandma Sorrel needed was to be led on, only to be let down. There was no way to spin this result: Janey's doll would have Janey's hair. Not a dog's.

23

It wasn't until Lis got out to the hospital parking lot, intending to drive to the DNA testing lab, that she remembered she'd left home in Vanessa's car all those hours ago. Her car was at home.

Lis sat on a bench by the main entrance of the hospital and called Vanessa, hoping to get her to come by and give her a lift. No answer. She texted. Still nothing.

Finally Lis called a cab. She had the cabbie take her home, and from there she drove herself to Laurel Bay Testing Services. The address turned out to be a nondescript storefront in a strip mall. A receptionist wearing a telephone headset sat behind a sliding glass window that had a row of stickers on it. MasterCard. Visa. American Express. And a sign: NO PERSONAL CHECKS. Beneath that in smaller lettering: NO REFUNDS. Lis could imagine that they had to deal with plenty of cases of buyer's remorse, customers who weren't pleased with what they found out.

Less than thirty minutes later, Lis had filled out the forms, submitted the samples, had her cheek swabbed, and charged $550 to her credit card. She drove home feeling a strange combination of queasy and elated. Laurel Bay's advertised "results in three business days" meant she'd have an answer Wednesday, at the earliest. More likely next Thursday. But compared to forty years, that wait seemed like a spit in the ocean.

Back at home, Lis parked her car in the driveway. She climbed the front steps, noticing that the front window had been repaired. She'd have to find out who to thank, Vanessa or Evelyn or Frank. Behind her, she heard a car pulling up and turned to see Vanessa's rental car. The rear tires still looked fine.

Vanessa got out of the car, carrying a shopping bag and a pizza box. Lis realized she was ravenous as she unlocked the front door.

"How's Grandma Sorrel?" Vanessa asked.

"I left her sleeping. The nurse on duty said she should be fine overnight, and Evelyn promised to come down and check on her later."

Lis followed Vanessa through the house and into the kitchen. Vanessa sct the pizza on the counter and Lis helped herself to a slice, wolfed it down standing. She started on a second slice before she'd even snagged a napkin.

Vanessa sat down at the table and helped herself to a slice of pizza. Took a bite and pulled a face.

"What? It's good," Lis said.

"It's mediocre. Next time you come to Rhode Island, I'll show you pizza." Vanessa set the slice down on a napkin. "Frank says he'll be sending Jenny's DNA to the state lab to see if it's a match for the sample they have from Janey. He said it's likely to take a while."

"You talked to Frank?"

Vanessa took the doll from the bag. "He asked me to bring this over, and I did."

Lis touched the doll's poor sweet battered face. "Your grandma's convinced it's Janey's doll."

"It's not," Vanessa said. "They looked at the hair. It isn't human."

Lis picked up the doll and examined its hair. The fine blond hair looked and felt like the real thing, though mohair, often used in doll wigs, was hard to tell from human hair.

"It's from a dog," Vanessa said.

Lis had often seen Miss Sorrel brush their dog's coat—Binty and the golden retriever, Sierra, that they'd had before—and save the hair to use for repairing doll's wigs. But dog's hair would never have been used in one of Miss Sorrel's portrait dolls.

So what were they looking at? Lis turned over the doll's foot. There was the mark of the sorrel leaf, but that wasn't hard to fake. The doll's face, though the features were distorted by the damage it had sustained, was subtly modeled and painted. That was the hallmark of Miss Sorrel's dolls, and a lot harder to duplicate. The arm, the one it still had, seemed right, though the legs seemed slightly mismatched. Maybe one had been replaced. The doll could be a fake, or it could be a genuine Miss Sorrel doll with a replacement wig.

The glass eyes in Janey's doll would have been blue. These eyes were so cloudy that it was impossible to tell what color they'd been. But Lis had learned a few tricks over the years helping Miss Sorrel repair dolls, and clearing cloudy eyes was one of them.

Lis went into the workroom where she found a bottle of white vinegar and a handful of Q-tips. She returned and got out a dish towel and laid the doll down on it. Its milky eyes clicked shut. She forced open one of the lids and started to swab the eye with vinegar. But even as she was removing a skim of grease and dirt, she realized the cloudiness wasn't only on the surface. Vinegar alone wasn't going to do it.

"Vanessa, honey, would you run up and get me the hair dryer?"

Vanessa ran upstairs and came back with Lis's blow-dryer, plugged it in, and handed it to Lis. Lis turned it on and blew hot air directly into one of the doll's eyes. As she held the doll's face into the heat, the tangy smell of vinegar with undercurrents of mold filled the air. When she turned off the hair dryer, the eye had cleared enough to see what color it was.

Brown.

Lis tilted the doll's face up to Vanessa. "Brown eyes and a wig made of dog hair. That clinches it. This can't be Janey's doll."

24

Lis was embarrassed to tell Vanessa about the DNA test she'd bought and paid for. Not only were the police running their own DNA test, but on top of that, the doll Maggie Richards had brought them couldn't have been Janey's. Now, looking at all the anomalies, it must have taken a mighty powerful dose of wishful thinking to convince Miss Sorrel that it was.

Over the weekend, Lis and Vanessa took turns sitting with Miss Sorrel. By Saturday evening she was complaining about the food. The next morning, she wanted her own bathrobe and nightgown and shampoo. Sunday she was walking—make that pacing—up and down the hall. Ready to be at home, she told anyone who'd listen. But her doctor said her heart rate and blood pressure were still stabilizing. Another day wasn't going to kill her.

The word from Evelyn was that Jenny Richards had come through withdrawal and emerged conscious and lucid. Now she was ready to be discharged. According to Frank, a background check on Jenny Richards had turned up tickets for loitering, the kind that police award for being homeless, followed by missed court appearances. Subsequent arrests for the no-shows and fines that she couldn't pay. No drug charges. No theft. No check kiting. No criminal charges of any kind. But there was the matter of her juvenile record. It had been expunged. Even Frank couldn't find out what charges had been brought against her before she turned eighteen, only that there had been some. Lis didn't know what to make of that, but Evelyn had weighed in. According to her, there could have been anything in that sealed record. Even criminal charges.

Monday morning Lis got to the hospital early and shampooed Miss Sorrel's hair and manicured her nails a translucent pink. Later that morning, wearing a fresh nightgown with a white lace collar, her hair pulled back in a ribbon at her neck, Miss Sorrel sat up in bed looking as if she were holding court with Lis, Vanessa, and Frank in attendance.

Miss Sorrel surveyed them with a jaundiced eye. "So which of you all is going to tell me what this is all about? It couldn't wait? I'm going home tomorrow, for goodness' sake." Her look turned anxious. "I am going home, aren't I?"

"Yes, you are," Lis said. "That's what the doctor promised. But there's something you need to know now. Before you get home."

"Who died?"

"No one died," Lis said.

"And it takes three of you to tell me?" When none of them answered, Miss Sorrel rolled her eyes in a gesture Lis knew well and added, "Is this going to be a short story or *War and Peace*? And why are *you* here?" She addressed the final question to Frank.

"To listen," Frank said. He was out of uniform in chinos and a dark blue polo shirt, but he stood like a cop. "In case you remember something that will help us with our investigation." He raised his eyebrows at Lis, who gestured for him to continue. "In addition to the carbon monoxide leak and kiln explosion, you were robbed."

"Robbed." Miss Sorrel took that in. "Well, that explains why you were here the other day asking me if I heard anything when I was downstairs in the middle of the night. What did they take?"

This was the moment Lis had been dreading. "Dolls," she said.

Miss Sorrel's eyes narrowed. "Which ones?"

"The ones in the china cabinets in the dining room."

"Oh, no." Miss Sorrel blinked. "All of them?"

"I'm afraid so."

"*My* dolls?"

Lis knew Miss Sorrel meant the dolls she'd made herself. "All of them, except . . ." Lis nodded to Vanessa, who showed Miss Sorrel the two dolls she'd brought with her—Lis's doll that Vanessa had brought home in her suitcase and the doll Maggie Richards had brought them. Vanessa sat them side by side on the bed, and as if in character the one in pristine condition sat stiff and upright while the other one, battered and soiled, flopped forward onto its face.

Miss Sorrel reached for Lis's doll. "My first." She could have been referring to Lis or to the doll. "I was pregnant with Janey when Evelyn and I took a class in ceramics. It's an ancient art form, porcelain. The Chinese were making it thousands of years ago. So delicate"—she ran her fingertips over the doll's face— "and responsive to the touch. I made four different heads before it felt right."

"Three." The voice from the doorway was Evelyn's. She didn't hesitate but marched right in. She was dressed in her nurse's uniform. "Don't you remember how frustrated you were at first, trying to capture Lissie's essence?"

"Was I?" Miss Sorrel said.

"When you did Janey, you got it on the first go. You never needed another do-over, right up until the end when we stopped making them."

"No, I never did," Miss Sorrel said. "Lis has been telling me about the robbery."

Evelyn gave a somber nod. "All those years we've been collecting. It's a devastating loss."

"I know," Miss Sorrel said. "You and I handpicked every one of those dolls, didn't we, dear? I think they mean even more to you than they do to me. And then there are the dolls we made."

"Irreplaceable," Evelyn said.

Vanessa asked, "Why did you stop making dolls?"

"Well," Miss Sorrel said. She and Evelyn exchanged a look.

Lis realized that she had no idea, either, when or why Miss Sorrel and Evelyn had stopped making dolls. She knew she'd been a spectacularly moody teen, preoccupied with her own angst and feeling like the perpetual odd girl out at school. Her brothers had left for college and her father spent all day at the marina playing poker and drinking, if you'd asked Miss Sorrel. If you'd asked him, he'd have said he was running Woody's Charters. Schmoozing was an essential part of doing business.

Most afternoons Lis would come home from school, slam her way into the house, grab a snack, and race upstairs to her room where she'd turn up some music, preferably something Miss Sorrel found horrifying, open the window, and smoke. At the time, it never would have occurred to her that her mother did anything that wasn't motivated by a firm determination to prevent Lis from doing exactly what she wanted.

"After Janey disappeared," Miss Sorrel said, "they ran pictures in the paper of her and her doll. A reporter wrote a feature story about us. Local interest or some nonsense. We started to get calls. I needed to keep busy, and it felt like a blessing to at least be able to make dolls that made little girls happy. Before we knew it we had more orders than we could handle. We were even talking about renting studio space and getting a second kiln and hiring, and then—"

Evelyn interrupted. "It was really a business decision. Too much of a good thing, I reckon you could say that. We just weren't prepared for any kind of volume. We were getting orders, but it was too much for the two of us to manage, and, well . . ." Her voice trailed off.

"But that's not why we stopped," Miss Sorrel said.

"Sorrel," Evelyn said, a note of warning in her voice.

"Evelyn. You know as well as I do that it was not a business decision. Good heavens, it's past time to bring it into the open."

The room fell silent as Evelyn and Miss Sorrel stared across the room at each other. Evelyn stood with her hands on her hips, Miss Sorrel with her arms folded across her chest. Lis had rarely seen them so much as disagree, and when they did, Miss Sorrel was usually the one to cave. So she was surprised when it was Evelyn who said, "All right then. If you must. You never could be talked out of a thing once you set your mind to it."

Miss Sorrel said, "One of the last dolls we worked on was for a darling, rambunctious little three-year-old." Her gaze traveled from Evelyn to Lis to Vanessa, stopping at Frank. "Her name was Abigail Verner."

Abby Verner. Of course Lis recognized the name. Everyone who'd lived in the area in the late '80s would have known it. There'd been signs hanging all over town: FIND ABBY, with the police hotline number. Abby herself stared down from the posters, her dark haunting eyes shadowed by a fringe of bangs.

There had been buttons and bumper stickers. All through town, yellow ribbons hung in store windows, on front doors, on lamp-posts, on car antennas.

"Her family lived on Lady's Island," Miss Sorrel went on. "They had five little boys, and her parents had been over the moon when they had a little girl."

Lis knew that. A picture of Abby's family had run in the paper. Lis had stared at Abby's older siblings and wondered if one of them had been charged with watching Abby.

"But by the time we'd finished the doll," Miss Sorrel said, her voice breaking, "there was no little girl to give her to."

Evelyn said, "Abby vanished. Right out from under their noses."

"Just like Janey, she was taken from her own yard." Miss Sorrel gazed up at the ceiling, her eyes filled with tears. Evelyn handed her a tissue and she dabbed at the corners of her eyes.

"About broke our hearts," Evelyn said. "Of course we helped with the search. Everyone did. Frank, you were there. Remember?"

"All too well," he said.

"We still have Abby's doll, don't we, Evelyn?" Miss Sorrel said.

Evelyn winced. "We did."

"Oh." Miss Sorrel's voice was tinged with dismay. "Of course. Stolen."

Lis knew how Abby Verner's story ended. Just like Janey's. But . . . "No one told me about the connection," she said. She looked at Frank. Her friend and lover for the last fifteen years. He'd never thought to mention it? Not once? And now he couldn't meet her gaze.

Evelyn said, "We . . . I . . ."

"That little girl disappearing just about finished me off," Miss Sorrel said. "The least I could do was protect you, darlin'. There'd already been enough guilt and woe piled on your little shoulders."

"Why open old wounds?" Evelyn added. "And for all anyone knew, there was no connection. Just a sad coincidence."

Miss Sorrel sank back against the pillows. "Long story short, that's why we stopped making dolls. Because what if my dolls were somehow connected with that little girl's disappearance? What if my hobby—that's all it was, really—was drawing some pervert's attention to vulnerable children? I couldn't risk it happening again."

"Did the police ever find that little girl?" Vanessa asked.

"No," Miss Sorrel said. "Not a trace."

"No one was arrested?"

"No. But . . ." Miss Sorrel looked across at Evelyn. Some message passed between them, a mutual understanding. "Let's just say the person responsible isn't going to do it again." She reached for the damaged doll that was lying facedown on the bed. But before she could pick it up, there was a knock at the open door, and then Maggie and Jenny Richards stepped into the already crowded room.

25

Lis barely recognized Jenny Richards. She had on a white T-shirt and drawstring pants that hung loose from her gaunt frame. The purple bruise on her forehead was yellowing at the edges, and black stitches marred the flesh beneath her lower lip. She seemed so much less formidable than she had when she'd been waving that shotgun around.

Jenny's gaze swept the room, pausing at Frank and coming to a full stop at Miss Sorrel. The two of them looked long and hard at each other.

"Sorrel, dear," Evelyn said, "this is Jenny Richards. You've already met Maggie. The doll belongs to Jenny. Her parents gave it to her when she was little."

Miss Sorrel extended her hand to Jenny. Lis could imagine her using the same gesture to lure a feral cat. "You don't know me, do you?" Miss Sorrel said.

Jenny furrowed her brow and tipped her head to the side. Her head shake seemed more like indecision than an outright no.

"Go ahead, dear," Evelyn said, nudging Jenny forward. "No one's going to hurt you."

Vanessa got up and Jenny took her chair.

"Evelyn told me that you made my doll," Jenny said to Miss Sorrel.

"I did. Do you remember how you got it?"

"I've just always had it."

"You don't remember sitting for it?"

Jenny shook her head, puzzled.

"It's a portrait doll. I'd have taken some pictures of you and drawn a few sketches. You would have been very young. Or maybe your parents brought me your photograph and I worked from that."

"That doll is supposed to be me?"

"Unless your parents picked it up somewhere."

"Picked it up? As if my mother would have been caught dead shopping at flea markets or rummage sales. She didn't buy used."

"Well then, she must have asked me to make it for you. Did you grow up nearby?"

With a shaking hand Jenny brushed a wisp of hair from her forehead. "Mount Royal."

Lis had often seen the highway turnoff for Mount Royal but she'd never been there, only seen billboards on the highway advertising its gated communities and golf courses. Girls who grew up there still had coming-out parties, although no one called them that anymore.

Miss Sorrel said, "What did your parents do?"

"My father was a doctor. My mother called herself a homemaker, only we had help with most of that."

Maggie was leaning forward, listening intently as if she were hearing this for the first time.

"Evelyn and I knew most of the families we made dolls for, especially the early ones. But I don't remember making a doll for a family in Mount Royal. Way back then, wasn't it still mostly farmland? An old cotton plantation that they turned into a to-mato farm—"

"That was near our house. It's got a little country store where they sell candy and Coke. I used to ride my bike over."

"You've come a long way from Mount Royal."

"As far away as I could get, and still it's not far enough. And just so you know, I'm not a junkie." Jenny's voice sounded tired but defiant. "I had a prescription for the pills I was taking."

"That's what I gather," Miss Sorrel said.

Evelyn sucked in her breath.

"I want to apologize," Miss Sorrel said. "I was unspeakably rude to your daughter, and I'm sorry for that." She gave Maggie a tentative smile. "If I hadn't run her off, we could have met in much more pleasant circumstances, without quite so much"—she gave a vague gesture around the room— "melodrama. And I'm truly sorry that you got frightened and hurt."

"I'll recover," Jenny said, gingerly touching her stitches.

"If you want to take the doll back, I'll understand. I gather that Maggie didn't clear it with you when she brought it to us. Or we'll keep it and give you the reward. You did know there's a reward."

Jenny picked up the doll. Her face crumpled as she took in the doll's cracked face. She fingered the hair. "What happened?" She looked across at Maggie. "What did you do to her?"

"It's my fault," Maggie said, her eyes hidden behind her sun-glasses. "They kept asking me questions about where you got it and I got mad. I'm sorry. I lost it and threw it at them."

"That's not what I mean." Jenny looked around the room. "Is this some kind of joke?" She held out the doll. "This is not my doll."

Lis took a step back.

"How could it not be?" Evelyn said.

"Let me see." Miss Sorrel patted the bed beside her and Jenny laid the doll down on its back. She gestured Evelyn over. Together they looked at the arm and legs, the soft body and dress. But most of all they examined the head. Smelled the hair.

"She's right," Miss Sorrel said at last. "It's not the same doll, is it, Evelyn? I might have made some of its parts. But look closely, and overall it's not even close."

"You don't think it's Janey's doll?" Evelyn said. She raised her eyebrows in disbelief.

"I don't think it's the doll that Maggie brought over to us. *That* was Janey's doll. At first glance this doll looks the same: the damage, the dress. But . . ." Miss Sorrel looked around the room. "For heaven's sake, everyone stop looking at me like that. Lis, you saw it. Tell them."

Lis didn't know what to say. This doll looked like the one Maggie had broken against their front steps. But she was the first to admit that she often missed what her mother's sharp eyes saw. There was a reason her mother was a doll expert and she was not.

Evelyn said, "Of course this is the same doll. I'm sorry to be the one to have to tell you this, but your eyesight's not what it used to be and your memory's playing tricks on you." Her voice rose. "You want it to be Janey's doll. I understand that. But it's not. It never was."

"Oh, be quiet, Evelyn," Miss Sorrel said.

Evelyn recoiled, her chin receding into her neck. "Well, excuse me."

Miss Sorrel pushed herself straighter in the bed. "I saw what I saw. I know what I know. Shouting at me's not going to make a darned bit of difference. Jenny?" Miss Sorrel took a deep breath and sat up forward. "I have something to ask you, and I want you to think about it before you reject it out of hand. Okay?"

She waited for Jenny to acknowledge with a nod.

"I know we're complete strangers, but would you consider staying with us? For a little while, maybe a week, maybe longer, until you're completely recovered. We have plenty of room. You won't be alone; Lis and Vanessa will be there and Evelyn is right next door. This way your daughter can start her job without worrying about you."

Evelyn folded her arms across her chest and shook her head in disbelief. For a change, Lis agreed with her, and Vanessa looked equally horrified. Miss Sorrel had barely begun to convalesce and she was opening their home to a woman who had a pathological fear of the police and threatened strangers with a shotgun?

Jenny looked across at her daughter, clearly dumbfounded. "Maggie? What do you think?"

Maggie took off her sunglasses and looked at Miss Sorrel. "Why would you do that?"

Miss Sorrel was quiet for a few moments, and Lis could almost hear her arguing with herself. "To be honest, my reasons are entirely selfish. I'm hoping you'll open up about where you got the doll. The other doll. Even if you don't think you know, I hope you'll help us find out. There's no doubt in my mind that the doll your daughter brought us belonged to my daughter Janey. It disappeared the day she went missing, and now it's disappeared again. We haven't got a prayer of finding out how it got from her hands to yours without your help. And the fact that the doll you brought us has been replaced with a clumsy replica tells me that finally"—she sent a meaningful look in Frank's direction— "we're on the right track. You may not think you know anything, but odds are, you do."

26

"I hope we're not making a terrible mistake," Vanessa said to Lis a short time later in the hospital cafeteria over cups of weak coffee. "We don't really know who she is."

"Your grandma's gone plumb crazy," Evelyn said as she bumped past Vanessa and plunked down into a chair opposite them. Tea sloshed from her Styrofoam cup when she set it on the table. She mopped up the spill with a napkin. "Bless her, she's blinded by wishful thinking." She swirled her tea bag. "I saw the doll her daughter brought over. Trust me, this is the same doll, and it was *never* Janey's doll." She took the tea bag out, squeezed it against the rim of the cup, and parked it on her napkin. "And trust me, Jenny Richards *is* a junkie. She's also a compulsive liar."

Lis said, "It sounded to me like she got addicted to painkillers prescribed for her by a doctor after she was in a car accident. That happens to lots of people who aren't junkies. Now she's clean."

Evelyn said, "People who take painkillers for a valid reason do not get addicted."

"That's a myth," Vanessa shot back. Also a myth, the belief

that everyone who took painkillers for long enough got addicted. The cycle of addiction was complex, and for anyone coming out of detox, spending day after day isolated in a trailer was a recipe for disaster.

"Well, Miss Smartypants," Evelyn said, "you go right ahead and bury your head in your scholarly journals. I'll tell you what I know from experience. She's a druggie, and anyone can see that it's left her a bit touched."

"Touched?" Was that her clinical diagnosis? Nothing in Jenny's behavior convinced Vanessa that she'd gone over the edge or was beyond help. Still, Vanessa wasn't convinced that help should come from them, though she'd never say so since it galled her to agree with Evelyn.

Lis put her hand on Vanessa's arm and said to Evelyn, quite a bit more calmly, "Oh? Touched in what way?"

"She imagines insults and slights and even conspiracies. Thinks Vanessa is trying to turn Maggie against her. Told me I was spying on her. Trying to read her thoughts. It's beyond me why your mother would invite a complete stranger—"

"She needs help," Lis said. "Anyone can see that. And Frank says she has no criminal record. It's the Christian thing to do."

"No criminal record that they *know* of. And don't you go telling me what's Christian and what's not. Y'all don't even say grace. You want to invite a drug addict into your home, that's your business. I'll just mind my own."

Right, Vanessa thought. *When pigs fly.*

Evelyn sniffed. "Do what you want, but keep an eye on her and be sure you count the spoons. Did Frank tell you that the woman's been living under a stolen identity?"

"You're kidding," Lis said.

"I don't," Evelyn said, staring hard at Lis, "kid. Are you forgetting my husband was chief of police? I still have my sources." She looked around and lowered her voice. "The real Jenny Richards died in a car accident. Miss I'm-Not-a-Junkie probably found her name on a gravestone. Probably stole her Social Security number. With a new identity"—Evelyn poured a stream of sugar into her tea and stirred it with a wooden stirrer—"you can walk away from a whole lot more than an unhappy childhood." She picked up her tea and squinted at Vanessa through the steam. "Sometimes I wonder if either of you have even the slightest idea what Miss Sorrel went through, all because someone didn't pay attention. And now you're letting a viper into her garden." She stood. "That's all. I've said my piece." She pretended to zip and lock her mouth, and then she marched off carrying her tea to the elevator.

"A viper in the garden?" Vanessa said. She didn't like to admit it, but Evelyn's certainty was unnerving, and it echoed her own misgivings.

Lis said, "The Bible. It's her go-to source for supporting her opinions. Besides, whether Jenny Richards comes home with us isn't really up to you or me. Or Evelyn, for that matter. Your grandmother's made up her mind. If all we lose is a few spoons, that's fine by me."

But Vanessa didn't feel as sanguine about dismissing Evelyn's concerns. As she was driving Lis home, she said, "Has Frank mentioned anything about Jenny living under a stolen identity?"

"Not a word," Lis said. "Why?"

"Because he got a fax when I was with him at the police station. All I saw was the heading. It was a death certificate. He seemed surprised when he read it. Then he sort of hid it. Folded it up and tucked it away. I didn't think anything of it. But now—"

"Why would he keep us in the dark?" Lis said. Then she

added as an aside, almost to herself, "And why not tell me about Abby Verner?"

Vanessa parked at the house. From the front, it looked as if nothing had happened. Inside it was getting there. Power to the workroom had been restored. The kiln had been carted away and the plumbers had been in to fix the gas, leaving behind a new carbon monoxide detector.

As soon as they got back inside, Vanessa went to her computer. Lis came around to the screen as Vanessa opened up a death records website. There were plenty of search parameters. Name she knew. Location, she could guess. Date of birth, the system allowed her to enter a range.

"Nineteen seventy-two," Lis said. "That was the date of birth on Jenny's insurance ID card."

First Vanessa tried looking up Jenny in Mount Royal. Nothing. But then she changed the location to Bonsecours, and there it was:

NAME: Jennifer Ann Richards
DATE OF BIRTH: September 9, 1972
DATE OF DEATH: April 8, 1977
MOTHER: Renata Fielding Richards
FATHER: Clive Francis Richards
DEATH PLACE: Bonsecours, SC

27

It was as cold and raw as it ever got in Bonsecours the next morning when Lis pulled into the hospital loading zone to pick up the woman who was calling herself Jenny Richards. Vanessa had come earlier for Miss Sorrel. Jenny was sitting in a wheelchair under an awning near the loading zone with Evelyn beside her, smiling benignly, her hand resting on Jenny's shoulder.

All night and on the drive over to the hospital, Lis had gone back and forth in her mind. One minute she had herself convinced that they were dealing with a scam artist who'd stolen the identity of a dead girl and tarted up a doll to look like Janey's, all so she could collect the reward. And when she'd found herself in deeper than she'd expected, she'd jumped at the chance to invade their lives. That was Evelyn's viper scenario, and one that Vanessa supported.

But then Lis would wonder if Jenny was Janey. Because if Janey had survived, she'd have to have been living all these years under an assumed name given to her by her new "parents." And if she was Janey, Lis would never forgive herself if she turned her back on her a second time.

When DNA test results came back, they'd know for sure.

In the meantime, Lis would salute and march to her mother's wishes, the way she always did.

They arrived at the house and Jenny got out of the car. Sun had broken through the clouds and shone off the angular planes in her face, making the hollows under the cheekbones look even deeper. In all the family photographs, Janey's face had still been padded with baby fat.

"Is that where Evelyn lives?" Jenny asked, indicating the big pink house next door. Evelyn's car wasn't parked in the driveway.

"It is," Lis said. "Though I swear, half the time it feels like she's living with us."

Miss Sorrel came out onto the porch. She was wrapped tightly in a shawl and looked as if a stiff wind could knock her over. Binty stood by her side, tail wagging furiously. Lis carried Jenny's bag into the house, leaving Jenny with Miss Sorrel.

When she came back out, Jenny was sitting on the porch swing, petting Binty. "I always wanted a dog," Jenny said. "We had one when I was little. Until my mother got rid of it." She bent close to nuzzle the dog and Binty licked her on the face. "The truth is I was too young for that much responsibility."

"Why don't you take Jenny inside," Miss Sorrel said to Lis. "Show her where she'll be sleeping."

Lis led Jenny inside and up the stairs to the corner bedroom where she'd made up one of the twin beds with fresh sheets. On the maple bureau was a cardboard box filled with Jenny's clothing and toiletries that Maggie had dropped off the night before. "Think you'll be okay in here?"

Jenny looked around, taking in the maroon and off-white history-of-transportation wallpaper. She crossed the room to the closet and opened the door, peered inside, and closed it. She crouched between the beds, raised one of the bed skirts and looked under it. Then she glanced at Lis. "Sorry. It's an old habit. Because you never know what you're going to find under a bed in a shelter. Rats. Roaches." She looked under the second bed, then stood and brushed her hands off on her leg. "Sometimes a person, even."

"All clear?" Lis asked.

"This wasn't her room, was it?"

"No. My brothers slept in here," Lis said. Back then the room had had a bunk bed and a twin. There were still marks on the door where tape had secured a sign: NO GIRLS ALLOWED, a rule that had been strictly enforced.

Lis went out onto the landing and pulled a set of fresh towels from the linen closet. "If you need more towels, they're out here." She put the towels on the hamper in the bathroom. "And if you need another blanket or—" she started, but when she went back out onto the landing, Jenny wasn't in the boys' room. Instead, she was silhouetted in the sunlit open doorway to Janey's bedroom.

Lis followed Jenny as she entered Janey's bedroom. Jenny looked all around, pivoting in place. Opened the closet and pushed aside Janey's clothes that were still hanging there. Knelt down and looked under the bed. She gave Lis a thumbs-up and sat on the bed, running her hand across the pink-and-white-flowered bedspread. She picked up the stuffed kangaroo that was sitting on the pillow.

"We lost Roo," Lis said.

"Roo?" Jenny said.

"There used to be a baby kangaroo in its pouch." When Jenny still looked puzzled, Lis added, "Kanga and Roo? Characters from *Winnie-the-Pooh?*" She picked up the copy of the book that sat on the bedside table. A faded cardinal feather one of the girls had found marked the place where Miss Sorrel had been reading the book before Janey disappeared. Now it was part of the mausoleum. Lis had had to buy a new copy so she could read it to Vanessa.

Jenny sniffed Kanga and dropped it back on the bed. She got up and went over to the low bookcase, its top shelf packed with children's books. "My mother subscribed to *Christian Women* and *Woman's Day*. We didn't have books, we had Bibles." She opened the pink leather jewelry box on the top of the bookcase. A plastic ballerina in a tutu popped up and music tinkled as she pirouetted. "I had one like this, too," she said. She picked through the gumball machine prizes and shiny jingle shells that Janey had collected, then looked across at Lis. "This was her room, wasn't it? Evelyn told me that her bedroom window overlooked her house."

"What else did Evelyn tell you?" Lis asked.

Jenny stood and gazed out the window at the big pink house next door. "Evelyn didn't have to stay with me the way she did. No one's ever done anything like that for me. Ever."

"She was Janey's godmother."

"She told me all about Miss Sorrel and Janey," Jenny said. "And you and your three brothers. I told her about my parents and growing up in Mount Royal. She really listens. I've never talked about any of that. Not to anyone. Maybe it was okay because she's a stranger. Made me think I should tell Maggie. She deserves to know where she comes from, don't you think?"

"Maybe," Lis said mildly. She'd never heard this much from Jenny Richards before. Was Jenny opening up now because she felt safe? Or because she wanted something from Lis? Or . . . was she a little manic?

"I grew up an only child. More than anything I wanted an older sister." Jenny put her hand over her heart. "It must have been hard to lose her."

Lis bit her lip and nodded.

"Do you have any pictures of her?"

"Let's go downstairs," Lis said. Truth be told, she wanted Jenny out of Janey's room.

In the living room, Lis showed Jenny the framed Christmas picture on the mantel. "That's me," Lis said, pointing to the little girl with dark straight hair cut short and blunt so that it cupped her face.

"And that's her," Jenny said. In the picture, Janey's hair was wispy and light and hung to her shoulders. Lis had heard it a million times: Rose Red and Rose White. Lis had dark eyes, like pots of ink, while Janey's were light. Lis was shaped more like a dumpling with soft fleshy cheeks and squeezable arms while Janey, even at two or three years old, was starting to get long and lean.

"I don't have pictures of me when I was little," Jenny said. "Or my family. That doll was the only thing I kept."

"That's so sad," Lis said, wondering how much of Jenny's story she should believe. "Do you know where your momma or—"

"*Momma*?" Jenny barked a laugh. "Let me tell you something. She'd slap you silly if you called her Momma. She was always Mother. Formal and proper and always grammatically correct. I'd ask, 'Can I go outside?' and she'd say, 'You can, but you may not.' Never went downstairs in bedroom slippers or a bathrobe. Hot as Hades, she'd have on nylon stockings."

That pretty much described Miss Sorrel, too. "That was the generation," Lis said. "Three-course meals. Cloth napkins." In a singsong she added, "Good manners never go out of style."

Jenny laughed and added, "Don't take food you don't eat.

Hush your mouth, Jesus can hear y'all. She used to look at the mess in my room and then at me, like I was some kind of heathen." Her look turned serious. "I was never quiet enough. Never neat enough. She used to put lemon juice in my hair to lighten it and scrub my face with scouring powder. But most of all I was never godly enough." Jenny laced her fingers together, her knuckles going white. "Always praying on this and praying on that. I swear, that woman was in that church every time the door opened."

Even if Jenny had taken someone else's name, there was no question in Lis's mind that this was a deeply held personal narrative, not a fabrication. "I can understand why you had to get out of there."

"Well, they threw me out. I'll admit I was a handful. Skipped school. Smoked. Drank. Stayed out past curfew with kids they didn't approve of. But basically? They got mad at me because I wouldn't drink the Kool-Aid. Father locked me out of the house in the middle of the night when I was fifteen."

Lis remembered what she'd been like at fifteen. Smoked: check. Drank: check. Hung out with the "wrong" crowd: check. If Miss Sorrel had known half of what she'd gotten up to, she'd have been grounded for months. No TV. No phone. But thrown out of the house like a piece of trash? Never. Nor could Lis imagine anything that Vanessa could have done, even when she'd been a monstrous mouthy fifteen-year-old, that could have induced Lis to lock the door behind her. "What did you do? Where did you go?"

"I stayed with my boyfriend for a few days until I realized that wasn't going to work. But he had cash so I helped myself to some of it and hopped a bus to Columbia. Minute I got there, know what I did? Got myself some Lady Clairol and dyed my hair.

Radiant auburn—I loved the name of that color, but it made me look like Raggedy Ann's wicked stepsister. Permed it, too. I didn't want anyone to recognize me." Jenny looked at herself in a mirror hanging on the wall, tracing the part in her dark brown hair where light roots were growing in. "A year later, I was pregnant. Which only would have proved to Mother that she was right to turn me out. Ironic, isn't it." Jenny shook her head. "Maggie's the best thing that ever happened to me."

"Your parents never came looking for you?"

"They probably thought I'd come crawling back. That I'd never survive without them. Lord knows it wasn't easy."

"Did you change your name?" Lis asked carefully. Maybe this was the opening Jenny needed to explain why the real Jenny Richards had died when she was four years old.

Jenny gave her an odd look. "I should have, you know. I really should have. But I didn't. What I did was what I had to do, and a lot of the time what I had to do wasn't very pretty, or legal, for that matter." She gave Lis a wry smile. "Now you're probably worried that I'm going to steal your family jewels."

Lis remembered Evelyn's warning about the spoons and felt her face go hot.

28

Vanessa stayed up that night long after Lis and Grandma Sorrel and Jenny Richards had gone to bed. Resigned to staying in Bonsecours long enough to convince herself that Jenny (or who-ever she really was) wasn't going to steal the spoons (or worse), she stayed up working on her grant proposal. Overhead she could still hear occasional footsteps. A door opening and closing. Water going on and then off. Less and less until silence settled and the only sound was the clicking of her keyboard.

She was logged in to the university library, finding citations to beef up her literature review and rationale. Aristotle had been the first to describe lucid dreaming, and there'd been plenty of junk science in the 1970s and 1980s to discredit it. But more recent work published in places like the *Journal of Sleep Research*, *Neurology Review*, and the *Journal of Nervous and Mental Disease* of-fered the support she needed for her grant proposal.

Vanessa was particularly interested in ways that investigators had attempted to induce lucid dreaming and then measure it. Neuroimaging. EEG. Transcranial direct current stimulation. As the house quieted and Vanessa got deeper into the research archives, her rationale for her own approach grew more solid.

Her own work was so much more practical than what had been done up to now, oriented as it was to problem-solving, not to measurement and analysis or discrediting straw men. She took lucid dreaming as a given and assumed it could be learned. Her goal was to teach people to use it to their advantage.

She was copying a few final citations when she heard a cry. At first she thought it was coming from outside. Maybe an owl or a nighthawk. She went into the front hall. Heard it again, followed by the distinctly human sound of sobbing. It was coming from overhead.

Vanessa climbed the stairs. Light spilled into the hallway from Miss Sorrel's room. Vanessa hurried to it, but found the room empty.

The sobbing was coming from the boys' room where Jenny was staying. Vanessa opened the door just enough to see in. There was Grandma Sorrel sitting on the edge of the bed, her arms wrapped around Jenny. Jenny was crying. Grandma Sorrel was talking to her, too quietly for Vanessa to hear.

Vanessa went into the bathroom for a box of tissues. "Can I do anything?" she whispered as she set the box down next to Jenny's bed.

Grandma Sorrel shook her head and motioned for her to leave.

A half hour later, just as Vanessa was dozing off in bed, there was a tap at her door. Vanessa opened it to find Grandma Sorrel on the other side. "I'm sorry to wake you, but I need your help," she said, and she pulled the little pink chintz-covered chair up to the side of the bed. She had a shredded tissue clenched in her hand.

Vanessa nodded and yawned, trying to clear her head.

"Jenny's having terrible nightmares."

Vanessa wasn't surprised. She remembered Maggie commenting on how much better her mother had been doing once she'd started taking oxycodone. Oxycodone kept you from reaching REM sleep, which meant you didn't dream at all. Go cold turkey and your brain would spew a bottled-up torrent of dreams—and nightmares. Eventually they would subside, but a pattern of disturbed sleep was one of the many reasons recovering addicts relapsed.

Grandma Sorrel went on, "She's terrified, poor thing. Afraid to fall asleep. She's finally dropped off. You can help her, can't you? Aren't you working on a cure for nightmares?"

Cure seemed too strong a word. It smacked of quack medicine. Vanessa's dream catcher wasn't a cure so much as a tool to harness nightmares. It was a powerful idea, and the grant would give her a chance to realize it. If Jenny tried using the prototype, it could help them both—Jenny with her nightmares and Vanessa with her research.

"For me to help her she'd have to trust me," Vanessa said. "Do you think she would?"

"Maybe we can figure out a way that makes it feel like it's her idea."

Vanessa woke up the next morning smelling the breakfast she'd been dreaming about. That's the way dreams worked; real-life sensations shouldered their way in. She really didn't want to get out of bed. By the time she got to sleep last night it had been after three. But the smell of breakfast sausage got her to pick her head up off the pillow. Coffee, too.

Vanessa got up and put on jeans and a T-shirt. When she entered the kitchen, Grandma Sorrel looked up at her from the table where she and Jenny and Lis were sitting. Evelyn was at the stove, cooking sausage meat. She turned to get some flour to make gravy. Vanessa could smell biscuits in the oven. Her mouth watered. Biscuits and sausage gravy were pure Low Country comfort food. ·

"Morning, 'Nessa," Grandma Sorrel said.

"Good morning, y'all," Vanessa said. She poured herself a cup of coffee and took the empty seat between Lis and Jenny.

Evelyn pulled the biscuits from the oven and popped a pair of them onto each of the five plates. "I hope this tastes all right," she said as she ladled thick sausage gravy over the biscuits.

"Oh, Evelyn, there's no one makes biscuits and gravy like you," Lis said, rolling her eyes at Vanessa.

"Some fool got the wrong kind of sausages," Evelyn said. "Musta been on sale. I did the best I could."

Vanessa got up to help Evelyn distribute the plates. She was about to dig in when Lis elbowed her from the side. Everyone else was sitting, head bowed, holding hands. Vanessa put down her fork and took Lis's and Jenny's hands.

Evelyn smiled and sighed, closed her eyes and began, "Bless us, O Lord, and these Thy gifts . . ." Vanessa didn't close her eyes. She noticed that Jenny didn't either.

In the middle of the blessing, a cricket chirped. And chirped again. A cell phone on the table in front of Lis lit up. Lis swiped it to ignore the call.

"Amen," Evelyn said. Lis's phone dinged with a message. Vanessa picked up her fork. The biscuits were fluffy, the thick gravy studded with tasty nuggets of sweet, salty sausage. If she'd been alone, she'd have run her finger across the plate to scrape up every bit of gravy. No one in Rhode Island understood biscuits and gravy.

"Vanessa was up late last night working on the computer," Grandma Sorrel said. "Weren't you, darlin'? She's a psychologist."

Grandma Sorrel nudged Vanessa under the table in case she missed her cue. "I study dreams," Vanessa said.

"I once saw a hypnotist," Jenny said. She'd barely touched her food, just poked at it with her fork. "He made this woman climb up on a table and squawk like a chicken."

"Actually, what I study are nightmares," Vanessa said. "Not ordinary, garden-variety bad dreams. Everyone has those occasionally. I'm talking about terrifying dreams that people get over and over again. They're so terrifying that you wake up in a blind panic, soaked with sweat, your heart pounding in your throat."

Jenny's eyes widened. Vanessa could tell the description was striking home.

"It can be so upsetting that you're afraid of falling asleep, which only makes things worse. Because if you can't sleep, you end up with all kinds of other physical and psychiatric problems."

"Tell us about your research," Grandma Sorrel said.

Vanessa felt everyone's eyes on her. "I watch people sleep," she said, trying to sound calm and confident. "I monitor things like their brain waves and heart rates and eye movements. And I'm working on a gadget that helps people gain control of their dreams. It can be lifesaving. No exaggeration. I've worked with trauma survivors who were so severely impaired by nightmares that—" Vanessa broke off, realizing that her voice was escalating and Jenny had dropped her fork, her portion still half eaten. "It's noninvasive. I've used it myself and lived to tell about it."

"Do you have nightmares?" Jenny asked.

"Sure. Everyone does. On a scale of one to ten, mine are about a five. Upsetting but not terrifying." Vanessa remembered that wave approaching, feeling her feet anchored in place. The panic she'd felt when Grandma Sorrel tried to thrust that bundle into her arms. "The point is, I've taught myself to control my dreams."

Jenny said, "How did you even know you're dreaming?"

"Ah. That is a brilliant question, because that is exactly the challenge. I've assembled a device"—she held her hands inches apart to show how big—"just a sleep mask with sensors in it connected to a little computer, just a souped-up cell phone. I go to sleep, and when the mask senses that I'm dreaming, it sets off a vibration just strong enough to penetrate the dream. It doesn't wake me up, but it alerts my subconscious. And if I'm having a nightmare, it tells me I'm dreaming."

"So?" Jenny asked, her eyes widening. "How does that help?"

"I direct the dream. Like it's my movie and I can bend it to my will. Rewrite the ending. Of course it takes practice, but it's empowering. Instead of being at its mercy, I'm in control."

Jenny looked intrigued, but Vanessa didn't press it further. Best to let her think about it, let the possibilities sink in.

Sure enough, after breakfast Jenny joined Vanessa at the sink, drying dishes while Vanessa washed. Keeping her voice low and masked by the water running, Jenny asked, "How hard is it to learn?"

29

After breakfast, Lis left Jenny and Vanessa doing the dishes and ducked out onto the porch to listen to her phone message. The caller ID said the call had come in from Laurel Bay, the DNA testing service she'd hired to perform a siblingship test.

She swallowed a wave of anxiety. She had to go somewhere private to listen to the message, so she grabbed her coat and scarf and jingled Binty's leash. The dog woofed and scrabbled to meet her at the front door. The poor dog may have been losing her battle with old age, but her hearing was sharp as ever.

"I'm going out to walk the dog," Lis called to Miss Sorrel and Evelyn, who were sitting in the living room. She snapped the leash onto the dog's collar and carried Binty down the front steps.

When they were around the corner, she sat on a bench in front of the library and stroked Binty as she tried to calm herself. She knew the results would be negative, still she felt apprehensive as she started playing the message.

A polite woman's voice. "This is Julia at Laurel Bay Testing Services calling Elisabeth Strenger. To collect your test results, please call back and schedule an appointment."

Schedule an appointment? She sat there for a few moments, staring at the phone and trying to imagine what it would be like if Jenny were Janey. It would be good, right? Really good, but complicated.

She was about to return the call when her phone rang again. A glance at the readout told her it was Frank. She'd already ignored two calls from him, and she wasn't sure what she wanted to say to him. She was still angry that he had never told her he'd been involved in the search for Abby Verner. He must have known that the little girl's parents had commissioned a Miss Sorrel doll. And Lis had had to learn from Evelyn that Jenny Richards was living under a stolen identity. What else was Frank keeping from her? Was she always going to be little Lissie to him, the girl who needed to be sheltered and protected? It was no basis for an adult relationship. But maybe she was the only one who thought that was what they had.

She let Frank's call go to voice mail and called the clinic back. A woman answered, "Laurel Bay Testing Services. This is Julie speaking. How can I help you?"

"This is Elisabeth Strenger. Calling about my test results."

"Of course. Strenger." There was a long pause and Lis thought she could hear a keyboard clicking on the other end. "Yes. Here we are. When would you like to come in and speak with one of our counselors?"

"Do I really need to drive all the way over there and talk to someone?" Lis said. "Can't you e-mail me the report or tell me over the phone?"

She thought she heard Julie heave a sigh, like maybe she had to explain this a hundred times a week. "We can FedEx the results to you. But our genetics counselor feels you'll want to go over the findings in person. It's our experience, even when results are straightforward, a clear explanation helps make for a clearer understanding."

Were her results less than "straightforward"? And what happened to *You provide usable DNA samples and results will be conclusive*? If she and Jenny weren't sisters, wouldn't that be a flat-out negative result? What could there be to discuss? "Is that really necessary? Because I don't really have the time and I can't afford—"

"There's no charge. As I say, we can FedEx the results to you if that's what you'd like. But I always advise our customers to take advantage of our in-house expertise. Rest assured, we don't make a penny more whether you do or don't." She paused, then, in a tone that sounded a lot less like she was reading from a script, she added, "You're going to want to go over these results with a counselor."

Now Lis's imagination spiraled off into doomsday scenarios. They'd taken one look at Lis's DNA and discovered that she was going to have early onset Alzheimer's. Or Jenny was going to get ALS. All she wanted to know was whether Jenny was her sister.

Lis made an appointment for first thing the next morning. The test center opened at eight. She'd stop in on her way to Woody's Charters. She'd promised Cap'n Jack she'd come in and get caught up on the work she'd missed.

When she hung up the phone, she was shaking.

Lis walked Binty back to the house and then ran to catch up with Vanessa and Jenny, who'd gone for a walk on Main Street. She joined them a block into the business district.

The sun had broken through and the wind picked up. Lis unbuttoned her jacket and Vanessa unwrapped her scarf from around her neck. Jenny was hunched over like a walking cocoon, her arms folded tight and her coat pulled tight around her. Every time a car whooshed by Jenny gave a start.

"Are you cold?" Lis asked. "I can go back and get the car."

"I'm not cold," Jenny said through clenched teeth.

"Have you been to Bonsecours before?" Vanessa asked.

"I . . . I don't think so." Jenny took in the cafés and art galleries and boutiques on either side of the street.

"This area's changed a lot in the last few years," Lis said. "It's basically an old port city, but ever since they built the waterfront park, the downtown's been getting fancier and fancier. There used to be a department store over there." She pointed to the cavernous antiques mall on the other side of the street beside what looked like an old five-and-dime.

Vanessa said, "I remember you used to take me there for shoes."

"And your grandma used to take *me* there for shoes."

Vanessa added, "And wasn't there a drugstore next door? I remember the giant apothecary bottles they had in the window. I was sure one of them was filled with red bug juice and the other one was mint-flavored mouthwash."

Lis remembered the pharmacy, an obligatory stop when she was little, too. Comics and candy under the register in front. A soda fountain in the back with a counter and red vinyl-seated stools that you could spin around on. At Christmas every year they'd have a bowing Santa and Mrs. Santa in the window next to a miniature tree.

"And that used to be a bank," Vanessa said, shading her eyes and looking across the street to a building that had a PANINI PALACE sign in the window but the words *PEOPLE'S BANK* embossed in the pediment over the entrance. Every Monday Lis used to go with Grandma Sorrel to the bank, where they would stand in line to deposit the weekend's receipts from Woody's Charters. These days, Lis was responsible for making their cash deposits, but she had to drive to a bank out on Route 28 to do it.

"What's out behind?" Jenny asked.

"A park. It's the reason the downtown has had such a comeback," Lis said. She led the way, down a brick path between the Panini Palace and an antiques gallery. Behind the buildings, a manicured expanse of park opened up, and beyond that, the broad Bonsecours River. When Lis and Janey were little, nothing had been there but mudflats, swamp grass, docks, and warehouses. Tons of cement had had to be trucked in to stabilize the riverbank so the esplanade could be built. It had opened not long after Lis had moved back to Bonsecours with Vanessa.

Jenny wrapped the borrowed coat even more tightly around her as they stood looking across the river.

"There's the hospital where you were." Lis pointed to the complex of green-roofed buildings on the opposite shore.

They walked to the far end of the esplanade, then cut back to Main Street and continued on into residential streets. Closer to the water's edge, the houses were raised, in recognition of Bonsecours's famously high water table. New houses were built to look old, and some of the oldest still had slave cabins on their property.

Down here the air turned sulphurous and the only sound aside from rustling branches was the occasional hollow thunk as a nearby overflow conduit filled and emptied. Lis stopped at the edge of an inlet that Lis used to call "the creek." She and Janey used to come here all the time, trailing after their brothers when Grandma Sorrel thought they were at the drugstore buying red licorice whips and cellophane-wrapped rolls of Smarties. In the days after Janey disappeared, Woody had brought in boats from Woody's Charters and nets to help the police drag the waters here. If Janey had fallen in, this was where she would have done it.

Lis stepped onto a crumbling low wall that had once functioned as a breakwater. Made of tabby concrete studded with broken oyster shells, it extended about twenty feet into the water. She used to load her pockets with stones, and then walk out to the end and skip them. Edging her way out, she was startled when, with an indignant cry, a dark heron with a white breast flew out from nearby reeds and flapped off.

Gingerly, Jenny sidestepped across the breakwater to join Lis. Vanessa followed, and the three of them looked out at the sun-dappled water.

"Oh, look," Jenny said, leaning forward. The base of the breakwater was alive with fiddler crabs, the males waving their one oversized claw. Beyond the crabs, the surface of the water looked like a matted carpet of flattened sweetgrass baskets, hanging there perfectly still. And then, with only the smallest sighing sound, the surface began to undulate. "Oh my," Jenny said, gasping. "Wow. Did you see that? It's like magic."

"It does seem like magic," Lis said, "but it was probably the tide turning."

"Or a boat's wake," Vanessa said.

"I hate boats," Jenny said. A pair of kayakers paddled past. So far off that its motor's roar was nothing but a muted buzz, a powerboat sped down the river. Farther out a shrimp boat chugged along, outriggers extended and nets ready to be lowered. "I *really* hate boats."

Lis laughed. "You know my family owns a sportfishing business. We're all about boats. Muscle boats." She remembered how

Janey used to love being on a boat. The faster it went, the more she liked it. She'd stand between Woody's legs up on the fly-bridge with her arms spread as the boat sped along, while Lis cowered on the lower deck, holding on for dear life.

"Did you grow up with boats?" Vanessa asked.

"We didn't live near the water, less'n you count the water hazard at the golf course or the baptismal font at church." Jenny crouched and picked out a stone from the crumbling concrete. She threw it far out into the water. "But the thought of going out on a boat makes me sick to my stomach."

"Are there boats in your nightmares?" Vanessa asked.

"What do you think?"

"But if there was no water nearby," Vanessa said, "and no one took you out sailing, I wonder why you ended up so terrified of boats? Phobias can usually be traced back to a trigger."

Jenny blinked a few times. "I wish I knew."

"Do you?" Lis said. "Because if we can track your parents down, it's one more question you can ask them."

Jenny narrowed her eyes at Lis, as if searching for a hidden agenda. "You think they'd remember?"

"Maybe," Lis said. "Can't hurt to ask. Show up on your parents' doorstep. Ask them what happened that made you so afraid." When Jenny didn't hunch over and retreat like a snail into its shell, Lis pressed further. "We could drive over there today."

Lis held her breath. How far was Jenny willing to go to sustain the past she'd dreamed up for herself? Or was she exactly who and what she claimed to be?

"All right," Jenny said, her lips tightening into a thin smile. "She'll be shocked that I didn't go to hell after all. At least not directly."

Later that morning, Lis drove Jenny to Mount Royal while Vanessa went to the library to work on her grant proposal. Jenny sat tense in the passenger seat. According to her, this was her first time back since she'd run away at fifteen. Lis had the address of the house where Jenny said she'd grown up loaded into the car's GPS.

Lis had looked up the property and knew that the house had been built in 1977. Clive and Renata Richards, the couple that Jenny said were her parents, were no longer listed as living there. The current homeowners were Dwayne Nash and his wife, Sheila Nevins-Nash. They'd bought the house on Enclave Drive for $385,000 in 2012. Sheila was a dental hygienist who must have had a thing about cats because her Facebook profile picture was a black-and-white tuxedo cat. Dwayne was an attorney who'd gone to Duke and specialized in personal injury. They were registered Republicans. It was scary how much you could learn about complete strangers in a matter of minutes.

Sadly, the Richardses had not sold the house to the Nashes, and Google didn't turn up any breadcrumbs leading to their current whereabouts.

The road forked east a few miles before Charleston, and Lis continued driving across a causeway. Ten miles farther along they passed a billboard that read "Welcome to Mount Royal," below that, "Not Your Average Place." *Talk about damning with faint praise.* A few miles past the billboard, a sign pointed to the town's "historic center."

Jenny said, "Didn't used to be a darned thing out here excepting swamp and fields and once in a while a farm stand." She pivoted in her seat as they drove past a Publix market and a Chick-fil-A.

"*Turn right on Enclave Drive.*" The GPS voice pronounced it EN-clave.

"Turn there," Jenny said. "That's my street."

The curving road was lined with substantial houses set on manicured lots. Each had an attached two-car garage, and each was just different enough from its neighbor so they didn't feel cookie-cutter.

"There it is," Jenny said. She put her hand over her mouth as she stared at the generous, two-story putty-colored house. "When we moved in, it was brand-new. Used to be white."

Lis parked in front of the house and cut the engine. When she rolled down the windows, the smell of bark mulch wafted in. She got out and went around to the passenger door. Jenny stared out the open car window. She looked pale, her eyes bright.

"That was my room." Jenny pointed to the window in the leftmost gable. "You can't really tell, but this is the highest point around, and that window's got a window seat. I used to love to sit there and imagine what it would be like to live somewhere else. Wishing I knew what the world was like beyond my rancid little corner of Mount Royal. Guess you should be careful what you wish for."

It did seem bizarre that the little girl who'd grown up in this

solidly upper-middle-class neighborhood would end up consid-
ering a move to a rent-subsidized single-wide upward mobility.

"Do you want me to see if there's anyone home? Maybe they'll
let us come in and look around." Lis didn't wait for an answer.
She went up to the front door and rang the bell. Heard it chime
inside. Waited. A painted slate hanging beside the front door
said WELCOME. The smell of potpourri might have been coming
from the wreath that hung on the door. It was heart-shaped,
made of red-and-white-quilted calicoes. Valentine's Day was in
two weeks. She rang the bell again. Nothing.

Lis returned to the car. "Looks like no one's home."

Jenny seemed relieved. She got out. "Think they'd mind if I
take a look around back?"

Lis walked with Jenny to the backyard. A broad awning covered a screened-in flagstone patio, and beyond that stretched a
weedless lawn. Jenny headed past Lis and ducked into a thicket
that separated the property from the one behind it. Lis followed.
"There used to be . . ." Jenny turned in a full circle. "There. That's
where I'd play. Like this was my Terabithia." She approached
a tall, arching shrub studded with the occasional explosion of
baby-blue flowers that looked like phlox. She pinched off a flower
at the base of the stem and offered it to Lis.

Bushes like that grew thick behind Miss Sorrel's house in Bonsecours. *Plumbago.* The name came to Lis, though she had no
idea how she knew it. Its branches created the perfect play space
to crawl underneath and set up housekeeping. In the summer its
branches would be loaded with flowers.

Lis took the flower from Jenny and pressed its stem to Jenny's earlobe, making a sticky-stemmed flowered earring, just
like she used to do when she and Janey played dress-up in
the yard, wrapping themselves in itchy boas of Spanish moss
and crowning themselves with chains of daisies. At first Jenny

pulled back, startled by the gesture. Then she smiled and patted her ear.

"I remember playing out here alone, except when I was real little and we had a dog," Jenny said.

"What kind of dog?"

"Black and white." Jenny smiled at the memory. "Short hair. Just a mutt. She had big brown eyes and floppy ears. Like velvet. Mother said she got too big so we had to get rid of her. I guess whoever sold them the dog promised she'd stay small and she didn't. Like me."

"Did she have a black patch over one eye?" Lis asked.

"The right one."

"And white on the tip of his tail?"

Jenny nodded.

The world, Lis reminded herself, was teeming with black-and-white short-haired pups with black eye patches and white-tipped tails. It was probably a coincidence that Jenny had just described exactly the dog that had run through their yard and lured Lis from Janey's side. Lis had not the slightest doubt that Jenny had grown up in Mount Royal in this house, believing herself to be Jenny Richards, the daughter of Renata and Clive Richards.

"I wonder where your parents moved. Were they friendly with their neighbors?" Lis eyed the houses on either side. "Did you have friends from school?"

"I was homeschooled until ninth grade. And their friends were at First Baptist. Church was their life. Mother was in the women's ministry and she sang in the choir. Father was a deacon. They thought the sun rose and set on the reverend, Dr. Mike."

First Baptist. Mount Royal. Lis keyed the search into her phone. Driving time from the house, ten minutes.

"Well, let's go pay a visit. Who knows, someone might still be around who can tell us what happened to them."

31

It turned out Lis didn't need a map. Jenny directed her to the church that she said had been the hub of her family's social life. The brick building with a tall, slender white steeple had a sign out front that read GOOGLE CAN'T SATISFY EVERY SEARCH. Lis took it as a good omen.

She parked the car in the near empty lot and followed Jenny into the church. Jenny paused in the lobby, closed her eyes, and sniffed. "I remember that smell."

Lis caught the cloying sweet smell of lilies over a layer of floor wax.

Jenny pushed open one of the doors to the sanctuary and Lis followed her in. Light streamed in through tall windows on both sides.

Lis was hoping they'd find Dr. Mike and, failing that, church records. "Where do you think the church office—"

But Lis realized Jenny had slid into one of the pews near the front. "This was where we always sat. I loved the preaching. I loved the praying. Most of all I loved the singing. *Sing joyfully to the Lord, you righteous.* I loved all of it, until I didn't."

Lis walked around the edge of the sanctuary, letting Jenny take her time absorbing echoes of her own past. In the back she found a sign with an arrow pointing down a corridor to CHURCH RECTORY OFFICES.

"There used to be Sunday school classrooms that way, too," Jenny said, joining her.

Lis followed Jenny down the hallway, which was lined with children's artwork and hand-lettered Bible passages. A tall, pale man in a dark suit and tie came striding toward them, then stopped, smiled, and tipped forward. "Can I help you ladies?"

"I was hoping to find Dr. Mike," Jenny said.

The man gave a formal bow and offered Jenny his hand. "I'm Reverend James." He smiled and shook his head. "I'm sorry to tell you, Dr. Mike passed. Ten years ago, maybe twelve. Before my time."

"I used to belong to this church," Jenny said.

"Did we lose you when you moved away?"

"You could say that. It was quite a while ago. I should have realized he wouldn't be with us any longer."

"Well, you're always welcome to come back. Why don't you and your friend stay for afternoon services?"

Lis said, "Actually, Jenny's lost touch with her family and she's trying to reconnect with them. Maybe they're still active in the church? Renata and Clive Richards."

"My father was a deacon," Jenny added.

"Well, I've been here going on eight years, but the name's not ringing a bell. We do have membership rolls going back to the early 1800s when this church stood across the street, pretty much just one room. Had about thirty members."

Lis hoped he wasn't going to give them chapter and verse on the congregation's storied past. He must have sensed that because he asked, "When did your family join the church?"

Lis answered. "Nineteen seventy-seven or thereabouts." To

Jenny she added, "That's when the house you grew up in was built. You said you moved in when it was new."

"Forty years ago," Reverend James said. "I'm afraid our member rolls from back then, such as they are, are handwritten. You're welcome to look." He turned on his heel and led them back down the corridor in the direction from which he'd come. He opened a door marked RECTORY CHURCH OFFICE and let them go in ahead of him.

The room had wall-to-wall bookcases and two big oak desks, one of them a rolltop, and a row of utilitarian gray file cabinets. The walls were papered with posters—landscapes with inspirational quotes.

Reverend James hauled a wide, old-fashioned accountant's ledger from a shelf. He set it on a wide slanted lectern and pulled over a floor lamp. Opened the ledger and flipped through to a page marked 1977. "You might want to start earlier and work your way forward. When you're done, just close the book and I'll put it back after you're finished."

"Thank you," Jenny said. "You have a blessed day."

Reverend James nodded and looked at his watch. "I'll leave you to it, then. And I'll check to see if there's any mention of your parents in our deacons' or Women's Ministry record books."

As Reverend James suggested, Lis turned back to 1974. She put on her glasses and she and Jenny stood side by side reading the ledger. Its pages were ruled into neat columns, each entry written in a crisp, clear hand. Scanning down the page, she saw the entries were limited to major milestones. Joining or leaving the congregation. Births. Baptisms. Marriages.

"Richards, Richards, Richards," Lis whispered to herself as she drew her finger down the page. And then one page into 1978, there they were. Renata Fielding Richards. Clive Richards. Jenny Richards. They'd all joined First Baptist March 15, 1978. Janey had disappeared January of that same year.

> Jennifer Richards. Joined 3/15/78. Baptized 10/26/86. EXCL 7/9/88.

"What does that mean?" Lis asked, pointing to *EXCL*.

"Excluded. Voted off the island." Jenny's voice was thick.

Just then Reverend James returned. He looked somber. "I'm afraid I have sad news." He handed Jenny a copy of a hand-drawn map labeled FIRST BAPTIST CEMETERY. On the map he'd marked a spot with a red X. "I'm so sorry for your loss."

Jenny's inhaled sharply. "They're dead. I wasn't expecting that." She put her hand over her mouth for a few moments. "And here I've been imagining what it would be like to face them. Practicing what I was going to say so I wouldn't break down. Wondering if they'd even remember who I was." She brushed away a tear.

"Such a shame that you didn't have a chance to reconcile with them before they passed," Reverend James said, handing Jenny a tissue. "Shall we go outside and you can pay your respects?"

Lis and Jenny followed him out and across the street to the small cemetery. A stone marking the entrance said FIRST BAP-TIST CEMETERY EST 1850. Reverend James led them down a path, past stones that dated back more than a century and on to newer single headstones and family plots. He stopped before a large stone that spanned several graves. Two names were en-graved on the stone.

CLIVE RICHARDS
MARCH 4, 1921–MARCH 15, 2000

RENATA FIELDING RICHARDS
MAY 16, 1931–JULY 23, 2003

After standing with them for a few minutes, his head bowed in respectful silence, Reverend James said, "Don't forget, you're welcome to join us for afternoon worship. It's about challenging ourselves to walk closer to God, leaving our rebellion behind." He smiled at Jenny.

When he'd gone back across the street and into the church, Jenny said, "My father used to rail against rebellion. Rebel and you were opening the door to demon spirits." Jenny blew her nose and wiped her eyes. "I don't know why I'm crying. He was full of shit." She gave a weak laugh, but tears kept coming.

Lis took a step closer and hooked her arm in Jenny's. She felt Jenny quaking. Heaving a sob. If they'd been sisters, Lis would have embraced her and they'd have cried together. Instead, Lis squeezed Jenny's arm and stood with her. Staring at the granite stones. At the grass littered with pecans. At the bare branches of the tree, etched like lace against a gray sky.

"I had a sister," Jenny said, unhooking her arm from Lis's. "She died a year before I was born."

32

"Maggie doesn't even know about her," Jenny said. "In their great wisdom, my parents gave me my dead sister's name. Jennifer Ann Richards. She'd been called Jennifer. I was Jenny. My parents never forgave me for not being her." Jenny pulled her jacket around her and crossed her arms. "I remember going with my parents to tend to her grave." She looked around, out at the street where traffic sped by. "Not here, I don't think. There was no road so close. Mother would weed and plant fresh flowers and leave me to wander. I tried to step between the graves, not on them. I didn't think dead people would like to be stepped on. And I looked for other children's graves. They weren't hard to spot because they had miniature headstones. I'd look for really old ones, children who'd lived a few days or a few years."

Lis looked at Jenny's parents' grave markers and the ones nearby. "But you're right, doesn't look like she's buried here."

"They moved to Mount Royal after she died."

"Did they ever talk about where they lived before they moved here? What church they went to before?"

"No. They tried to avoid talking about life with Jennifer, except for the grave tending. Once a woman visited us, someone my mother said she'd gone to school with. I remember she lived on an island. And she'd had to take a ferry to get to us." Jenny shuddered.

There were a ton of islands off the coast of South Carolina and Georgia.

"I remember the name was from the Bible. Saint something."

"St. Helena?" Lis said. "St. Simons?"

Jenny shook her head.

"St. Bridget?"

"Maybe."

Lis felt a tremor of excitement. St. Bridget was an island, a suburb of Bonsecours. Same county. Protected by the same police force. And accessible only by ferry until a bridge was built about ten years ago. Lis took Jenny's hand as a new, more detailed scenario unspooled in her head. Maybe the Richardses had been living on St. Bridget when their four-year-old daughter Jennifer was tragically killed. They buried her and grieved. If they'd been offered a needy little four-year-old girl to replace the one they'd lost, wouldn't they gladly have taken her? Paid whatever was asked? Convinced themselves that it was an act of grace, giving a lost (or abused, or abandoned) little girl a good home? It was, in fact, God's will.

But on some level they must have known it wasn't legitimate. Otherwise, why had they moved to the mainland? Started over in a new community, joined a new congregation, made new friends, and most of all avoided awkward questions about how they'd acquired their new little Jenny?

"What?" Jenny said. "Stop looking at me like that."

"Jenny, your parents didn't just name you after your sister. They gave you her identity."

Jenny stared at her parents' gravestone. Turned and looked

across the street at the church. She did have the palest of blue eyes, and the same shadows Lis had underneath them. They were faint, but they were there. Lis was sure of it.

"Think about it," Lis said, giddy with excitement. "According to your sister's death certificate—"

"Death certificate?"

Lis felt her face flush. Surely, when all was said and done, Jenny would appreciate why they'd been investigating her. "She was born in 1972. She died when she was four. Look at the stone. If you were born *after* your sister died, your mother would have been forty-five when she had you. I suppose it's possible. But unlikely."

Jenny blinked as this information sank in. Good news or bad, Lis couldn't tell.

"So my parents . . ."

"Seems unlikely that she was your biological mother. Maybe they took you in and gave you your sister's name. Adopted you legally. Or maybe not."

Jenny gave Lis a long searching look. "Am I Janey?"

"Do you want to find out?" Lis asked, though she already had herself convinced. Tomorrow morning when she went to collect the test results at the DNA lab she'd have proof.

Jenny hesitated. But when she spoke her voice was strong. "Yes. I do."

That night, after Jenny had gone up to bed, Vanessa took up
to her the sleep mask and the rest of the paraphernalia that she
used to catch dreams. She tapped lightly on the bedroom door
and found Jenny sitting up in bed. In her lap was one of their
family photo albums.

"It's amazing how everyone's baby pictures look so alike,"
Jenny said. She rotated the album so Vanessa could see the photograph of a newborn with saucer eyes and a squished newborn
face framed with wisps of fair hair.

"I'm pretty sure that's Janey," Vanessa said.

"Thing is, it looks a whole lot like a picture my parents had of
me as a baby." Jenny gave her a probing look.

Vanessa tried to keep her expression neutral. Lis had come
back from Mount Royal flushed and excited. She wouldn't say
why. Not until she was sure, she said. Vanessa was dreading the
crash, the emotional letdown if Jenny turned out to be a fraud.

"You're right, babies do look alike," Vanessa said, shifting her
gaze to a bowl with pink camellias floating in it that sat on the
bureau. "Those are lovely."

"Aren't they?" Jenny said. "I guess white ones were planted

for your momma and pink ones for Janey." Vanessa hadn't known that. Once again she was reminded of how little Janey had been mentioned. Vanessa had conspired in the silence, content not to ask.

"Evelyn brought them over," Jenny added.

"How sweet of her," Vanessa said, though the gesture surprised her. When Vanessa had been working in her bedroom earlier that day, she'd overheard Evelyn and Grandma Sorrel arguing, Evelyn insisting that Jenny was running a con; Grandma Sorrel saying, so what if she was.

"She brought the flowers over and we chatted," Jenny said.

"Really? About what?"

"That woman's nosier than a pig's snout. She wanted to know all about Mount Royal. Whether we found my house. Tracked down my parents. I told her we found the churchyard where they're buried. That shut her up."

"My mother told me about that. I'm sorry."

"Don't be. Like I told Evelyn, far as I'm concerned they died long ago. And no, I really don't want to talk about it."

Changing the subject, Vanessa asked, "Ready to face off with your nightmare?"

Jenny pushed herself up straighter in bed. "It can't be any scarier than what I was afraid I'd have to face in my hometown."

"First, full disclosure. This gadget can't discriminate everyday vivid dreams from nightmares," Vanessa said, handing Jenny the sleep mask and the cell phone to which it attached. "So we might have to toss the first couple of dreams you catch back."

"Well, I didn't think it was going to be like shooting fish in a barrel." Jenny held the mask at arm's length, eyeing it warily. "This all there is to it? I thought it was going to look like something out of Frankenstein."

"That's the whole deal, and, no, we don't have to wait for lightning to strike," Vanessa said. "No drugs. Nothing gets stuck in you or to you. You change your mind, you just take this thing off."

Jenny turned the mask over.

"So, there are sensors in there," Vanessa said. She had Jenny rub the mask, inside and out, so she could feel the wiring. "They measure your eye movements and brain waves to tell if you're in REM sleep and dreaming." She attached the leads to the cell phone on which data would be recorded.

"What happens to my brain waves?"

"They get measured and the data stored on this little device. I transfer the numbers to my computer, erasing anything that makes them traceable back to you."

"And then?"

"Crunch the numbers and incorporate the results in a federal grant proposal."

"Giving it to the government." Jenny gave Vanessa a long, hard look, and Vanessa could feel her wavering from trust to distrust.

"All they get is my analysis. There's no way anyone can trace the numbers back to you. And no one's going to be able to crawl around inside your head."

Jenny looked unconvinced.

Patience, Vanessa told herself. She wasn't about to overcome decades of hard-earned distrust of authority in a matter of minutes. "I am applying for a government grant," Vanessa said. "If my approach works, it's going to help people like combat vets who keep reliving their worst nightmares. Like rape victims who dream that their attackers come back. Or people like you, tormented by nightmares from some past trauma they've long ago forgotten."

Jenny seemed to soften. "It works?"

"Not for everyone. But unlike most interventions, it won't hurt you, either. You're not going to overdose or get addicted. Why don't you put on the mask and see how it feels?"

Jenny stared at the mask like it was going to rise up on its hind legs and bite her. Irrational fear was just that, irrational. Vanessa knew she'd have to reassure Jenny, and keep reassuring her at every step along the way. Make it feel as if nothing was being forced on her. At least she was holding the mask. Baby steps.

"The only way I can show you how it works is if you put it on," Vanessa pressed. "I promise I won't collect an ounce of data until you say it's okay."

Jenny mumbled something about *Goddamn guinea pig* but she put on the mask.

Vanessa started the app in test mode. Adjusted the mask's tension so it was firmly settled over Jenny's eyes. The readout showed brain waves. High frequency. Conscious and on high alert.

Jenny lifted the bottom of the mask and peeked out.

"It's working," Vanessa said, showing her the readout. "Those are your brain waves. Now just sit back and try to relax."

Jenny lowered the mask and leaned back against the pillows, though from the lines of tension in her face she was anything but relaxed.

"Just breathe. In. Out. Try to relax from the top of your head right down to your toes." Vanessa watched as Jenny settled. She waited. Jenny's brain waves moderated slightly. Then a bit more. "Good. Now I'm going to play the vibration that will go off when you're dreaming. I want you to be able to recognize it."

Vanessa turned on the vibration. She could barely hear it, but Jenny jerked to attention.

"I'm going to turn it down a bit. We don't want it so strong that it wakes you up." Vanessa adjusted the intensity. "Okay? Raise your finger in time with what you feel."

Jenny leaned back, and when Vanessa triggered the vibration, she raised and lowered her finger, *quick quick slow, quick quick slow*. . . .

Vanessa fiddled with the intensity, raising and lowering it until she found the least intrusive level at which Jenny could still feel the signal and locked it in.

"It's a dream. It's a dream," Vanessa said in time with the vibrations. "That's what I want you to say to yourself when you feel that."

"It's a dream," Jenny said, her finger pulsing. "It's a dream. It's a dream."

"And that," Vanessa said, turning off the test program, "is all there is to it."

Jenny pushed up the mask and rubbed her eyes. "So it won't go off until I'm dreaming?"

"Not until you're in deep REM sleep. It may take some adjusting until I find the right frequency for your most vivid dreams."

"And you think this is going to help me."

"I can guarantee it won't hurt. There's one more thing we need to do before you go to sleep, and that's talk through your nightmare. Kind of like a dress rehearsal for how you're going to redirect it."

"Dress rehearsal." Jenny chewed on her bottom lip.

"Right. Actually talk through the dream, play it out while you're wide awake. Are you up for that?"

Jenny glanced toward the open door and Vanessa got up and shut it. She pulled the shades and sat back on the edge of the bed. She disconnected the wires to the mask so no data would be collected. "It's just you and me. Promise."

Reluctantly Jenny lowered the mask over her eyes again and Vanessa led her through a series of relaxation exercises. "Steady breathing. Inhale . . . Exhale . . . Relax." As Vanessa repeated the instructions, slowly, chanting, lines of tension eased in Jenny's brow, and the cords in her neck relaxed. Her hands unclenched.

"Now I want you to imagine that you're in the dream. Visualize." Vanessa paused. "Try to see it in your mind's eye." She paused again. "Are you there?"

Jenny nodded.

"Good. Now look around. Take in the details. Where are you?"

"On the water."

"Good. Can you tell how big the boat is?"

"We're sitting in a closed compartment. Behind glass."

Sounded like they were in the cockpit behind the windscreen. "Who's with you?"

"Someone . . ."

"Someone who?"

"No mouth. No eyes. A faceless face. I don't even know if they can hear me. Shiny buttons." Jenny's voice went flat and she reached her hand across, like she was touching them. "I'm afraid."

"Are you standing up or sitting?"

"Sitting."

"And is the boat moving?"

"Fast." Jenny clutched the quilt. Vanessa had been worried that Jenny would just be going through the motions, but instead she was fully engaged.

"What are you afraid of?"

Jenny flinched. "The water's ending and we're not slowing down. And I know we're going to get to the edge and crash and fall in and drown. Faster. And closer." Jenny's voice kept rising and in genuine distress. "And I don't know how to make it stop."

Vanessa took hold of Jenny's hand. "You know you're safe right now, don't you? You can whip off that mask and you'll be right here with me in this bedroom with the world's most hideous wallpaper. Right?"

Jenny gave a tight smile.

"Okay then. We're almost done. Hang in with me."

Jenny clenched her jaw and swallowed hard.

"You're on the boat. I want you to hear the motor roaring." Vanessa paused. "Feel the spray. Taste it?" She waited again. "Feel the wind rushing by."

Jenny squeezed Vanessa's hand. Beads of sweat glistened on her forehead.

"You can't let the boat go off the edge. You're not going to let that happen. So make up a new ending."

"A new ending." Jenny bit her lower lip. "Like what?"

"Imagine that your dream is a movie, which is sort of what it is, only it keeps rerunning itself. You're editing this movie and you can change the ending to anything you want. You can draw a face on that faceless person and make him tell you where he's taking you and what's happening and make him stop the boat. Or make the boat sprout wings and lift off. Or make yourself sprout wings. It's your dream. What's your safe ending?"

"Safe." Jenny was quiet for a few moments. Then she smiled. "I just want to stop the boat. How do you do that? Are there brakes? There'd have to be."

"You pull the throttle to neutral."

"Throttle?"

Vanessa realized that with all her fear of boats, Jenny had never spent any time on one. "You've driven a car with a stick shift?"

Jenny nodded.

"Imagine that the boat has a gear stick alongside the steering wheel. It comes up out of the floor and right now it's tilted forward, toward the front of the boat. Can you visualize it? Okay. That's the throttle. Put your hand on the throttle."

Jenny put out her hand.

Vanessa triggered the vibration on the smartphone. *Quick quick slow. Quick quick slow.* "Hear that? Recognize that pattern that you felt earlier? Imagine that's the throttle vibrating against your hand, up your arm." She waited. Jenny nodded. "Now imagine that you are looking at that throttle and repeat to yourself, 'It's a dream. It's a dream. It's a dream.'"

"It's a dream," Jenny whispered. "It's a dream."

"Now pull the throttle so it's pointing straight up. That puts the engine in neutral."

Jenny closed her fist and pulled back.

"Feel the boat slowing down. Slowing down. Water's backing up and foaming in front of the boat. Splashing on the glass. You come to a full stop and the boat rocks, back and forth, back and forth."

Jenny raised a hand and splayed her fingers.

"And now tell yourself that it's okay to wake up."

Jenny sat forward, pushed up the sleep mask, and gasped for air. She looked flushed.

"How are you feeling?" Vanessa asked.

"I'm okay." She sounded surprised.

"Take your time," Vanessa said, waiting for Jenny's breathing to slow. She took the mask from Jenny, reconnected it to the little computer, and set it on the bedside table. "Of course it won't be nearly as one, two, three when I'm not sitting next to you giving you cues."

"And I'm not awake."

"Exactly. But promise me you won't give up if it doesn't work the first time you try it. Or the second. And it will help if you practice while you're awake, the way we just did. I'll take you over to the marina and show you what the cockpit looks like. You can go on board and feel—"

"No way."

"Or not. One more thing." Vanessa handed Jenny a small notebook. "Here's your dream diary." She opened it to one of the blank pages. "Write down your dream. Do it the minute you wake up. You think you'll remember later but you won't."

"Will this be part of your data?"

"No. It's your personal story and no one else's business." She snapped the diary shut. "But many people find writing it down helps. Like taking it out of your head and putting it on a shelf where it can't hurt you again."

"Are you saying that I dream it because it really happened?"

"Dreams aren't memories. Not literally. You didn't fall off the deep end of the ocean, but something happened that left you traumatized. Maybe it wasn't even about a boat, but it will keep playing itself out as a nightmare until you do something to make it stop."

34

Lis was up during the night, anxious about what she'd learn in the morning when she got the DNA test results. She left the house early before anyone else was up and about, leaving a note on the kitchen counter saying she'd be at the marina working all day.

She arrived for her appointment at Laurel Bay a half hour early and waited in the car, flipping the radio between news and music stations. Unable to settle. When someone unlocked the storefront door a little before eight, she went in and used the ladies' room before taking a seat in the empty waiting area. Fluorescent lights seemed to bounce off the white walls and shiny vinyl tile floor. Lis tried to read a back issue of *People,* but reading it just made her feel old. She barely recognized any of the celebrities.

At last the door to the inner area opened and a young woman with long dark hair wearing a white doctor's coat came out holding a file folder. She looked at Lis. "Elisabeth?" she said. It was a good bet, since Lis was the only person in the waiting room.

Lis stood, dropping the magazine. She picked it up and placed it on a table before following the woman down an antiseptic-smelling corridor and into a tiny office every bit as bland and anonymous as the waiting area. On the wall behind a bare desk hung a half-dozen framed diplomas, too far away for Lis to read.

"I'm Dr. Lieu," the woman said. She looked even younger than Vanessa. "You're here for the results of a siblingship test."

Lis tried to read her polite smile. Dr. Lieu pulled a sheet of paper from the folder and placed it on the desk, rotating it to face Lis.

"Before I go through the results, I want to explain a little about how genes work." She smiled, and with a black Sharpie she drew two stick figures, one male and one female. Under the male figure she wrote XY, and under the female XX.

"Siblings get one chromosome from their father and one from their mother. Sisters will always have in common the same X chromosome that they inherit from their father." She circled the male stick figure's X. "They inherit their second X from their mother. But since women have two X chromosomes, simple law of averages, half the time both sisters will inherit the same X and half the time they won't." She drew a question mark over the two Xs below the female stick figure. "That's why we need maternal DNA to be able to say, with any statistical certainty, that two women have the same mother and father."

Lis shifted in her seat. Where was this heading?

Dr. Lieu went on, "We analyze the value of the markers in a handful of standard locations and look for matches. We don't always get a clear result, but in this case we did. We did a statistical analysis of the data from the three samples you brought in, and we can say that there's a 99.8 percent probability that these women are related versus not being related at all."

Related versus not related? If she and Jenny were sisters, then why not just say so? Lis put on her reading glasses and tried to make sense of the columns of numbers on the printout. The columns were labeled SIBLING 1 ALLELES, SIBLING 2 ALLELES, and KNOWN PARENT ALLELES.

"These are genetic markers, genes with known locations on a chromosome," Dr. Lieu explained. "An allele is the form that a gene can take." She pointed at various numbers, anomalies as she called them. Lis felt as if a hive of bees had taken over the inside of her head. *Jenny. Janey. Jenny. Janey.*

"The combined siblingship index is over 500, which signifies a very strong result."

That sounded good. So? Lis waited for the punch line.

Ms. Lieu's enigmatic smile was loaded with sympathy. "There's a very high likelihood that these two individuals have the same mother"—Lis relaxed a notch—"but different fathers."

What? Maybe she'd misheard. "Excuse me?"

"The samples you submitted. They're half sisters."

Lis sat in her car in the test center's parking lot, reeling as she stared at the printout. *My Rose White and Rose Red.* Well, now that made sense at least. The idea that Lis's father wasn't Woody Woodham seemed impossible. Who, if not Woody, had Miss Sorrel loved?

Lis scolded herself for letting the results cloud the one certainty: Jenny Richards was Lis's sister. So what if they had different fathers? Miss Sorrel had been right about one thing. All this time Janey had been alive, enduring an intensely unhappy childhood just hours away. Adopted but never told that she was. Made to feel like an alien growing up in a household where she didn't belong. Lis crumpled up the DNA report and was reaching across to shove it in the glove compartment when her cell phone rang. It was Frank. She'd have to talk to him sometime. She took the call.

"Didn't you get my messages?" he said. Not a great conversation starter and his timing sucked.

"I'm sorry, did you call?" Lis knew she was being passive-aggressive, but she couldn't help herself.

"Where are you?"

"At work." The lie slid out. "Where else would I be?"

"What's wrong?" he said. "You don't return my calls and now you sound royally pissed. I thought we were long past playing games with each other. Is it something I did? Just tell me and let's talk about it."

More like a million things he didn't do. Where to start? "I've been getting the impression that you never really wanted us to find Janey."

"Uh-huh." A long pause. She could imagine his jaw freezing, his expression turning to stone. "How's that?"

"You wouldn't run Maggie's license plate."

"But I did," Frank protested.

"Then you practically arrested me when we went looking for her car at the college. Are you going to tell me that you weren't following us?"

"You were playing detective, you could have gotten yourself arrested for stalking, and if you'd gotten on the highway with those tires you could have gotten yourself killed."

"Yeah, and about those tires. You didn't think I'd find it a little odd that *both* rear tires were flat but there was no puncture?"

Silence on the line. Then, "You seriously think I'd let the air out of your tires?"

Lis felt a pang of guilt. Letting air out of her tires was just the kind of nasty trick Frank, of all people, would never pull. "What I seriously think is that you should have told me that another little girl disappeared."

"What are you talking about?"

"Abby Verner."

"Abby? . . . What's she got to do with Janey?"

"So you remember her?"

"Of course I do. She went missing years ago."

"Right. Back when the police were actually following up leads instead of obstructing."

Frank didn't have a snappy comeback to that.

"She was never found, was she?" Lis asked.

"You know she wasn't." After a long pause, "Lis, I'm tired, and I don't want to fight with you. There was no connection—"

"Oh, but there was," Lis said. "Abby posed for Miss Sorrel for a portrait doll right before she disappeared. Maybe she's been out there all this time, just like Janey, waiting for the police to pull their heads out of their asses and—"

"Abby Verner?" Frank said, cutting her off. "Posed for a Miss Sorrel doll? If we'd known that . . ." Lis could almost hear Frank's wheels turning as this piece of information dropped into place.

"The police knew," Lis said. "Evelyn would have made sure that they did."

"Well, maybe she told Buck but no one told me."

"Are you sure? Because sometimes it seems like you and Evelyn have some kind of connection. Like there's a direct line from your mouth to her ear, and vice versa. She's the one who told me that you think Jenny Richards is living under a stolen identity. Did you know that that death certificate you have is actually her sister's?"

"Her sister's," Frank repeated, his voice flat. "Explain."

"Jenny told me that she had a sister who died, and Jenny was named after her."

"She told you that? What evidence—"

"I think you'll find her sister buried in a cemetery near First Baptist on St. Bridget. I'm pretty sure the family lived there before they moved to Mount Royal."

There was silence on the line, then what sounded like a keyboard tapping. "There's no birth record for a second Jenny Richards."

"Uh-huh. Are you surprised? Jenny *says* she had a sister. She believes she did. But what if she was given Jenny Richards's identity, but they weren't sisters."

More keyboard tapping. "So you think Jenny is Janey."

"Do you?"

"I think we need to wait and see what the DNA test results tell us. Which is why I called you in the first place. I'm picking them up this morning in Columbia and I can bring them by this afternoon."

That was the last thing Lis had expected to hear. "I thought it was going to take a while."

"Thank Evelyn. She knows someone at the state lab and managed to get the test fast-tracked."

Lis smoothed out the private test lab results she'd been about to put in the glove compartment. The official DNA results from the state lab would have only two columns: Jenny's and Janey's. And the results would be a match. No wrinkles. No loose ends and unanswered questions regarding siblingship to stir up a hornet's nest.

Maybe no one needed to find out what Lis now wished she didn't know.

35

That morning, Vanessa had woken up when she heard Lis's car pull out of the driveway. She padded down the hall to Jenny's room. The door was open a crack. She peered in.

Jenny was sitting up in bed with Vanessa's sleep mask pushed up over her forehead. She was writing in the notebook. A leftie, she had the notebook turned nearly upside down.

Vanessa tapped lightly on the door. Jenny looked up. "Morning," she said, putting the pen down.

"Were you able to sleep?" Vanessa asked.

"Off and on."

"So the mask didn't bother you too much?"

"It's kind of annoying. I've never slept with a mask before, and I usually have trouble falling asleep anyway. But I managed. Waking up was weird. You open your eyes and it's pitch-black."

Vanessa pulled a chair up to the side of the bed. "And?"

"I caught a dream," Jenny said, "but I didn't catch the nightmare."

"That would be too easy, wouldn't it? No one does on the first try."

"Still, it worked. The buzzing. I heard it in my dream and

woke myself up." She turned the notebook page and showed Vanessa the words and phrases she'd written: *Riverbank. Tent. Waiting for Maggie. Trying to pack. Police. Dogs.*

Vanessa said, "Do you feel like talking me through it?"

"I guess." Jenny glanced at the notes she'd taken. "Riverbank. Maggie and I are homeless and we're living"—Jenny squinted—"in a tent. On a riverbank. Under a highway. There's a place like that in Columbia. And we have to move. Again. Maggie's not there and I'm getting worried, trying to check the time because the police have warned us to clear out. Everyone around me is packing up and getting the hell out of there. They're saying that the police are coming to round everyone up and bulldoze the place. They used to do that all the time, like it's against the law to be homeless."

Made sense that Jenny would dream about being displaced, and this sounded like a typical anxiety dream, not the stuff of posttraumatic stress. Vanessa's own anxiety dreams were much milder and usually revolved around school—not being able to find a class she'd signed up for or the room where they were giving an exam she was supposed to take but hadn't studied for.

"I'm trying to pack up our blankets and clothes but things keep spilling out of my buggy," Jenny went on. "And I keep finding more stuff that we need to take with us. I can hear the dogs. They're coming for us. We need to go, but I can't leave without Maggie because how will we find each other? She told me where she is but I can't remember. I wrote it down but I can't find the piece of paper I wrote it on.

"And then I hear this buzz. And it's really terrifying because it sounds so close to me and I think they've brought in choppers, which I know is ridiculous. Because this isn't a movie and Maggie and I aren't terrorists. And I'm trying to figure it out, like maybe we're camped out over a hornet's nest or under some power lines.

"And then it hits me: It's a dream. It's a dream. And I can make anything happen." Jenny took a deep inhale, exhaled. "I can make the police go up in a puff of smoke. I can change the dogs into butterflies. I can transform our tent into a room at the Days Inn."

"And what did you do?"

"I pulled an AK-47 out of my buggy and mowed them all down." Jenny chuckled. Then she started to laugh. Hysterically. Like a dam had broken inside her. When she stopped, she had to wipe tears from her eyes. "Sorry, honey, didn't mean to freak you out. Don't worry, I haven't even got ammunition for that old shotgun. Only thing I ever shot at was a beer can, and most of the time I missed."

Vanessa cracked up. Jenny had nailed it, and on the first try. On top of that, she'd been able to joke about a pretty scary anxiety dream. It wasn't until Vanessa was in her bedroom getting dressed that the thought occurred to her: How come Jenny could easily imagine firing an assault rifle but she couldn't conjure a way to stop a boat?

Frank offered to bring the DNA test results to Miss Sorrel's house that afternoon, but Lis realized that Evelyn would likely "pop over," and for once Lis wanted her family to find out first. Instead, she suggested that he bring the results to the marina. Lis called Vanessa and asked her to make up an excuse to get Miss Sorrel and Jenny there, and see if there was any way Maggie could get there, too. The results affected them all.

After she hung up, Lis folded the siblingship test report and stuffed it into her bag. Then she started the car and blasted the radio, trying to turn off the voice in her brain that kept murmuring *half sister, half sister, half sister.*

Woody's Charters was in the Bonsecours Marina building, and they owned a half dozen of its sixty or so slips. Back in the early days, when Lis's father started the business fresh out of the military, the marina was nothing more than a few docks and a Quonset hut. Miss Sorrel ran the office from a corner of the makeshift building, and Woody did everything else, from boat maintenance to fishing guide. Now their office was in a bright, airy corner of the second floor of the marina's two-story brick building. Cap'n Jack met her at the door. "Lis, well, aren't you a sight for sore eyes," he said.

Still tall and trim, now heading into his seventies with his chiseled jaw going to jowl, Cap'n Jack had taken to growing a full beard. He still had a warmth and charisma that made the wives of their clients fall all over him. Husbands paid a premium to get him as their guide regardless because he knew every corner of the Bonsecours River and the waterways connected to it, which lures worked best, and where the fishing hot spots were at any given time of day or season.

Lis reached out to shake his hand but found herself enveloped in a bear hug. Then he pulled away and gave her a big smile. "When I heard about what happened, I didn't know what to think. So good to see you looking no worse for the wear, if you don't mind my saying so. How's your momma? Is she back home?"

"She's coming over later so you can see for yourself. And by the way, she thanks you for the lovely flowers. How are things here?" She eyed the pile of what looked like mail and messages on her desk.

"Just fine," Cap'n Jack assured her. "You know it's the quiet time of year."

"But it's a busy time ahead. We need to keep things moving. I can't expect you to do everything." Lis took a seat at her desk and started working her way through the mail and messages that had accumulated. It was a comfort to keep her mind busy with paying bills, updating spreadsheets and their online booking system, and returning calls.

Around noon Lis took time out for a quick trip to the restaurant across from the marina to grab a sandwich. She was back at work and almost caught up when she heard Miss Sorrel's voice. "Yoohoo, comin' up!"

Cap'n Jack went out into the upstairs hall, and a few moments later came back, linked arm in arm with Miss Sorrel, the pair of them looking for all the world like an old married couple.

"Oh my, I am winded," Miss Sorrel said. "Can't even manage a flight of stairs. That is pitiful." She took another few moments to catch her breath. "Lis, 'Nessa's out there giving Maggie and Jenny a tour. Poor thing, Jenny went green around the gills just looking at a boat setting in the water. 'Nessa says she needs to see how the throttle works. Don't know why if she's determined never to get on a boat." She cast a critical gaze around the office and rocked back on her heels. "Y'all rearranged."

Miss Sorrel rarely came to the marina, not since she'd handed the reins over to Lis. She hadn't been there since before Lis moved her desk, the one from which Miss Sorrel had once presided, to the window. The lounge area that Lis and Cap'n Jack had set up in a corner with a couch and comfortable chairs and a microwave and coffee machine was new, too. They'd installed corkboard panels on the inside wall and tacked up nautical maps and tide tables. On the opposite wall Lis had put up shelves to show off their fishing trophies, as well as a striped bass mounted on a piece of driftwood. The fish shone like fiberglass, or at least it did when Lis remembered to dust it. It was the real deal, a prizewinner, caught so long ago that no one could recall who'd caught it.

"We shifted things around a bit," Lis said. "Wanted to impress the public and offer customers a place to relax and get settled. And Jack needed his own space."

"Jack, you never said you wanted a desk," Miss Sorrel said. "You'd have had one long ago."

"Didn't need one. You took care of all the sitting down that needed doing around here," Cap'n Jack said with a wry smile. Their easy rapport reminded Lis that between them they'd run Woody's Charters for the twenty years after Woody died right up until Lis started coming in part-time. It had never occurred to her until now, with those DNA test results taunting her, that their friendship might have been something more.

A few minutes later Vanessa and Maggie and Jenny arrived. Jenny looked windblown. Her eyes seemed alive with curiosity as she looked around the office. She marched right up to the mounted striped bass, the one thing that had hung on the wall when Woody's Charters was in the Quonset hut. Janey used to scream whenever she saw that fish. Jenny didn't seem to be in the least bit bothered by it now.

"Jack," Miss Sorrel said, "you remember Lis's daughter, Vanessa?"

" 'Course I do." He and Vanessa shook hands. "How you liking it up north?"

Coming from a deep-rooted southerner, that was a loaded question. "It's different," Vanessa said.

"When y'all movin' back?"

Vanessa laughed.

"And that's Jenny Richards and her daughter, Maggie," Miss Sorrel said. "Friends of the family."

Not friends *of the family*, Lis thought. *They* are *family*.

Miss Sorrel gave her a narrow look, her head tilted and her brows furrowed. "Why are we here?" she asked under her breath.

"Excuse me?" Lis said. Sometimes she thought her mother was one part witch.

"You tell me with a straight face that the only reason we're here is so Vanessa can show Jenny how to stop a boat," Miss Sorrel whispered.

Lis was saved from having to answer by the ping of her cell phone. Stepping away from her mother, Lis read the message. It was Frank.

Be there in 10.

"I'll see you ladies later," Cap'n Jack said, waving a pair of work gloves. "I've got some outboards to service and a bilge pump to clean." He grabbed a hooded slicker and left the office.

"Was that your father?" Jenny asked Lis. She was pointing to a photograph that showed Evelyn's husband, Buck Dumont, squinting at the camera from under the rim of a baseball cap and holding an enormous sleek cobia, brown with a white belly and an impressive dorsal fin.

"No. That's my dad." Lis pointed to another picture that showed Woody waving from the flybridge of a boat in open water. So what if he might not be Lis's biological father? In every other conceivable way he'd been her dad. Made sure she knew how to fish *and* cut bait. Taught her where the most coveted fish hung out and how to spot their presence. How to assemble a rod and load a reel. To read nautical charts and tide tables. He'd hammered into her that just because she was a girl didn't mean she couldn't pilot a boat. Made sure she knew he thought she was pretty, too.

Below the picture was the framed certificate recognizing Woody's Charters for sponsoring a Police Athletic League baseball team. Every one of her brothers had played in that league and Woody had coached. In those days they didn't let girls play with the boys, but Woody had taught Lis to play regardless. He'd died before Vanessa was born, but Lis had honored his memory when she taught Vanessa to catch and throw, overhand and underhand.

"That's one big fish they got there," Maggie said.

"Oh, they caught bigger fish than that," Miss Sorrel said. "Landed a five-foot, eighty-six-pounder in the Broad River. Broke the record for a saltwater fish. Heckuva job, wrestling that thing into the boat. Woody got his picture in the paper for that.

I'm sure we've got that clipping lying around somewhere—you should frame that article, too, Lis."

Lis nodded. Better that her mother not discover quite how many of their old files and clippings she'd shredded when she "rearranged."

Miss Sorrel stepped to the window. "None of our boats out?"

This was why Lis dreaded her mother's visits to the marina. She couldn't help putting her oar in. Lis was about to point out the obvious, that cold water wasn't great for fishing, when she noticed Jenny was looking closely at another photograph. Jenny leaned into the picture, then took a step back. Lis squinted to see what Jenny had been looking at. The photo showed Woody receiving a certificate from Buck, who was smartly turned out in his dress uniform.

Lis heard footsteps on the stairs, and a moment later Frank came in, holding a large mailing envelope. He unzipped his battleship-green jacket and nodded to Lis, to Miss Sorrel, to Vanessa, and to Maggie.

"Frank's brought DNA test results," Lis said. "I wanted us all to find out together since it affects us all."

37

"We sent a sample of Jenny's DNA to NamUs, a national missing persons' database," Frank said.

Maggie and Jenny sat on the couch, while Lis perched on its arm. Miss Sorrel sat ramrod straight in the wing chair and Vanessa stood behind her.

"We asked them specifically to see if it matched Janey Woodham's DNA, which we'd sent them years back when they were setting up the database. The results are still sealed." Lis knew Frank was making that point for her benefit. He handed the envelope to Lis.

"You open it," Lis said, handing the envelope to Jenny.

Lis could feel all of them leaning in as Jenny tore open the envelope and extracted a set of stapled pages. How would she feel, Lis wondered, seeing it confirmed. That the past she'd believed was hers had been a fiction her parents made up to mask how she'd come to them.

As Jenny read, her face fell. "Negative," she said, the paper trembling in her hand.

. Miss Sorrel's hand flew to her mouth. She hunched over and let out a sob. Vanessa crouched in front of her and held her hand.

"Negative?" Lis said.

Jenny looked at Maggie and gave a weak smile. "It's official. I'm not Janey." She turned to Lis. "I never said I was, but I confess, I was hoping for a different result."

"No match? No way." Lis tugged the report from Jenny's grasp. Sure enough, there it was, at the end of a short paragraph on the top sheet:

Probability of a match: 0

She turned to the attached pages. There was a table with columns of numbers, like what had accompanied her other test results. One table was labeled EVIDENCE SAMPLE. A second table was labeled SUBJECT SAMPLE. Even to her unschooled eye, it was obvious that the values didn't match up.

"I'm sorry. I know you're disappointed," Frank said under his breath to Lis.

Disappointed didn't begin to describe the torrent of emotions coursing through her. Surprise. Disbelief. Outrage. "Those *official* test results—and I use the words loosely—are simply wrong. Bull. Shit." The words seemed to hang in the air like the bleat of a foghorn.

"Elisabeth, dear," Miss Sorrel said, wiping her eyes, "I know you're upset. We all had our hopes up and—"

"This is not me and my naive wishful thinking. How do you explain this?" Lis crossed the room to her desk and pulled out the private lab's DNA test results. "I collected samples myself. I took them to a testing lab. And their results"—she unfolded the pages and shook them at Frank—"show that Jenny is my mother's daughter. My sister."

Miss Sorrel inhaled sharply and placed her hand over her heart.

Frank shook his head. "Private testing labs aren't held to the same standards as a state lab. Who did your test? Let me have a look at that."

Lis handed him her report. Slowly and deliberately, he laid her test results on the coffee table alongside his official report. "Laurel Bay has a solid reputation. We use them sometimes." He traced down the columns on each sheet with his fingers, then squinted across at Lis. "You ran three samples?"

Lis guessed he'd gotten to the bottom line. *Same mother. Different fathers.* Lis pressed her lips together, hoping he'd get the message and keep that detail to himself for now. "My mother's hair. Jenny's blood. My cheek swab."

"My blood?" Jenny said. "How did you get that?"

"I'm sorry," Lis said. "I stole a used bandage from the ambulance. You were unconscious, and then you were in the hospital. I couldn't wait. I'd already waited too long."

"And how did *you* get a sample of my DNA?" Jenny asked Frank.

"A cheek swab," he said absently, his attention focused on the two reports. "When you were in the hospital."

"Really? I have no memory of that. None whatsoever."

"You were in and out of consciousness," Miss Sorrel said. "No wonder you don't remember."

"Wait a minute," Frank said. "Look at this." He pointed to the SUBJECT SAMPLE column in the official NamUs report. "Here's Janey's DNA from a sample we sent in years ago. And here"—he pointed to the adjacent column labeled EVIDENCE SAMPLE—"we have the sample my office sent NamUs a week ago. A sample that was supposedly Jenny's DNA."

Supposedly Jenny's DNA? Lis felt the flicker of hope.

"They found no match," Frank said. "But look at this." He

took Laurel Bay's test results and aligned the values from their sibling samples with the evidence sample that had been sent to NamUs.

Again, Lis could see no apparent match.

"Don't you see?" Frank said. "Both your sibling sample and the NamUs evidence sample were supposed to be Jenny's DNA. And yet, they don't match each other."

He went on. "Now compare this sibling DNA from Laurel Bay with Janey's DNA profile in NamUs." He aligned the sibling sample from Laurel Bay with the subject sample from NamUs. Even to her unschooled eye, Lis could see that the values matched.

Lis tried to make sense of what he was saying. The DNA from Jenny's bloody bandage matched Janey's DNA that had been submitted years ago to the government database. "What happened? Someone screwed up?"

"Someone sure did. The sample my people sent to NamUs wasn't Jenny's. If it had been, they'd have found that Jenny's DNA matches Janey's."

"So you're saying—" Miss Sorrel started.

Jenny said, "Would someone please explain—" She looked confused and upset.

Lis walked over to Jenny. "We've found Janey."

Jenny blinked a few times and for a long moment, no one moved. Then slowly Jenny rose to her feet. "This time you're sure? I'm . . ."

"My Rose Red." Miss Sorrel stood, too. She smiled. With tears glistening in her eyes, she came over to Lis and Jenny. She stared from one to the other, then opened her arms and hugged them both.

When Miss Sorrel finally pulled away, she wiped her tears

and blew her nose. "Maggie?" She turned to face her. "Can we start over?"

Maggie said, "I'm afraid we got off to a rather bad start."

"I didn't understand," Miss Sorrel said, "but now I do. And I'm so grateful to you. If you hadn't brought us Janey's doll . . ." She shook her head and wiped the corner of her eye.

"And you, Elisabeth," Miss Sorrel said, giving her a kiss on the cheek. "If you hadn't tracked her down . . ."

Lis's vision blurred again and she could barely swallow the lump in her throat.

"And Janey—" Miss Sorrel started.

"Jenny," Jenny said.

"Jenny. Of course. No one can wave a magic wand and erase all the lost years."

Lis said, "Miss Sorrel never gave up. She always knew you were out there."

"I did. I knew," Miss Sorrel said. "And deep down, the minute I saw you in the hospital, I felt a connection. I couldn't let you walk out of our lives. My sweet girls. I have imagined this moment so many times. How I'd be ecstatic. Overwhelmed with gratitude. And I am. But you know?" Her voice turned hard and steely. She took a few steps to the window and stared out. "I had no idea how angry I'd be. All these years you were lost to us and we were lost to you." She turned back to face Jenny. "And you were not even an hour away, being raised by . . . those people who had no idea how special you were. Who had no idea how precious—" Miss Sorrel's voice broke and she sobbed. "And while I don't think of myself as a vengeful woman, all I can think of now is that I want to find out who stole you from us"—she looked directly at Frank—"and make them pay for what they did."

·⋇·

Later, after Frank had gone, Lis stood out in the parking lot with the rest of what was now her family watching the sun set.

"Know what I used to pretend when I was little?" Jenny said. "That I was a princess who'd been stolen by a wicked fairy."

"So maybe you always knew?" Miss Sorrel said.

"I'm sure I didn't know. Quite the opposite. Not until a few days ago when I was looking through your photo album. There was one picture in there of Janey when she was a newborn, a close-up of her being held? I know hospital baby pictures all look alike, but that picture in particular looked just like a photo my parents had framed on their piano. And here's the thing. It wasn't the baby that I recognized. It was the ring." She took Miss Sorrel's hand and turned it over, running her thumb over the delicately carved cameo ring. "My mother wore a plain gold band. She used to say that jewelry was wasteful. The devil's playthings. And Dr. Mike railed against wasteful indulgence in his sermons. 'Beauty should not come from outward adornment.' I heard that a lot."

"Why didn't you tell us you recognized the picture?" Grandma Sorrel said.

"I was afraid you'd think that I'd read about your loss and was after your money."

Lis stared down at her shoes and felt her face flush, because that's exactly what would have occurred to her, and Evelyn would have piled on.

Jenny went on, "And it's not like I actually remember living here or recognize any of you. I don't. But I do feel a kind of peace in your house, a feeling of belonging that I've never felt anywhere."

"Your home is with us," Miss Sorrel said. "I hope you'll stay."

"Maybe," Jenny said. "Maggie and I need to talk and figure things out. This is a lot to digest."

It wasn't until later, when Lis was driving home, that it occurred to her to wonder: How had a copy of their picture of baby Janey in Miss Sorrel's arms found its way onto Renata and Clive Richards's piano in Mount Royal?

That night after supper, Lis, Maggie, Jenny, and Vanessa followed Miss Sorrel upstairs and into Janey's room.

"I guess it's time to put this out," Miss Sorrel said, her voice choked with emotion. She lifted the candle lamp from the windowsill and handed it to Jenny. The light from under her face cast deeper shadows under her eyes. "You were my sweet angel. A delicious bonus baby that I didn't deserve and never expected to have."

A tear trickled down Jenny's cheek. Miss Sorrel wiped it away with her thumb.

"And now." Miss Sorrel bent down and yanked the plug from the wall. The light went out and they all cheered.

In the silence that followed, Lis flashed back to the moment she thought of as between *before* and *after*. She'd returned to the house, her arms loaded with Spanish moss and goldenrod, to find Miss Sorrel frantic. "Where have you girls been?" Miss Sorrel had demanded. "You scared me half to death. You know you're supposed to stay in the yard."

Lis had tried to explain about the puppy, but Miss Sorrel was having none of it. Instead Lis got a scolding. She was supposed to be the big sister, Momma's big girl. She was supposed to stay in the yard, not . . . That was when Miss Sorrel realized and everything changed.

"Janey?" Miss Sorrel had said. Then, "Janey!" Then she'd started to scream. "Janey! Janey! Janey!" So loud that within moments neighbors were out of their houses wondering what was wrong, and within moments after that they were all searching.

Over and over the police had asked Lis whether she had seen any strangers hanging around the house. And over and over again she told them she hadn't seen anyone she didn't know. Only a black-and-white puppy that she'd wanted for her very own.

They all went down to the kitchen, where Lis popped open a bottle of champagne she'd picked up on her way home. She got out juice glasses and poured some for each of them. Miss Sorrel raised her glass. "To my family," she began.

Just then there was a knock at the door. "Yoohoo!" called a familiar voice.

Vanessa opened the door and Evelyn burst in. "I noticed it right away," she said, out of breath as if she'd run over. "The light in the window is out."

"Evelyn," Miss Sorrel said, "she's home. Janey's home." She reached over and hugged Evelyn.

Evelyn pulled away first. "But how . . . I don't understand."

Lis said, "DNA test results."

Evelyn said, "Really? So fast?" Lis couldn't read the look that passed between her and Miss Sorrel.

Miss Sorrel said, "Lis did it. She went to an independent test lab."

"Well, weren't you resourceful," Evelyn said. She clapped her hands together. "So our Janey is back. That's wonderful news."

She kissed Jenny on the cheek and turned to Miss Sorrel. "We all should have trusted your instincts."

Later that night, Lis and Miss Sorrel sat together, alone in the kitchen. Vanessa had taken her computer to the workroom, Jenny had gone to bed, and Maggie and Evelyn had gone home.

Miss Sorrel loosened her bun and shook out her braid as Lis poured herself the last dribble of champagne. What Lis really wanted was a cigarette, a yearning she considered a sign of returning health since she hadn't craved a smoke since she'd gone into the hospital. She'd been dreading this moment since she'd left Laurel Bay Testing Services. Now she couldn't put it off any longer.

"There's something I need to ask," Lis said. "I should have asked you ages ago. It's about when Janey disappeared."

Miss Sorrel returned Lis's steady gaze. "What do you want to know?"

"Did you blame me?"

Miss Sorrel drew back, her eyebrows raised. "Did I blame *you*? Have you been thinking all these years that it was your fault?"

"But it was," Lis whispered.

"No. It was not." Miss Sorrel reached out and touched Lis's face. "The person who is to blame is the person who took Janey. You were seven years old and you wanted a dog in the worst way. Brandy had died just a few weeks earlier."

Brandy? Lis had not forgotten that Brandy, their brown-and-black mutt with a feathery tail and ears that stood up when she was excited, had been hit by a car. Her father had blamed himself. He'd been putting off installing a pen in the yard. Janey's disappearance had eclipsed Brandy's death.

"Of course you chased after that stray, if that's what it was. I wonder now if it wasn't a lure."

"You think someone deliberately—"

"Released that puppy. Staged it. Might have even known about Brandy, though all children love puppies. One of you would have been sure to take off after it. Maybe they meant to take you but you were too quick." Miss Sorrel shook her head and stared toward the window. "If anyone is to blame, it's me. I was here in the kitchen when I should have been watching you. You girls were my responsibility and I was"—she paused—"I was on the phone. Talking to . . ." She grimaced, as if she were trying to erase the memory. "It was an unhappy time and I was desperate for a little attention. Hungry for adult conversation. Which is no excuse."

Miss Sorrel gave Lis a sad smile and a long look. "So, no, my darling. I never blamed you. It was never ever your fault." She reached out and touched the side of Lis's face. "Does that answer your question?"

If only. Lis tried to smile. "There's something else I need to ask."

"Do we have to talk about it now?" Miss Sorrel yawned and stretched and started to rise.

"It's about the DNA test results."

Miss Sorrel turned pale. She sank back into her chair and folded her hands on the table. "Go on."

"First thing," Lis said, "is that I love you. You know that, right? And I'll love you no matter what."

Her mother sat there like a pinned moth.

"I'm just going to blurt this out," Lis said, "because I can't figure out how to make it any less awkward to ask. When I called the DNA lab to see if I could bring in my DNA sample and

Jenny's, they said I needed yours, too, to tell if Jenny and I were sisters." Lis swallowed. "And I found out a bit more than I bargained for. Jenny is your daughter. And so am I, of course. But she and I are half sisters."

Miss Sorrel squinched her eyes shut and clapped her hands over her ears.

"We have different fathers," Lis said, though she knew from Miss Sorrel's reaction that she got it.

Miss Sorrel shook her head. Lis would have given anything not to press her mother, to allow her to keep her secrets. But this one was too big. She pulled Miss Sorrel's hands from her ears and waited until she opened her eyes.

"It's not my place," Lis said, "and you have to believe me when I say that I am not judging you. Everyone has things that are nobody's business. But I need to know. Jenny needs to know. Maggie, too."

"But she's just come home. Does it have to be now? I need time to figure out how to explain it. How to make her understand."

"What about me? I don't want to wait until . . ." *Until you've figured out how to explain it away.* It was an angry thought and not fair, but there it was.

"You know who your father is. Of that there isn't the slightest doubt. You were Woody's pride and joy. His baby. He thought Janey was his, too. When Janey went missing, he'd have fallen on his sword if it could have protected you and Janey from what you went through."

"But Janey isn't his daughter," Lis said.

Miss Sorrel winced and looked away. "Honestly, I never knew for sure. I suspected, of course. It was not a casual fling. I would never do that. But your father was preoccupied, spending more and more time at the marina. I was overwhelmed with the four of you. I was lonely and desperately unhappy, and he was . . . kind. Charming. Or so I thought. I was flattered. I had no idea that I wasn't his first affair and I wouldn't be his last. I'm not making excuses. There are none. I believed no one knew.

"When I found myself pregnant, I was stunned. I thought I was too old. Then I told myself the baby was your father's, even though that seemed unlikely. I broke it off right away and I never told him why, but eventually he guessed. How could he not? When Janey was taken, I told myself it was God's punishment."

Lis said, "When are you going to tell Janey who her father is?"

"Don't you think Jenny and Maggie are dealing with enough right now? At this point does it really matter?"

"It matters. You know as well as I do that it does."

Miss Sorrel heaved a sigh. "All right then. Just let me do it in my own way, in my own time. Trust me when I tell you it's complicated."

"Does this man know he's Janey's father?"

A pause. "He did."

Did? "Did the police know about him?"

"The police?" Miss Sorrel gave a bitter laugh. She got up, carried her glass to the sink, and poured out her remaining champagne. She turned back and looked at Lis straight on. "He *was* the police."

"Evelyn is the one who put it together," Miss Sorrel told Lis. She rinsed out her empty glass in the sink, then turned and leaned against the counter. "When Abby Verner disappeared, she came to me. Said she knew Buck had been cheating on her for years. From the way she said it, I figured she knew that I'd been one of his conquests. But I was wrong. She told me that Abby Verner's mother had been one of Buck's"—she shuddered—"whores. Mrs. Verner was a clerk in the municipal court. I guess that's how she and Buck met. As you can imagine, Evelyn was livid. She didn't think it was right that Buck was heading the investigation into the Verner girl's disappearance when he'd been involved with her mother.

"And of course he'd been the one who'd headed up the investigation into Janey's disappearance, too. And I'd been one of his 'whores.' So I had no choice. I had to tell Evelyn about Buck and me. It was just about the hardest thing I've ever had to do. Evelyn was my best friend and I'd betrayed her. It seemed especially cruel because I knew how desperately she wanted children and there I'd gone and had four of my own and conceived a baby girl with her husband.

"I wept. Begged forgiveness. She said she understood. Didn't blame me, she blamed him for taking advantage. She even cried a little, too. I could never have been that generous, had our roles been reversed.

"Then, in the back of Buck's closet, Evelyn found a pair of children's overalls and a little pink-and-purple top." Miss Sorrel choked up for a moment. "The clothes Janey had on when she disappeared. That's when we knew he'd taken Janey. And if he'd taken Janey, he'd taken Abby, too. The police were never going to find either of those girls, not as long as Buck and his buddies were leading the investigations. So we hatched a plan to make him tell us what he'd done."

A small smile played across Miss Sorrel's lips. "Buck always was crazy about sportfishing. But after Woody died, he couldn't just tag along the way he used to, and of course he didn't have the money it took to go out as often as he'd like. So Evelyn and I decided we'd give him a little birthday gift. A day of fishing. His own personal charter."

Miss Sorrel hugged herself and shivered. "It was an unseasonably warm February morning. When Buck got to the marina, I made up something about how Cap'n Jack had called in sick so I had to take him out. Evelyn said she'd come along, like it was just then occurring to her. I remember she had a big picnic basket with sandwiches and coleslaw. There was cold beer on the boat in a cooler. Soon as he boarded the boat, Buck cracked one open. Half hour later he started another one. Later I gave him a third. Lamb to the slaughter."

As Miss Sorrel spoke, her face seemed to grow younger, softer, and Lis could imagine her at about Lis's age in the cockpit of one of their charter boats. In those days, Miss Sorrel wore her hair in a long braid down her back. Evelyn wore her hair long, too, parted in the middle, and back then she was a brunette. It was only after it started turning gray that she went blond.

Bookkeeping had been just one part of Miss Sorrel's job, and as often as not she went to work at the marina wearing jeans and steel-toed work boots. All those years working alongside Woody, she'd learned everything there was to know about running and maintaining their boats. She wasn't an intuitively gifted fishing guide the way he was, but that day she and Evelyn weren't really taking Buck on a fishing expedition—at least not with the goal of catching fish.

"He suspected nothing," Miss Sorrel said. "Not even when we stopped out in a spot where the water was deep, too far from the seawall for fish to be cruising."

Miss Sorrel had left the boat idling and come around with Evelyn to confront Buck. He'd been stunned when Evelyn told him she knew about his whoring. How it had come to her in her prayers that the little girls who'd been abducted were his children. There was no use him denying it.

"Well, you could have knocked him over with a feather," Miss Sorrel said. "He didn't deny the affairs, but insisted that he knew nothing about what happened to Janey or Abby, and how could either of us suggest that he did. Flat out told Evelyn that she was crazy. Well, you know Evelyn. She lit into him. Told him he wouldn't know the truth if it bit him.

"But he wouldn't admit to taking the girls. Evelyn got angrier and angrier. Finally she picked up the boat hook and swung it at him. She meant to scare him, but he grabbed onto it. The momentum carried him overboard." Miss Sorrel shuddered. "I can still hear that splash when he landed in the water, and the moment of silence after when we realized what had happened.

"He kept going under and coming up thrashing. He'd had

those three beers, remember, and his rubber boots kept pulling him down. When he could sputter a few words, he kept saying that he didn't know. He didn't know. He didn't know. What kind of a man did we think he was? Janey was his goddaughter. How could we think that he was capable of something like that?

"Finally, it was obvious to both of us that he wasn't going to crack. He went under again and Evelyn extended the boat hook to where he could grab on to it when he came up. But instead it hit him in the head. It must have knocked him out because after that, he didn't come up.

"I went in after him. I kept diving down, over and over, but the water was murky and I was fighting the current. Finally I gave up. His body washed in on the next high tide."

"Do you still think he took Janey?" Lis said.

"I'm sure he did. How could he have had her clothes if he had nothing to do with her disappearance?"

"You never told the police?"

"I wanted to, but Evelyn convinced me that would backfire. Buck was chief of police. Frank was his second in command and he'd been Buck's protégé. Buck had hired and trained most of the other officers. They were loyal to him. And then there was Evelyn's widow's pension to consider. If Buck were implicated, she'd lose it, and what would that have gained us? We realized we couldn't rely on anyone else, we had to do our own investigating. That's when I start placing classified ads, every year on the anniversary of Janey's disappearance.

"So you see, it's not your fault that Janey disappeared and we couldn't find her. It never was."

The next morning Vanessa was awakened by a knock on her door. When she called out a groggy "come in," Jenny came through the door dressed in a flowered nightgown. Vanessa recognized it as one of Miss Sorrel's.

"It worked! I did it!" Jenny said.

Vanessa sat up, her sleepiness gone. "You had the dream?"

"The nightmare. And you were right. It helped to know what the boat actually looks like."

"You visualized the throttle?"

"There wasn't one. No steering wheel, either. Just seats and windows and water. The engine was going and someone had their arm around me, holding me in my seat. It was like I was being held in a cage. And there was this humming sound. I thought it was the motor of the boat, but then I realized it was pulsing. *It's a dream. It's a dream.* The words just floated into my head. And then I heard my own voice, in my dream, telling me I was dreaming."

That was exactly how it was supposed to work. Vanessa wanted to jump out of bed and cheer. "And?"

"I'm afraid nothing very original. I woke myself up. And then I wrote it all down."

"That's fantastic. And on the second try." It was actually nothing short of amazing, because it usually took at least several failed attempts. Vanessa was eager to see if the data that had been recorded would support Jenny's account. She tried to take the cell phone and sleep mask wired to it but Jenny held on to them.

"What exactly is it that's in there now?" Jenny said, eyeing the cell phone.

"Numbers. That's all."

"Like my DNA? Those DNA reports were just numbers. But that's how the government knew it was me."

Vanessa forced a pleasant, sympathetic smile. The last thing she needed was for Jenny to refuse to let her analyze the data. Even Jenny's two nights of directed dreaming would strengthen Vanessa's grant proposal. Show that her ideas weren't pie in the sky. The deadline for her grant proposal was a week away, and even if she flew home tomorrow, she had barely enough time to pull together what data she had, and no time to collect more.

"It's not the same kind of numbers," Vanessa said, trying to keep her voice calm. "The numbers I have are more like reading a temperature. Or blood pressure. One person's looks like anyone else's. Your DNA numbers are uniquely yours."

Jenny turned over the cell phone. The screen lit up. DISCONNECTED. "You promise? No one will be able to use this to get into my head?"

"Seriously, there's no way. After I transfer the data, it will be anonymous. And I'll delete it from there."

"Permanently?"

"Forever and a day."

Jenny released the mask and cell phone. "Thank you."

"Thank *you*. And Jenny—" Vanessa knew she needed to say more, because it was folly to think that a single success at short-circuiting a nightmare was going to make all of Jenny's problems vanish. "I don't understand what all you've been through, but I do know that it takes more than a dream catcher for most people to move past the kind of trauma you've experienced. You really need to talk to someone, moving forward."

Jenny said, "But Social Services—"

"I'm not talking Social Services. Private counseling—"

"Which I can't afford."

"Which you *can* afford. Now."

"I'm not taking charity—"

"It won't be charity. It's what families do. They help each other. Just like you're helping me with my research."

Jenny shook her head, as if she were about to keep arguing. Instead she turned and started for the hall. Vanessa pushed off her bedcovers. "Promise me you'll at least think about it."

Jenny turned back in the doorway. "I will. Could you do me a huge favor?"

"Of course," Vanessa said.

"I need a ride home so I can pick up a few more of my things."

"Today?" Vanessa said. "I guess." Though in truth she was anxious to transfer the data before Jenny changed her mind. She wondered why Jenny didn't ask Maggie.

As if sensing the question, Jenny said, "Maggie's been so busy or I'd ask her. And Lis has already done so much for me. And Evelyn's driving scares me."

Vanessa laughed. She'd only ridden with Evelyn a couple of times, but it had been memorable. Evelyn was one of those drivers who drove with one foot on the gas pedal and the other foot on the brake, as if hedging her bets.

"I'm sure my mother would lend you some clothes. Isn't that Grandma Sorrel's nightgown?"

"I really want my own things. If you can't do it, just say so and I'll figure something else out." She turned to go.

"Sure. Okay," Vanessa said. "No problem." The drive to the mobile home park wouldn't take long, and it wasn't likely that Jenny had too many things to pack since only weeks earlier she'd been homeless. "So you've decided to stay?"

Jenny turned back. "For a while at least. It's been so long since I've lived in a proper house."

"You could move back into your old room."

"*My* room." Jenny looked toward the hall. "I'll have to get used to that idea."

"Grandma Sorrel never threw anything away. You can go through what's in there, see if it shakes loose any memories."

"Do you think your mother would go through it with me?"

Vanessa wondered if there'd ever come a time when Jenny would think of *your mother* as *my sister*. "I'm sure she would. Ask her."

"I will," Jenny said. "You have to forgive me. All this takes some getting used to."

"All what?"

Jenny gave her a long look. "People being nice to me."

Later that morning, Vanessa found Lis in the workroom. A new kiln had been delivered and was waiting to be hooked up. Lis slid a cardboard box with gallon jugs of slip across the floor. When she saw Vanessa, she stood and ran the back of her arm across her forehead.

"Can I help?" Vanessa said.

"I'm almost done," Lis replied. "Making a working space in here for Jenny. Heard you offered to drive her over to the trailer so she can pick up her things."

"I didn't offer, exactly. But I'm happy to do it. Did she tell you about last night?"

"About the nightmare? She's"—Lis paused for a moment—"soothed, seems like the best word for it. Unburdened and smoothed and a whole lot less jangly."

"Did she tell you about the nightmare?"

"She said it was about being trapped on a boat that wouldn't stop. Looking out the window and seeing water rushing by and feeling terrified."

That was how Jenny had described it to Vanessa, too. But listening to Lis's retelling, Vanessa realized that Jenny might not have been riding in the cockpit of a boat. It was just as likely that she'd been cargo. Human cargo. It was something she needed to talk to Jenny about.

"What?" Lis said.

"Nothing." Vanessa took a breath and looked around, impressed by how clean and orderly the workroom had become. "Amazing, isn't it, that she's a ceramics artist, too."

"I know," Lis said. "Spooky." She started wiping down the baby food jars that held Miss Sorrel's paints and varnishes and moved them to one side of a shelf above the worktable. "There's plenty of room for her."

"Of course there is," Vanessa said.

Lis looked across at her and smiled.

"Mom, I need to get back," Vanessa said.

"I know." Lis straightened Miss Sorrel's paintbrushes, then turned to Vanessa. "I get that."

Vanessa was about to explain how imminent the deadline for her grant proposal was, how up shit's creek she'd be if she didn't submit it in time, how many fill-ins she was racking up and would have to pay Gary back, when she realized Lis was agreeing with her.

"Thanks for understanding," Vanessa said.

"Thanks for being here," Lis said.

·⽊·

With things starting to settle down, Vanessa booked a flight home for Sunday, day after next, and sent an e-mail to Gary saying she'd work her shift Monday night. Later, in the afternoon, she drove Jenny back to Palmetto Court. The street was quiet when she pulled up in front of the mobile home.

"I've been thinking about your nightmare," Vanessa said. "Remember, you asked me if you keep dreaming it because it really happened? And I said probably not literally, but that recurring nightmares are related to past trauma. So the obvious question: Does it go all the way back to when you were abducted?"

"Could it?"

"You were four. That's early to be laying down permanent memories, but people do. The way you described the dream—being trapped in a compartment and seeing the water through a window—that's an interesting detail and it got me thinking. Maybe you weren't in the cockpit of that boat."

"Then where was I?"

"Maybe in a car—"

"But the water—"

"—on a boat. A car ferry."

Jenny blinked, silent for a few moments as she absorbed the possibility.

Vanessa went on, "What if the Richardses were living on St. Bridget when you were abducted? The only way to get from the mainland to St. Bridget back then was by ferry. You would have been taken there after you were abducted. It would certainly explain why you hate boats."

Jenny said, "What about the shiny buttons?"

"Still no clue what that's about," Vanessa said. "But if I had to guess, I'd say whoever had taken you was wearing them."

"The faceless person."

"Maybe someone wearing a mask?"

"A mask." Jenny was quiet for a moment. "Maybe someone I would have recognized."

"Makes sense."

Jenny turned her attention to the mobile home. "Bet you've never even been in one of these. I hadn't, not until we got the rent subsidy."

"It looks fine from here," Vanessa said.

"Depends on what you're used to. For us, it's more than fine. It's really nice. Come in. It won't take me long, and I think there's some Coke in the Frigidaire."

Vanessa had long ago stopped drinking soda, but she was curious to see inside, and if she could help carry Jenny's things, they'd get back sooner. She got out and followed Jenny to the front steps.

"Shoot," Jenny said, crouching in front of the geranium by the front door. She pinched off some wilted leaves. "Why can't Maggie remember to water my flowers?"

Vanessa noticed that still lying around the base of the plant were smooth lumps of glazed pottery incised with the heads of winged cherubs. "These are so sweet," she said, picking one up to examine it more closely. Turning it over. Like the one she'd taken, the bottom was incised with the initials JR.

"Those are my angels," Jenny said. "I sell them on Etsy."

"The design reminds me of engravings on old tombstones. Only they had skulls instead of faces."

Jenny looked pleased. "They were called death's heads. A skull because the person is dead, wings because they've ascended into heaven. People were pretty literal in those days."

"But the faces on yours look angelic, and anything but dead. I hope you don't mind that I took one last time I was here."

"You're welcome to it. Hitting me on the head with it I minded," Jenny said. She unlocked the door. Vanessa startled at the sound of voices emanating from within the trailer.

"TV," Jenny said, holding the door open for Vanessa. "We keep it on all the time so it looks like someone's home. Not sure it fools anybody, but we haven't been broken into. Come on in. Get yourself something to drink. It shouldn't take me long to get my things."

The mobile home was snug but surprisingly pleasant inside. The front door opened into a kitchen with wood-grained cabinets. The kitchen, in turn, opened onto a living area with a brown plaid couch and a brown velour recliner. More pieces of terra-cotta glazed pottery with the angel-wings design were everywhere. Pitchers. Tiles. Vanessa could imagine an entire line of home goods with the same gentle folk-artsy image.

Vanessa waited in the kitchen while Jenny packed. The small, flat-screen TV affixed to the wall was playing *The Price Is Right.* Vanessa hadn't watched that show since she'd stayed home sick from elementary school. The blaring theme music hadn't changed, but Bob Barker had been replaced by Drew Carey. The crowd seemed louder and more frenetic. Vanessa found the remote and notched down the sound.

Jenny emerged from the bedroom carrying a cardboard box filled with paintbrushes, chamois skins and sponges, spools of wire, hand tools, and other art supplies. "Can you take this out to the car for me?" She set the box by the front door. "And there's two tubs of clay under the front porch. Miss Sorrel said I can set up a work area in her workroom."

Vanessa took the box out and put it in the trunk. Then she found the two large plastic tubs. She peered under the lids. Both were half filled with what looked like reddish clay under a layer of about an inch of water. It occurred to her that Jenny might have dug and processed her own clay. With considerable effort, Vanessa dragged each tub to her car and lifted them into the trunk, too.

When she got back, Jenny was watching the TV, a plastic bag stuffed with her belongings at her feet. "Those tubs weigh a ton—" Vanessa started, but Jenny shushed her. It was only then that Vanessa noticed Jenny was standing rigid, her face ashen.

No more *Price Is Right.* On TV a pair of talking heads looked serious, the logo at the bottom of the screen: NEWS AT 3. A headline crawled across the top. *BREAKING: Girl found 40 years after kidnapping.* Vanessa's stomach dropped. This was the last thing Jenny needed.

The video on the screen flashed to Miss Sorrel's house, a crowd of people gathered on the sidewalk out front. A man was standing on top of a parked car, taking pictures. In the foreground, a male commentator stood next to the pink camellia bush, squinting into the camera and speaking in hushed tones. "Forty years, that's how long ago four-year-old Jane Woodham was abducted in broad daylight from the backyard of this, her family home in Bonsecours. Today she's home." The announcer seemed to take a ghoulish relish in those facts.

The background changed to a shot of a front-page newspaper story about the original kidnapping. Up came a picture of Janey, taken on her birthday just a few weeks before she disappeared. Also pictured were Grandma Sorrel and Vanessa's grandfather, Woody Woodham. The pair were speaking into a microphone, looking distraught, obviously asking for the public's help finding their little girl.

"A spokesman for the police said the investigation is far from closed," a voice-over reported. "Authorities now believe that the individual or individuals who abducted Janey Woodham were trusted persons in the community and may still be at large."

The image was now back to the somber, on-air commentator. "Where has little Janey been all these years? A neighbor told this reporter that until recently she has been living in a trailer park not far from . . ."

Oh, shit. A chill went down Vanessa's back. She rose and stepped to the window. Sure enough, a media van was now parked outside. As Vanessa watched, another van pulled up. A man hopped out and began taking pictures of the mobile home.

Jenny came up behind Vanessa. "How the hell did they know where to find me?"

"Who knows. But you need to get out of here right away. Is there a back door?" Vanessa grabbed the plastic bag Jenny had packed. "And we need to get a message to Maggie so she's not blindsided when she gets back here. Where are your house keys?"

Jenny didn't move. Vanessa looked around, frantic, and spotted the keys lying on the kitchen counter. She pushed Jenny through the kitchen and was relieved to find a back entrance to the trailer opposite the front door. She opened the back door cautiously and peered out.

"Cut through there," Vanessa said, pointing to the lot that backed up to Jenny's trailer. "Continue out onto the next street. I'll go out the front door. Give them something to look at. Then I'll drive around and pick you up. Okay?"

Vanessa held the door open, but Jenny just stood there, that same cornered look on her face that she'd had when she'd first confronted Vanessa and Lis from the front steps of the trailer. "I can't—"

"Of course you can. Just go. If it helps, tell yourself it's a dream. Don't worry about anyone spotting you. Just act as if you're out for a walk. Or running an errand. They weren't showing your picture, which means they probably don't know what you look like. I'll distract the reporters."

Jenny stared down at her feet. "I really don't know if I can do this. It's not a dream."

"You've survived much worse." There was a knock at the trailer's front door. Jenny startled and grabbed Vanessa's arm.

Vanessa gave her a long, hard look. "Jenny, I'm going to have to answer that, and meanwhile you have to get away. The door's not locked and it will just be a minute before whoever's on the other side tries to open it. You don't want to be here when he does."

Jenny blinked. Slowly she loosened her grip.

"You can do this," Vanessa said. "Go. Now. I'll pick you up in just a few minutes and we'll get the hell out of here."

Jenny took a sharp breath and slipped out the back door. Before she could change her mind, Vanessa bolted the door behind her. Then she picked up the plastic bag Jenny had filled with her belongings and went to the front door. She opened it and backed out, locking the door behind her, and then feigning surprise as she turned to face the reporter who was waiting there.

"Ma'am? Excuse me," the reporter said. He looked painfully young, maybe an intern, his collared shirt a size too big. "I'm looking for Jane Woodham."

For a moment Vanessa actually felt sorry for him. This was the kind of assignment editors gave to newbie reporters: get in the faces of people who are living their worst nightmares and squeeze out sound bites to feed a voracious news cycle. "I'm sorry, who did you say you're looking for?" She held the bag in front of her and pushed her way past him.

"Jane Woodham."

Vanessa was surprised that the reporter knew this was the address but apparently not that Jane Woodham was now Jenny Richards. "There's no one here by that name. Excuse me." She held the stuffed plastic bag in front of her face to block the cameras. "You're wasting your time." She made her way past another two reporters, a photographer, and folks who were probably just curious neighbors before a microphone was thrust in her face.

"Jane Woodham?" the man wielding the microphone said.

"Who?" Vanessa said. Surely he'd know that she was far too young to be Janey.

"Jane Woodham. She lives at number twenty-five." He pointed.

Vanessa shaded her eyes and looked back at the mobile home. Then up and down the street. "Woodham? There's no one living there by that name. Not as far as I know. Are you sure you've got the right address?" She opened her car door and heaved the plastic bag of Jenny's belongings into the backseat. Heart pounding, she got in and started the car. The first reporter she'd spoken to was at her window, the second one standing in front of the car. She put the car in gear and let it roll slowly forward. Once she was clear of the visitors she accelerated and continued out the entrance to the mobile home park onto the main road, checking that no one had followed her. She pulled into the nearest gas station, waited a few minutes, then turned the car around and drove back in to the trailer park. It took her just a minute to find Jenny.

"I don't understand why anyone still cares what happened to me," Jenny said, clutching the dashboard and looking back over her shoulder as Vanessa drove home. "This is insane."

"Forty years missing makes it a huge story." Vanessa checked her rearview mirror. "I read somewhere that when a child goes missing, the first hour is critical. After a few days, police start expecting the worst. To turn up after forty years is pretty much unheard of. People are going to want to find out what happened."

"And gawk at me like I'm some kind of sideshow freak."

That wasn't even remotely paranoid. Vanessa turned onto the main road, checked her rearview again. No one was following them. "They'll be curious. They'll want to see what you look like. If you turned out normal, whatever that means. If you decide to talk to the press, you can still protect your dignity and your privacy. Look at Elizabeth Smart. She told her own story, and she told it her way."

"Right. Elizabeth Smart. They'll think I was abused. Molested. Kept in a cage. But that's not what happened. My parents weren't the best, but they weren't evil monsters, either, and I don't want people to think that about them. And I don't want people to think about me at all." Jenny twisted in her seat and looked behind them. "I hate this. I should have thrown away that damned doll when I had the chance."

"Really?" Vanessa said, rolling through a stop sign.

Jenny turned back around. "No. Of course not."

"I hope at least you'll talk to the police. Maybe you know something that can help them find Abby Verner. She could still be out there, too."

"I've never heard of Abby Verner. And I *don't* remember anything. At least not anything useful."

"You recognized the picture of you and Miss Sorrel that your parents had in their house. You could know something you don't even know you know." It was only after she'd said it that Vanessa realized it was just that possibility that could mean Jenny was in danger.

Just then, Vanessa's cell phone rang. "Can you dig that out of my purse?" she asked Jenny.

Jenny found Vanessa's purse on the floor and pulled out the phone. She looked at the readout. "It says MOM."

"Put her on speaker."

41

"Vanessa, honey, are you there?" Lis spoke into the handset as she lifted the curtain in the front window and peered out. The crowd had started gathering an hour ago, prompting Lis to pull the shades and curtains and double-lock the front door. The landline kept ringing, so she'd taken the phone off the hook. Ignored the doorbell and knocks at the doors. How long could this go on?

"I'm in the car," Vanessa answered. Her voice sounded distant, like she'd turned on the speakerphone.

"Is Jenny with you?"

"I'm right here." Jenny's voice.

Lis flashed a thumbs-up to Miss Sorrel and Evelyn who were sitting at the dining room table, listening anxiously.

"Thank God," Miss Sorrel said.

"We know about the news leak and the reporters," Vanessa said. "Saw it on TV and there was a swarm of them at the trailer. We barely got away. We're on our way back now."

"I'm not sure that's such a good idea," Lis said. She peeked out the front window again, as if things could have changed in the minute she'd been on the phone. If anything, the crowd outside had grown, and a continuous stream of cars crawled past. "Jenny, can you hear me?"

"I hear you." Jenny's voice.

"Don't freak out when you get here. Okay? There are police officers out front. They're protecting us. Keeping anyone from getting to the house." One officer was blocking access to their front walk. Another was standing at the foot of their driveway. Frank was out in the street directing traffic, encouraging rubberneckers to move along.

"We should be there in about ten minutes," Vanessa said.

"You'll be swarmed. Go to Evelyn's house instead. She'll be waiting for you."

"Okay," Vanessa said. "I'll call you when we get there."

"Take care," Lis said and hung up the phone.

"Thank God you reached them before they got here," Evelyn said. She tore a sheet off the yellow pad on which she and Miss Sorrel had been writing a statement to send to the press.

"They should be here soon," Lis said.

"I'd better get back. But first, how does this sound?" Evelyn adjusted her glasses and started to read from the page. "The Woodham family thanks the police and our friends and our community for their support in reuniting our family. We are extremely grateful. We ask that the media and the public respect our privacy. Thank you for respecting our wishes."

"Sounds perfect," Lis said. "Though I doubt it will make a lick of difference. Reporters are paid to be disrespectful. Leave it on the table. I'll type it up and e-mail it to media outlets."

A soft rap at the back door stopped her. *Shave and a hair . . .* no cut. Frank's knock. She went to the door to let him in. Frank looked worn out, like he'd been up the night before. He tried to squeeze Lis's hand but she pulled away.

"Is that Frank?" Miss Sorrel called through from the dining room. Without waiting for an answer, she came and joined them in the kitchen. "Isn't there anything you can do to get them to go away? Isn't there some law about trespassing?"

Frank said, "I'm afraid what they're doing is not against the law. As long as they stay off private property. Free press and all that."

He turned to Lis and lowered his voice. "Can we talk? I've only got a minute." He tipped his head toward the back of the house and started to walk toward Miss Sorrel's workroom.

"Secrets?" Miss Sorrel said. Lis could feel the hint of anxiety beneath her smile.

"I'll let you know," Lis said and followed Frank.

When they were in the connecting passage and out of earshot, Frank turned to face Lis. "First, I need to know." He raised her chin with his finger until she was looking at him. "Are we okay?"

She pushed away his hand. "What do you mean?"

Frank scowled. "Please don't pretend you don't know what I'm talking about."

"Don't patronize *me*, either. Honestly, I don't know if we're okay. This has been a confusing couple of days. I thought I knew I could trust you."

Frank gave a slow nod. "What makes you think you can't trust me?"

"You must have known that Abby Verner's mother worked for the municipal court."

"Everyone knew that."

"And that she was having a relationship with Buck Dumont?"

The flicker in Frank's eyes said he wasn't surprised. "That's why Buck put me in charge of the investigation into her disappearance. He didn't even sit in on status meetings until we'd ruled him out as a suspect."

"But you did rule him out?"

"We had to. He'd been leading an internal investigation that eventually took down some court clerks and traffic officers who had been taking bribes. The day Abby Verner disappeared Buck was in the Columbia courthouse, waiting around to testify before a grand jury. Many eyewitnesses placed him there. Believe me when I say we didn't just look the other way. No one gave him special treatment. There's really no way he could have taken Abby Verner."

"But Buck had Janey's clothes. Evelyn found them in his closet before he died."

"We found Janey's clothes washed up on a riverbank a little ways downstream from here. We never made that public, but they were booked as evidence. I don't know how they ended up in Buck's closet. Someone must have . . ."

Someone must have planted them there. Lis groaned. Miss Sorrel would be horrified if she realized that when Buck wouldn't say where Abby had been taken, even as he was drowning, it might have been because he really didn't know.

"Buck died soon after Abby disappeared, remember?" Frank went on. "I didn't have the slightest twinge of conscience paying my respects and speaking at his funeral. He might not have been perfect in his personal life, but he was an honorable cop, committed to public service. He did a lot of good for this community. Life's complicated. Look closely and no one's a saint. Start by looking in the mirror. That's something you learn, first week on the police force."

Lis stared into Frank's eyes. Did he know that Buck had had an affair with Miss Sorrel, too? That Buck was probably Janey's and Abby Verner's father? "I don't get it. If Buck didn't . . ." Lis shook her head. "Just when I think I'm starting to understand, the whole thing gets turned inside out."

"Lis, we investigated the disappearances of both girls. Thoroughly. The extent of it was not made public. We've never given up. I've been following up on the leads you uncovered in Mount Royal. Jenny's older sister, also named Jenny Richards, who supposedly died before Jenny was born? I found her birth certificate. Found her death record, too, and the story in the news. Hit by a car when she was four years old. On life support a week before she died. She lived on St. Bridget and was buried there."

Lis winced.

"But there's no record of Mrs. Richards giving birth to another child," Frank went on. "Nevertheless, six months after Jenny died, Mr. and Mrs. Richards moved to Mount Royal with a daughter, Jenny. You found her in the church rolls. She's also counted in two decades of census records. We didn't find her enrolled in public school until high school. She went to Mount Royal High but didn't graduate. And now the Richardses are both deceased. Natural causes."

"All that matches what Jenny says and what I've figured out in the past couple of days," Lis said. "So the Richardses lose their daughter and somehow acquire a little girl the same age to take her place. They have a ready-made identity and maybe even a wardrobe for her to step into. Along with enough grief and despair to convince themselves that it's okay to adopt a child through unorthodox channels. A little miracle, even. Jenny told me her parents were devoutly religious."

"Here's something you may not know," Frank said. "When Janey was taken, the Richardses belonged to Bonsecours River Baptist Church." Lis had been there many times. Her parents didn't belong but Evelyn did. It had one of the largest congregations in the region. "I've sent an officer over there to poke around, see what he can find out about who their friends were and why they moved. There's got to be a link between Abby Verner and Janey. Something else besides Buck Dumont that connects them."

Lis heard the kitchen door close. She glanced up the passageway, back toward the kitchen. Must have been Evelyn leaving. She looked at Frank, suddenly afraid. What if the police investigation uncovered that Evelyn and Miss Sorrel had killed the city's vaunted police chief? Two elderly women charged with murder? She could only imagine that media circus—*Arsenic and Old Lace II*. Was that going to be the cost of finding Janey? The shame and scandal would utterly destroy Miss Sorrel. Lis couldn't bear for that to happen.

Frank's cell phone rang. He turned away from Lis and took the call. "I'll be out in a minute." He pocketed his phone and turned back. "There's one more thing I need to tell you, but it isn't going to make anything less complicated. It's about Jenny's DNA. That sample that my office submitted to NamUs? Our procedure is to FedEx a DNA sample to their office in DC. But that's not what happened, or at least no one seems to be able to find the receipt, if it did."

"But the sample got there," Lis said.

"*A* sample got there. But the chain of custody was broken."

"So it could have been tampered with."

Frank gave a somber nod.

"So someone else's DNA got sent with Jenny's paperwork?"

"It would explain why our DNA test results don't match yours."

"But who—?"

"Exactly."

Cars were parked on both sides of Grandma Sorrel's street when Vanessa and Jenny arrived back from the trailer park. The sun was low in the sky. Police barriers blocking Miss Sorrel's drive-way kept people from spilling in from the street. Beside a media van that was parked in front of the house, workers were setting up portable lights. Digging in for the night.

Jenny sank down in her seat as Vanessa waited for oncoming traffic to clear before she could drive past. She didn't dare try pulling into their driveway.

Evelyn darted out of the crowd and came up to the driver-side window. Vanessa rolled it down.

Evelyn said, "Go around the corner and pull in behind my house. Come in through the yard and I'll meet you at the back door."

Vanessa continued down the street and parked around the corner. She and Jenny got out of the car and slipped through a side gate to Evelyn's backyard. As promised, Evelyn was waiting for them. "Come in, quickly," Evelyn said, ushering them inside and closing the door behind them.

Though Vanessa had run errands and ferried items between

Grandma Sorrel's and Evelyn's kitchens many times, she'd never come in through this entrance. As she followed Evelyn up a dark hallway to the kitchen, she peered into a back parlor, past pocket doors with etched glass. Lace curtains, an oriental rug, and an uncomfortable-looking settee with matching upholstered chairs. On every surface sat open dishes filled with scented rose petals and dried lavender. And you'd have to be careful turning around for fear of knocking over a doll. They were everywhere. On shelves. In cabinets. By the fireplace in a little circle of hand-painted, doll-size rocking chairs. And Vanessa had thought Miss Sorrel's passion for dolls was a little extreme.

Vanessa turned to say something to Jenny, only Jenny wasn't there. Vanessa retraced her steps and found her standing in the back entryway. "Is everything okay?" Vanessa asked.

"There's something about this house. It feels . . ."

"Familiar?" Evelyn said, materializing in the passageway behind Vanessa and giving her a start.

Jenny gave an uncertain nod.

"You used to come here when you were little," Evelyn said.

"Is there a powder room?" Jenny asked.

Powder room? There was a euphemism you didn't hear much these days. Evelyn led Jenny to a half bath off the downstairs hall, Vanessa trailing behind. Jenny stood in the doorway for a moment, then went inside and closed the door behind her.

Vanessa followed Evelyn to her roomy kitchen. The modern stove and refrigerator and dishwasher were anachronisms next to the massive double-basin cast-iron sink anchored to the wall and the white Hoosier cabinet alongside it. Dishes were neatly stacked behind glass doors on shelving over the sink.

"I promised Miss Sorrel that I'd feed you," Evelyn said. "Are you all right with an early supper?" Not waiting for an answer, she set a pot of water on the stove to boil. She already had two cans of tuna open. She dumped them into a mixing bowl and added a can of evaporated milk and breadcrumbs.

"What can I do?" Vanessa asked as she watched Evelyn rinse a stalk of celery and some sprigs of parsley.

"You can set the table, dear. Silverware's in there," she said, pointing to a drawer in the Hoosier cabinet. "Then you and Jenny can relax. There's a television in the back room." The phone rang. "And don't answer the doorbell and ignore the phone. It will just be those reporters."

As Vanessa finished setting the table, Jenny emerged from the bathroom. When she saw Vanessa, she put her finger to her lips. Then Vanessa followed her as she slowly retraced her steps, as if something there was drawing her to the back of the house.

Jenny paused at the back parlor, slid a pocket door open, slipped inside, and turned on the TV. She adjusted the sound so it was audible in the hall. Then she rejoined Vanessa in the hall and continued to the back entryway. Turned. As Vanessa came up alongside her, Jenny opened one of a pair of heavy mahogany doors to reveal a coat closet. Jenny closed the closet door and opened the adjacent door. Beyond were dark narrow back stairs.

Vanessa hadn't known it was there, this back staircase. But of course when Evelyn's house was built, the family that lived there would have had live-in help that needed to invisibly navigate to the upper floors without being seen.

Jenny motioned for Vanessa to follow and started to climb. Vanessa took a quick look toward the kitchen. She heard Evelyn close the oven door, run water in the sink. Then she crept up the stairs, following Jenny.

The air grew cooler as she climbed, and the staircase doubled back on itself at a landing on the second floor before it ended at a door on the third floor. The door creaked as Jenny pushed it open and stepped out into a narrow hallway with a low ceiling and small windows at opposite ends.

Jenny started down the hallway, moving determinedly as if she knew exactly where she was going, past what Vanessa was surprised to discover were small attic bedrooms. Once upon a time these must have been servants' quarters, but with their hidden access they might as easily have provided safe refuge for fugitive slaves. Or in a different era, a hiding place for bootleg liquor. But as far as Vanessa knew, Evelyn and Buck were teetotalers. They'd never had live-in help—Evelyn prided herself on doing for herself even before she'd retired and had to make do with a limited income. And though Evelyn had hosted plenty of church groups, her guests were always white.

Vanessa followed Jenny into one of the little rooms. It was sparsely furnished, just a child-size bed and a small oak bureau with a mirror hanging over it. The sloped ceiling was stained, and the wallpaper—bunnies scampering across a cream-colored background with sprouts of grass—was coming loose at the seams. A framed pastel drawing of a manic mommy teddy bear holding a birthday cake hung on a wall.

"I've never been up here," Vanessa said.

"I think I have," Jenny said. She stooped beside the little bed. Just as she had in the bedrooms at Miss Sorrel's house, she looked under the bed. She glanced across at Vanessa, then knelt, reached underneath, and pulled out a large plastic bin. She lifted its lid. It was full of doll parts. That didn't surprise Vanessa. She'd grown up surrounded by dismembered dolls, damaged dolls, bodiless heads of dolls with eyes that seemed to follow you around.

Jenny shoved the bin back under the bed.

"Evelyn and her husband were your godparents," Vanessa said. "They—" She broke off at the sound of footsteps.

Evelyn appeared in the doorway, her hand to her chest, breathing heavily. "There you are. I wondered what y'all had gotten up to. Casserole's baking in the oven."

"Jenny thinks she remembers being up here," Vanessa said.

"Of course she does," Evelyn said. "We used to keep a lovely dollhouse right here in this room. Buck built it for me, a replica of our house, to scale and accurate to the last detail. It was even wired with lights and it had a working doorbell. You and Lissie used to come over and play with it."

"I don't remember a dollhouse," Jenny said.

"I don't remember one, either," Vanessa said. She didn't remember ever being up here in the tippy top of the house at all. She would have loved the hidden feeling of it, tucked into the eaves like you were in a tree house.

"Of course you don't, 'Nessa," Evelyn said. "By the time you and Elisabeth moved back, I'd donated the dollhouse to the historical society. Not much reason to come up here now." Evelyn wrinkled her nose and covered a dainty sneeze. "Room needs a good turning out and scrubbing, top to bottom. And this old wallpaper." She took hold of a corner and peeled away a good-size strip. "On its last legs." She smoothed the piece and set it on top of the bureau, then smiled at Jenny. "What else do you remember, dear?"

"I don't remember a dollhouse," Jenny said. "I do remember . . ." She lay down on the bed, her feet hanging off the end. *Like Alice*, Vanessa thought, *after she ate the mushroom.* "Angel wings." She pointed to the ceiling.

Sure enough, the water stain that bloomed on the ceiling looked like a pair of wings. Like the wings of the death's-head images Jenny used to decorate her pottery.

Evelyn brushed her hands off on the front of her skirt. She stepped to the narrow window that was set into the wall just below the sloping ceiling. "Oh my land, how much longer are they going to be out there?" She turned back to Jenny. "Miss Sorrel suggested it might be wise for you to stay here overnight. Not up here, of course, but in one of the proper bedrooms. What do you think?"

"But my things—" Jenny started.

"I can bring in your bag from the car," Vanessa said.

"And I've got a spare toothbrush if you need one," Evelyn said.

Jenny stood and looked out the window. "Doesn't look like I have much of a choice. I go out there, I'll be mobbed."

"You're welcome to stay, too," Evelyn said to Vanessa.

Vanessa waved away the offer. She was not eager to spend the night saturated with potpourri, surrounded by families of teddy bears and even more battalions of dolls. Besides, the reporters weren't interested in her.

Vanessa went out to her car. From the backseat, she hefted the plastic bag Jenny had packed for herself. The twist tie came undone and the bag rolled over on its side. A T-shirt and a nightgown slipped into the gutter before Vanessa could catch them. She was stuffing them back in when she spotted a glasses case that must have fallen out, too. She picked up the case. It was much heavier than she'd have expected it to be. She squeezed the top open and tilted the case. Out slipped a silver revolver with a wooden grip, small enough that it could be hidden in the palm of her hand.

Vanessa remembered Jenny waving around that shotgun. She checked the cylinder. Like the shotgun, this gun wasn't loaded. But jingling around in the bottom of the eyeglass case were . . . Vanessa peered in and shook them out. Bullets. Three tiny ones.

She gazed across to the big pink house where Jenny would be taking refuge for the night. It was really none of her business whether Jenny had a gun. Women did, especially here in South Carolina. But was Jenny emotionally stable enough to be trusted right now with a firearm? Was she likely to have another meltdown? See threats where there were none?

Vanessa was ill equipped to make that call. What she did know was that Jenny was a grown-up. She'd survived on the street and, against all odds, raised a daughter who was completing a college degree and working. She didn't need a gun to protect herself at Evelyn's house, but maybe that wasn't the point. Maybe it was *having* the gun, as opposed to using it, that mattered. Peace of mind.

But what if . . . Vanessa's argument with herself was interrupted by the garden gate creaking open. Jenny was headed toward the car, looking completely calm and collected.

"Hey, y'all," Jenny said as she approached the car. "I wondered what was taking you so long."

"Just being clumsy," Vanessa said, slipping the gun back into the glasses case and returning the case to the bag. The bullets she dropped into her own pocket. "Sorry, I managed to drop your shirt in the street."

She picked up the plastic bag, closed the car door, and followed Jenny back into Evelyn's house.

43

Before dawn the next morning, Lis was awoken from a sound sleep by a siren. She waited for the noise to pass but instead it got closer and closer. Lis ran to the window. It was still dark out, and an ambulance, lights flashing, was slowing down right outside. *Red. White. Red. White.* Lights silhouetted the tree branches.

Her heart in her throat, Lis's first thought was that something had happened to her mother. She ran to Miss Sorrel's bedroom, only to find her pressed against the window just as Lis had been. The ambulance had continued past their house and stopped under the streetlight in front of Evelyn's.

Lis started back to her room, passing a sleep-befuddled Vanessa in the hall. Lis had talked to Vanessa when she returned home after having dinner at Evelyn's. She'd told her that Jenny had gone to bed early, opting to stay overnight with Evelyn.

"There's an ambulance at Evelyn's," Lis told her.

Vanessa looked in the direction of Evelyn's house, suddenly alert. "Did you hear anything? A gunshot?"

Lis froze in the doorway of her bedroom. "A gunshot?"

"Jenny has a gun," Vanessa said, avoiding Lis's gaze.

"She has a gun? Why didn't you tell me?"

"I took all the bullets, or I thought I did—"

"Never mind. I didn't hear any gunshots." Lis ran into her bedroom and pulled on a pair of sweatpants. "I'm going over there."

She threw on a fleece pullover, jammed her feet into sneakers, and raced down the stairs and out the door. When she got to Evelyn's, the doors of the empty ambulance were flung open as was the front door to the house. The wheeled metal frame for a stretcher sat at the foot of the stairs.

Lis slipped into the entryway, listening to sounds from overhead. Men's voices. A woman's. Lis crept up the stairs, listening intently. She overheard occasional words and phrases. "BP eighty over sixty. Bradycardia . . . Hypotensive . . . Nonreactive . . ."

Lis got to the second floor. The voices were coming from a bedroom at the rear of the house. The door was open and a black backpack with a bold label, BONSECOURS EMS, was lying in the hall. Lis was afraid to approach the doorway, afraid to find out who was *nonreactive*. Evelyn was the one in her seventies, she reminded herself. The one with diabetes and a heart condition. The one who huffed and puffed when she climbed stairs.

"One two three . . ." she heard from inside the room. Then a grunt. Some scuffling sounds. One of the paramedics backed out of the room holding the end of a stretcher. It was Jenny, not Evelyn, who lay strapped to it.

Lis gasped. Jenny's eyes were closed and she looked deathly pale. An IV needle was taped to the tender skin of her inner arm and an oxygen mask had been placed over her mouth. Her hand rested on the blanket, two of her fingernails broken down to the quick.

A second paramedic walked alongside the stretcher holding the IV bag. In his other hand he had a plastic bag. Lis got only a quick glimpse of it as he moved past, but it looked as if the bag contained prescription pill containers, not a gun. A third paramedic took up the rear, holding the other end of the stretcher. Lis pressed herself against the wall as they jostled past and continued to the stairs.

Evelyn followed the stretcher out of the room. She was wearing a pink bathrobe with a chiffon scarf wrapped around her hair and knotted over the forehead. Her face was shiny, unmade-up, and she looked flushed. Oddly triumphant, in fact, until she saw Lis.

"What happened? Is she going to be all right?" Lis asked. She followed Evelyn down the stairs, trailing the stretcher.

"I'm so sorry, dear," Evelyn said as they stood in the front hall, watching the paramedics carry Jenny to the ambulance and load her in. Miss Sorrel and Vanessa were outside, Miss Sorrel fluttering over Jenny and Vanessa talking to the ambulance driver. "I'm afraid Jenny tried to take her own life. I found her unconscious and unresponsive, surrounded by empty pill bottles. Medications I can't even imagine how she got her hands on."

Lis realized Jenny must have picked them up yesterday at the trailer. It had seemed odd yesterday when Jenny had insisted Vanessa drive her over *today* when she could easily have borrowed what she needed and waited for the weekend when Maggie had time to drive her.

"But why would she try to kill herself now?" Lis asked.

The ambulance back doors slammed shut. The driver jumped into the front seat and the emergency lights started flashing. Vanessa backed her car to the start of Miss Sorrel's driveway and waited while Miss Sorrel got in, rolled down the window and motioned Lis over.

"We'll call as soon as there's news," Miss Sorrel said.

"But I want to go to the hospital," Lis said.

"One of us needs to be here." Lowering her voice, Miss Sorrel added, "Promise me you'll stay with Evelyn. You hear? She's not as strong as she seems."

The ambulance took off, its siren wailing.

"Promise me you will," Miss Sorrel said.

"All right, all right," Lis said.

Miss Sorrel rolled up the window and Vanessa drove off. Seconds later their car's taillights disappeared around the corner.

In the silence that followed, Evelyn said, "I think she was starting to remember. Little bits, coming back to her. She was excited about it. She even looked out the window into your backyard and seemed as if she had a moment of insight. A flashback." Evelyn shook her head. "But that's when a photographer who'd climbed a tree outside took a picture of her through the window. Jenny screamed. It gave me a terrible shock. After that she shut down. All I can think is that she couldn't face the notoriety. The shame."

"What shame? Jenny has nothing to be ashamed of."

"Really?" Evelyn stared at Lis, long and hard. "Only Jenny knows the answer to that. She hasn't told any of us what really happened."

It was so appalling and unfair, Jenny being kidnapped in the first place. Now she was going to be victimized again by supposition and innuendo? Then a thought occurred to Lis. Why had the photographer been in a tree in Evelyn's yard instead of Miss Sorrel's? "Evelyn, I don't understand. How did that photographer find out that Jenny was here with you?"

Evelyn didn't answer.

Lis reached out and grabbed Evelyn's forearm. "How did they know she was here, or where her trailer is?"

Evelyn gasped and turned pale, pulling away and cradling her arm. Lis looked down. Evelyn's arm was already marked with bloody half-moons, oozing scratches dug into her flesh.

"Did she hurt you?" Lis asked. Even as she spoke she wondered if that was the right question to be asking.

Evelyn's eyes widened. Then her lower lip quivered and she nodded. "I was only trying to help. I tried to get her to tell me what she'd taken, but she wouldn't say. I could see she needed medical care so I ran downstairs and called an ambulance. By the time I got back, she was unconscious." She stared off down the street. "I only hope it's not too late."

With that, Evelyn wheeled around and went back into her house.

44

Stay with Evelyn. Lis had promised Miss Sorrel she would. She was about to follow Evelyn into her house when a vehicle turned into the street. Its headlights blinded Lis until it got close enough and she could see that it was a media van. It pulled up alongside her, the driver squinting through the windshield at Miss Sorrel's house. All the lights were on and the front door was standing open. The driver already had a camera out and was snapping pictures.

Lis sprinted up the steps, into the house, and locked the door behind her. Turned off the outside lights. She checked that all the curtains were pulled, windows closed and locked downstairs. Then she ran upstairs and turned the lights off there, too. Finally, she exited through the kitchen, cut through the yards, and knocked at Evelyn's back door.

There was no answer.

Lis put her face to the window in the door and peered inside. The light was on in the back entryway. When she knocked again and there was still no answer, she tried the door. It was unlocked.

She opened it and stepped inside. "Evelyn," she called out.

The only sound was a shrill whistle. In the kitchen she found the source—a kettle of water had been left boiling on the stove. She turned off the burner and walked through the downstairs. No Evelyn. To the foot of the stairs. "Evelyn? Are you up there?"

No reply, but Lis heard movement. Like furniture being shoved about. The sounds were coming from the back of the house. She retraced her steps and stood by the back door, listening. Looked up at the ceiling. The sounds seemed to emanate from a door that was ajar. She pulled it open. Beyond were the back stairs. The sounds were from overhead.

She climbed the first step and pulled the door shut behind her. The sounds were louder. She groped for a wall switch and turned it on. A bare bulb on the landing above came on. As Lis climbed, scuffling sounds grew more distinct.

She continued past the second floor and on to the top-floor landing. A pool of light from a bedroom spilled out into the dark hallway. Lis was halfway to the room when Evelyn emerged from that doorway and into the hall. She wore purple latex cleaning gloves and shoved a lidded plastic storage bin along the floor with her foot. She froze when she saw Lis. "You're back. I thought you'd be at the hospital."

"Miss Sorrel's orders," Lis said. "I'm here to help you. Here, let me." She reached for the bin.

"No, no." Evelyn gave a vague gesture, brushing back hair that had escaped from her headscarf. She winced, cradling her arm, which looked discolored and swollen. "I can manage." Her face was pale, her forehead glistening with perspiration.

"Are you all right?" Lis asked. She'd never seen Evelyn looking so discombobulated. Without makeup, her face resembled an unfinished portrait doll, fresh from the kiln.

"I guess . . . I guess I'm not myself."

"Of course you're not," Lis said. "This has to be very upsetting. But why are you moving things around? Surely that can wait. And you should probably get that arm looked at."

"I'm a nurse," Evelyn said. "I can tell when I need treatment."

"Well, you should at least ice it." Lis picked up the bin. "Where should I put this?"

Evelyn tried to take the bin back. "No! I can—" She stiffened in pain and the bin dropped with a thud. The lid came off and doll parts spewed onto the floor.

"Now look what you've done," Evelyn said, her color rising. "Didn't I tell you? Let me do it myself."

Evelyn's imperious tone of voice might have worked on Miss Sorrel and maybe Evelyn's coworkers at the hospital, but Lis ignored it. She started to pick up the scattered doll parts. Only after she'd tossed some bodies and a head in the bin did it occur to her what an odd collection it was. Parts of porcelain dolls were mixed together with parts from composition and plastic dolls. Soft bodies and hard, arms and legs. These were dolls made decades apart by different makers. A jumble, really. A composition leg. A kidskin body. A porcelain bisque shoulder plate. An articulated wooden body. A socket head with painted hair and features. Miss Sorrel never would have stood for such a chaotic mix, and Evelyn was even more anal. How would she ever find anything?

Lis picked up a bald doll's head, a beautifully painted bisque with rosy cheeks, a Cupid's-bow closed mouth, feathered brows, and pierced ears. She recognized it instantly as a baby Jumeau— the red stamp on the back of its head confirmed it. Miss Sorrel had had a baby Jumeau. Hers had had a blond mohair wig.

Lis glanced across at Evelyn. Her mother's best friend had backed up and stood leaning against the wall, holding her hand to her throat.

Lis scanned the floor and then looked in the bin. A blond doll's wig lay half buried under a plastic arm. She pulled out the wig.

"I'll take those," Evelyn said and held out her hand.

Lis handed her the head and the wig. Evelyn set the wig on the baby Jumeau's head and smoothed it, staring at it with what felt like reverence before placing it carefully in the bin. If that wasn't Miss Sorrel's baby Jumeau, Lis thought, it was its doppelgänger.

Lis reached for a pair of porcelain legs. One of them had Miss Sorrel's sorrel-leaf stamp on the sole of the foot. She placed them in the bin. Next she picked up a doll's dress, robin's-egg blue with white polka dots, the dress Miss Sorrel's Alice in Wonderland doll wore, *original and surprisingly intact,* as Miss Sorrel liked to tell its admirers. On the skirt's inside seam, Lis found the tag she expected to find: MME ALEXANDER.

Lis sat back on her heels. Miss Sorrel's dolls hadn't been taken by some random burglar. They'd been taken by her best friend.

45

"I told you, I don't need help." Evelyn's voice was barely audible.

Lis ignored her. She picked up more doll parts, cataloguing them in her mind. The legs of six dismembered Miss Sorrel dolls. Another Jumeau baby. The heads of two German bisques.

Among the legs and arms and bodies was a plastic pen with a white label around its middle. "I'll take that," Evelyn said. Lis gave it to her and Evelyn tucked it into her hair, inside her scarf.

Lis piled all the doll parts back into the bin, then took stock of what she hadn't found. Only about half of the Miss Sorrel dolls were accounted for. No Judy Garland doll. No Cherokee rag dolls. No baby Dionne Quint. Of course there hadn't been room in a single bin for all the dolls in Miss Sorrel's china cabinets.

Lis looked through the doorway into the small bedroom. A second plastic bin sat on the floor. The rest of the supposedly stolen dolls were most likely there.

What was going on? Evelyn was Miss Sorrel's oldest and dearest friend. Had she heard the explosion, broken into the house to save Miss Sorrel and Lis, and then seized the opportunity, helping herself to dolls she'd always coveted?

Slowly Lis rose to her feet. She brushed her hands on her

pants. Trying to keep her voice even and not confrontational, she said, "Evelyn, I recognize these dolls. They're my mother's. Why are they here?"

Evelyn just blinked back at Lis.

Lis crossed the bedroom to the second bin. She reached for the lid, ignoring Evelyn's "Don't." More doll parts.

But still, it didn't add up. How to explain the gas leak or the kiln explosion? And what about the remnants of an arm and leg from a Miss Sorrel doll that had been cremated in the kiln? Why destroy one doll but save the rest?

Unless the theft had been a distraction. The real question was not about the stolen dolls or even the destroyed doll but about the one doll that had been left behind. The doll Jenny Richards had brought them, the doll that Miss Sorrel had at first been certain was Janey's and a few days later was just as certain that it was not.

"Where's Janey's doll?" Lis said. "The real one."

"I . . . You don't understand. I was only trying to protect your mother."

"By poisoning her and blowing up her kiln?"

"I didn't mean for the kiln to explode. Sometimes I get confused. I must have set it wrong and forgotten to check that the exhaust was working properly. Miss Sorrel always managed the technical details."

"So you faked a break-in, faked a robbery. Switched the doll. Why?"

"I had to." After a long pause Evelyn added, "I was afraid that if the police found her, your mother would have ended up facing murder charges."

"Found Janey?"

"Found Janey's doll. That doll could have led to their discovering that Buck took your sister, and that Miss Sorrel killed him. Of course it was justifiable homicide. She had no choice."

You *had no choice*, Lis thought, remembering the version of events she'd heard from Miss Sorrel. "Would Miss Sorrel kill the only person who knew what had happened to Janey?"

"Because you never know what juries will do," Evelyn went on, ignoring Lis's question. Her voice was becoming more steady. Back to the imperious Evelyn Lis had always known. "The notoriety would have killed her. Besides, it wasn't her fault."

"I know. She told me."

Evelyn's jaw dropped. "What? What did she tell you?"

Lis paused, choosing her words. "She said that it was an accident."

"Of course she did. And it was." Evelyn's words rushed out. "She never meant for him to drown. She never meant to hit him." *She. She.* Never *I* or even *We*. "Do you want your mother arrested at this point in her life? There's no statute of limitations on murder. I'd be forced to testify. Under God's oath, I'd have to tell the truth."

What would Evelyn testify to a jury, if it came to that? How far would she go if protecting herself meant sacrificing Miss Sorrel? "You're saying that my mother killed Buck, and Buck kidnapped Janey and then he sold her—"

"Sold her? Heavens no. He'd never do that. Or hurt her. The Richardses were a fine family. They had a lovely home."

"You knew them?"

"Well, I . . . not personally. I . . ." Evelyn hesitated. "Someone must have told me about them?"

There she went, trying to distance herself. Lis wanted to get in her face and shriek, *This is total bullshit.* Instead she said, "So you're saying that Buck took Janey and gave her to this family? Did he take Abby Verner, too?"

Evelyn folded her arms. "I know you think it's a terrible thing, but yes."

"So where is Abby Verner now?"

"He wouldn't tell us."

"Wouldn't? Or couldn't?" When Evelyn twitched and looked away, Lis went on, "Because Buck wasn't anywhere near Bonsecours when Abby Verner was taken. He was waiting to testify before a grand jury in Columbia."

"Is that what Frank told you? Well, what do you expect? He was like a son to Buck."

"Like the son he never had?" Lis said.

Evelyn flinched again.

46

Lis's phone pinged with a message:

@hosp pumping stomach more when we know -V

Lis turned her cell phone to show Evelyn.

"So they're pumping her stomach," Evelyn said. "That's the protocol. Good."

It was the tiny smile and sigh of relief that leaked out with it that gave Evelyn away. "Why is that good?" Lis asked.

"Emergency rooms can be busy. Trauma victims receive treatment before someone who . . ."

Someone who what? Lis thought. *Someone who was trying to die?* "Are you saying that suicides go to the end of the queue?"

"In an emergency room there are limited resources. Of course there are always hard choices to be made. It's a blessing, really, that she's unconscious."

"Is it? Miss Sorrel's not unconscious. I'm not."

Evelyn's gloved hand clenched.

"What I don't understand," Lis said, "is why. Why would she try to kill herself now? Just when she seemed to be settling in.

Bits of her memory were even coming back." Lis stepped to the window and looked out at their yard next door. "After Janey disappeared, the police kept asking me if I'd seen any strangers. I told them there weren't any."

"But now you're not so sure," Evelyn said, leaning in, "are you?"

But Lis was sure. There had been no strangers. No one but Miss Sorrel and a black-and-white puppy. And Evelyn.

"You were the one who raised the alarm," Lis said. It was a guess. Because of course Evelyn would have. The good Samaritan. Friend of the family.

Evelyn went still.

"Is this where you brought Janey? Up here? Is that what she remembered? Is that what upset Jenny so much?"

"Me? Why would I—"

"Why would you take Janey? Same reason you took Abby. How could you let Buck's children be raised by women who were sluts?" Lis paused, thinking it over, the pieces falling into place. "For years you thought you'd gotten away with it. Then, the doll came back. You couldn't risk anyone finding out what you'd done. So you destroyed the doll in the kiln. Replaced it with a replica. Maybe you even used one of the heads Miss Sorrel made for my doll, one that had been almost but not quite right. You did your very best to keep me from finding Maggie. Maybe you let the air out of our tires. Enlisted Frank to follow us when Vanessa and I went looking for Maggie's car. You haven't been trying to protect Miss Sorrel. You've been protecting yourself." Before Evelyn could respond, Lis rushed on, "And then there was the DNA test the police ran. The sample from Jenny didn't match the DNA they had on file for Janey. How was that possible? Maybe a nurse with longtime ties to the police department collected Jenny's DNA sample. After all, you were taking care of her in the hospital. One sample looks like any other one. Who would know?"

Evelyn rubbed the bloody scratches on her injured arm. "That's a tall tale if ever I heard one. Just goes to show, no good deed goes unpunished."

Lis ignored her. "We'd never have known that it wasn't Jenny's DNA that got submitted if I hadn't had my own test run. A test that showed, by the way, that Jenny and I are half sisters. We don't have the same father. When we find Abby, I'm guessing that we'll find out that she and Jenny are half sisters, too. They have the same father. Buck."

Evelyn bent over one of the bins of doll parts, straightening and rearranging. "She went to a God-fearing home," Evelyn said, "where her mother wasn't a harlot and her father wasn't an adulterer."

Lis felt as if the air had been knocked out of her. There it was, the admission so matter-of-fact and Evelyn so convinced of her own righteousness. "Did these God-fearing parents know they were getting a stolen child? Or were they so grateful," Lis said, anger boiling up inside of her, "for bringing them a beautiful little girl that they didn't press for answers? Was it sweet, your revenge?"

Evelyn stood. "Sweet?" She spit the word back at Lis. "What do you know about anguish and betrayal?"

Anguish and betrayal. That was a subject Lis knew quite a bit about, and she had Evelyn to thank for it. There hadn't been one day when she hadn't agonized over how losing Janey was her fault.

"Tell me," Lis said. "Where did you take Abby?"

Evelyn folded her arms across her chest.

"Or how about I go to the police right now and tell them you abducted her and Janey, too."

Evelyn shot back, "How about I go to the police right now and tell them your mother killed my husband."

"Go ahead. I don't care if it means you both have to face charges, and my mother doesn't care, either. She told me what happened. Of course she doesn't know that you took Janey. She's quite certain, though, that you killed Buck. The way she tells it, it's pretty convincing. I wonder which of you a jury will believe."

Evelyn set the lid on the bin of doll parts she'd been straightening. She pushed the bin into the corner of the room. Then she rocked back on her heels and brushed away a tear. The gesture brought to mind the Tiny Tears doll Lis had once had. She could cry on command, too.

"You're right," Evelyn said. "It was wrong to try to save Abby, and I'm tired of trying to cover it up. I'll tell you where I took her. Take the information to the police or go find her yourself." She pulled out the pen she'd tucked into her headscarf and removed the cap. The pen's orange label seemed to glow against her purple gloves. "I just need a piece of paper."

It seemed too easy. Lis couldn't remember Evelyn ever flat-out admitting that something she'd done was wrong. Nevertheless, Lis cast about the room, looking for a scrap of paper Evelyn could write on. There on the bureau was a strip of wallpaper. She glanced in the mirror over the bureau as she approached to pick up the scrap. Behind her, Evelyn was shaking the pen, nib pointed up to the ceiling. Then she pressed the button at the opposite end.

That wasn't how you primed a balky ballpoint pen. It was more like . . .

Before Lis could complete the thought, Evelyn had lunged at

Lis, sinking the needle-sharp point of the pen into her arm. Not a ballpoint pen. An EpiPen, the kind used to administer drugs.

She's a nurse, Lis thought as Evelyn stabbed Lis with the EpiPen again. The second stab snapped Lis out of her paralysis. She jammed her elbow into Evelyn's throat and Evelyn dropped the EpiPen. Evelyn reached for it but Lis kicked it away. Then she grabbed Evelyn by her injured arm. Evelyn screamed.

"What did you just give me?" Lis demanded. "What was in that?" She twisted Evelyn's arm.

Evelyn pressed her lips together and shook her head, her face contorted in pain.

Still holding on to Evelyn, Lis reached for the EpiPen with her foot and nudged it closer. Strained to pick it up. The orange label read: HUMALOG insulin. The words below seemed to swim. *Fast-acting injection.*

"You injected me with insulin? Is this what you gave Jenny? But they're pumping her stomach."

Evelyn smirked. "Don't worry. They'll figure it out eventually. But it's already too late. A competent medic would have checked her blood sugar right away. But with a history of addiction and a bag of empty prescription drug containers, well, they go along like lambs."

"Lambs." Lis didn't realize she'd repeated the word until she heard it as if coming from a distant foghorn. She remembered how Evelyn had produced an unmarked vial of Endocet from Jenny's cosmetics bag back when Jenny had first been in the hospital. Later Jenny had insisted she wasn't addicted to any medication and they'd all assumed Evelyn knew otherwise. No wonder Evelyn had let herself be recruited to provide round-the-clock nursing, positioning herself as an insider so she could fake Jenny's drug-test results, then fuel the myth that Jenny was a druggie who'd do whatever she needed to do to get her next fix. Evelyn had monitored Jenny through drug treatment that she didn't need. When Jenny regained consciousness, the benevolent, self-sacrificing Evelyn would be right there at her bedside, the first to know if Jenny remembered anything that could prove inconvenient.

"You're feeling it already, aren't you?" Evelyn said. "Soon you'll start to shiver and sweat. You'll feel disoriented and confused. That's because your heart will be slowing down. Don't worry. It's not a bad way to go. Drowsiness, unconsciousness, coma, and death."

Lis felt as if she were out on a boat, rocking in a choppy sea. She was at the beginning of the continuum. How far along was Jenny? "How long?" she asked, swallowing a lump in her throat. Were her hands already shaking?

"Not very." Evelyn wrenched free and backed away.

Lis reached into her pants pocket for her cell, but Evelyn knocked it out of her hand. The phone skittered under the bed. Lis went down on her hands and knees and went after it. Evelyn grabbed hold of her shirt and tried to pull her back.

Lis flipped over onto her back and kicked at Evelyn as hard as she could. Her foot connected with Evelyn's chin. Evelyn staggered back.

Lis reached under the bed for the phone. Got it. The EpiPen was there, too. She grabbed it. She was afraid to try to stand so she sat and scooched herself back into the corner of the room, next to one of the bins of doll parts. There at least Evelyn couldn't come up behind her. "Stay back!" She waved the EpiPen in front of her.

"That's not going to do you any good. It's empty," Evelyn said.

Lis eyed the label. It read *200 units*. She held it point up and shook it, the way she'd seen Evelyn do. Touched the button on top and a drop of clear liquid formed at the tip of the point. "Doesn't look empty."

Evelyn held her ground, too far away for Lis to reach her but close enough that she could lunge for Lis if she let down her guard. It was just a matter of time before Lis lost consciousness. She had to act.

Lis kicked the lid off one of the bins and reached into it. She took out the bald head of a beautifully painted porcelain doll. Miss Sorrel's handiwork, for sure.

Evelyn stared at the head as if mesmerized. Here was a woman who could have gotten away with everything—kidnapping two little girls and murdering her husband—betrayed by her own inability to destroy these dolls that weren't hers. She could have buried them. Or burned them. Instead she'd taken them apart and hidden them where she thought they would be safe. Just like she'd done with Abby and Janey.

Lis summoned all the strength she had and threw the doll's head at the opposite wall. It shattered on impact.

"Stop!" Evelyn screamed.

Lis reached into the bin again and picked out the head of an antique china doll with pink cheeks and blue eyes. As she held the head out in front of her, making sure Evelyn's attention was absorbed, Lis entered her pass code into her cell phone. The room was spinning.

Lis threw the second doll's head. It crashed into a picture of a teddy bear's birthday that hung on the opposite wall. The picture fell to the floor, the glass cracked, but the doll's head was still intact. Evelyn scrambled after it, picked it up, and held it to her chest.

All Lis wanted to do was put her head down and close her eyes. Taking a deep breath, she willed herself to hang on, to remain conscious. She rummaged in the bin for another head. This time she grabbed the baby Jumeau. She aimed the doll's head at the window, reared back as if about to throw.

"No! You can't," Evelyn said. "It's irreplaceable. It's your mother's favorite—"

"My mother's favorite? You already destroyed my mother's favorite."

"Just give it to me." Evelyn extended her hand and took a timid step forward.

Lis sidearmed the doll low across the room. It hit the floor and rolled out into the hall. Evelyn whirled around and followed it. With all the strength Lis could summon, she crawled across the room and slammed the door shut. *Have a blessed day,* she muttered to herself as she pressed herself up against the door and fumbled with her phone.

911 was just three numbers. Behind her she could feel Evelyn trying to press the door open. Pounding on it.

If she dialed 911 and lost consciousness before dispatch picked up, the police could use GPS to find her. But they wouldn't know how to save Jenny, or even that she needed saving. No, Lis had to call Vanessa and hope she picked up. She had to tell her to make the hospital treat Jenny for an insulin overdose. Then hope she was still lucid enough to tell Vanessa to get the police and an ambulance dispatched to Evelyn's house.

Lis found Vanessa's number and waited for the call to connect, praying that she'd pick up in time.

Lis was in pieces and the elastic was too short. Her eyes clicked open and she watched as Miss Sorrel tried to reassemble her, running an elastic from her head through her body to hook onto her legs. But her legs weren't her own, Lis noticed with detached interest. These legs were charred black and the soles of her feet were blank where they should have had the imprint of a sorrel leaf.

"Can you hear me, Elisabeth Grace?" Lis heard her mother's hushed voice coming to her through what felt like layers of cotton batting. Not *darling*. Not *dear*. Her mother was actually calling her by her given name. She had to be dreaming.

"I think she's waking up." That was Vanessa's voice.

The room seemed to emerge from a fog around Lis. Too white. Too bright. A hospital room.

"Draw the shade." Miss Sorrel's voice sliced through the blinding whiteness.

Lis heard footsteps and the room around her grew shadowy. From the shadows emerged shapes, and from the shapes, faces. Miss Sorrel sat on one side of her bed, Vanessa on the other. Both of them looked tense and anxious.

"Who died?" Lis asked, her voice little more than a whispery croak. Her throat was sore and her limbs felt as if they were encased in cement. Then it hit her that the question was anything but frivolous.

Miss Sorrel waved a hand in front of Lis's face. "Lis, dear, can you hear me?"

Lis blinked and tried to speak, but all that came out was another harsh croak.

"She's back," Miss Sorrel said. "Thank God."

Lis licked her cracked, dry lips and tried to sit up. Vanessa reached across and raised the bed. Miss Sorrel held a straw to Lis's mouth. Water. Lis couldn't remember anything feeling as soothing as its coolness in her mouth and down her raw throat.

Miss Sorrel set the water on the bedside table. She helped Lis lean forward while Vanessa plumped pillows behind her. On the windowsill was a vase filled with a virtual explosion of pink roses and an envelope with a card waiting to be read.

"What happened?" Lis asked.

"We almost lost you," Miss Sorrel said. "You've been in a coma"—she glanced at her watch—"going on eighty hours."

Eighty hours? Lis closed her eyes and tried to translate that number of hours into days. It had been Saturday morning when she was up on Evelyn's third floor, fumbling with her phone, calling Vanessa. Twenty-four, forty-eight, seventy-two was three days. Eighty was eight hours more. Which meant? Her brain felt like mush. The other bed in the room was empty. Where was Jenny? Had her call gotten to Vanessa in time?

Lis forced herself to ask. "Jenny?"

Vanessa said, "She's fine. Now. Thanks to you. I barged into the ER and raised a ruckus until someone listened. They stopped trying to pump her stomach and put her on dextrose to counteract the insulin. She was released yesterday morning."

"What day is it?"

"Tuesday," Vanessa said. "Three in the afternoon."

Tuesday? "Why are you still here?"

"It's okay. I canceled my flight," Vanessa said with a tight smile. She looked like she was on the verge of tears. "I couldn't leave, not until you could look me in the face and tell me to go home."

Lis reached out her hand and Vanessa took it. Lis cleared her throat. "Listen to me." Vanessa nodded. "Go. Home."

"But—"

"Shhh. I mean it. Today." Lis did not want Vanessa to look back and realize that she'd missed her big chance because of Lis.

Vanessa said, "But how will you manage without Evelyn . . ."

Of course Evelyn would be gone. Fled? Arrested? No more biscuits and gravy and tuna casseroles. No more deception and self-sanctified villainy. "We'll manage, won't we?" Lis turned to Miss Sorrel.

Miss Sorrel's eyes widened and her lip quivered as she shook her head. "Evelyn wasn't at her house when the ambulance got there for you. That's why it took so long for them to find you. All we knew was that you were somewhere in the house. She still wasn't there later when the police came looking for her. I found her the next morning in her kitchen. Dead. An insulin overdose. She wrote out a full confession, and her will was right there on the table. She'd revised it so the house, everything passes to Buck's children."

Children? *Plural.* Lis tried to sit forward, but the room started to spin and she fell back against the pillows. It was almost too much to absorb. Janey *and* Abby found? Evelyn gone?

"Evelyn . . ." Lis's throat went dry. She took another sip of water. "She was going to tell the police that you killed Buck."

"She told you that? Hmmm." Miss Sorrel rested her chin on the heel of her hand. "I was so sure Buck had taken Janey, I would never have killed him. He was the only one who knew what happened to her." Miss Sorrel's gaze drifted toward the window. "I didn't know he wasn't the one who took her. Evelyn did. If I'd known that, and that she was never going to tell me what she did with Janey, I'd have killed her. In a heartbeat."

"But you didn't," Lis said.

"You need your rest," Miss Sorrel said. She lowered the bed and tucked the blanket in around Lis. "We'll talk more later."

Lis felt a wave of exhaustion, like a heavy blanket weighing down on her. "Did you?" she forced the words out.

"I . . ." There was a long pause. "I couldn't stop her from killing herself." Something about the smile on Miss Sorrel's face—grim satisfaction, if Lis had had to put a name to it—would make Lis return to that moment and wonder. Because Miss Sorrel hadn't answered Lis's question.

Lis napped on and off through the afternoon. Nurses came and went. Lis got out of bed once to read the card tucked into the pink roses. The note in Frank's handwriting read:

Love you. (Like a needle needs a vein . . .)

Shivers crawled across her shoulders as she read the lyric from a love song they'd listened to for the first time maybe ten years ago when they were first dating and moving from old family friends to something else.

Lis took the card back to bed, tucked it under her pillow, and lay there, staring up at the ceiling. It was downright heroic that he hadn't up and given up on her with all the distrust she'd piled on him. Her head filled with the smell of leather, wood, pipe tobacco, spicy thyme—his aftershave—as she drifted back to sleep.

It was dark out, and she was starving by the time a dinner tray arrived. Thin slices of chicken floating in pallid gravy, a few carrot rounds, and tasteless mashed potatoes had never tasted so good. She was finishing off a dish of red Jell-O cubes when there was a light tap at the door. Jenny poked her head in. "Can I come in?"

Jenny was alone. She'd cut her hair supershort and it was growing in blond and bristly. That made her eyes' otherworldly color, the palest of blue, even more startling. She wore tight jeans with the knees ripped, and a T-shirt with a stretched-out neck. She looked rested, the shadows under her eyes barely visible.

Lis pushed aside the tray table and Jenny pulled up a chair and sat. "Thank God you're okay," Lis said.

"I don't think God had much to do with it," Jenny said, reaching for Lis's hand. "You're the one who saved my life."

"This time," Lis said, squeezing Jenny's hand back.

"Would you stop," Jenny said. "Seriously. You need to stop beating yourself up. Because it's about to get even more complicated and you can't go all *poor me* on me. Yesterday Frank drove me to meet my other half sister."

"He found Abby Verner?"

"Andrea Pines. That's her name now. He said to let you know he couldn't have found her without the information you discovered about what happened to me."

"Where was she?"

"Mount Royal."

"No."

"Not more'n a mile from where I grew up. Our families even

knew each other. Same church. Same Sunday school. She was homeschooled, too. Of course she's a lot younger. Frank's bringing her over so you can meet her, too. She's pretty stunned. Still making sense of it all. Like me."

But Jenny didn't look at all stunned. The events of the last few days should have further traumatized her, and yet she seemed settled, calm, for once comfortable in her own skin.

"What happened between you and Evelyn?" Lis asked.

"Evelyn?" Jenny grimaced. "Bless her heart, that was one evil bitch. When we were upstairs in that weird little bedroom, she kept asking me questions about when I was little. Like she was testing me. I realized that she was trying to figure out whether I remembered anything. I didn't. Honestly, I still don't. But I told her I remembered the stain on the ceiling. When that got her rattled, I kept making things up. Looking at old photographs. Dolls. I told her about my nightmares, and how Vanessa was helping me make sense of them. That she'd figured out that the boat was a car ferry. That really got her going. I told her that we were close to figuring out what it all meant."

"That was brave."

"Or foolish. I thought I could protect myself because I had a gun. But I never even got it out of my bag. We were clearing the table when she bumped up against me. I felt a prick, like a bee sting." She rubbed her hip. "I dropped a pitcher. I was mopping up the spill when I started feeling weird and sleepy. Light-headed."

"I know exactly the feeling," Lis said.

"She told me to sit. Took my pulse. Gave me a glass of water. The last thing I remember is her sitting there. Her eyes were closed, her lips moving, her hands clasped." Lis knew that pose. Evelyn had been praying.

There was a knock at the door and Frank appeared. "Okay if we come in?"

A woman followed Frank. At first, Lis thought she was Maggie Richards—something about her size and the way she carried herself. But that impression was dispelled the instant Lis got a good look at her. She was older than Maggie, and Maggie would never have been caught dead wearing precisely parted hair with Dutch-boy bangs or a blouse with a big bow at the neck. This woman most certainly would not have had a tattoo, even an angelic one, anywhere on her body.

Jenny said, "Meet Andrea Pines." She pronounced it On-DRAY-ah. "She was born Abby Verner. Andrea, this is my sister Lissie."

My sister Lissie. Lis savored the moment and the words she never thought she'd hear. Jenny got up and gave Andrea her seat. Andrea sat, smoothing her skirt and clasping her hands on her knees. "I . . . It's . . ." Her shoulder slumped. "I guess I don't know where to begin."

"You must be in shock," Lis said.

"I am," Andrea said. "And my poor parents are devastated. I just met my birth mom. She seems like a nice enough person. But I don't feel as if I know her at all." She spread her hands in a helpless gesture. "I thought I was an only child, and now it turns out I have a sister"—she smiled at Jenny—"half sister, I guess. And five half brothers. A passel of nieces and nephews that I've never met."

Poor thing, she seemed completely at sea. Lis said, "You were so little when you were taken, it's no wonder you don't remember."

Jenny said, "Evelyn connected with Andrea's parents the same way she did with mine, through the church. And they moved to Mount Royal after they took her in."

"At least I knew I was adopted," Andrea said. "I never thought much about it. My parents couldn't have children of their own. They told me I was a special gift. Of course they had no idea that I'd been abducted. They couldn't have." She closed her eyes and shook her head. "Abducted." Her eyes opened, blue but not as pale as Jenny's. "I'll need to say that about a million more times before I get it. My parents are good people, and they raised me with so much love. They're as shocked as I am."

Jenny said, "As I told you, Andrea and I went to the same church, same Sunday school. And she was homeschooled, like me."

But that was where the similarities ended, Lis thought as she looked back and forth from Jenny to Andrea, one so tentative and traumatized by parents who never accepted her for who she was, the other confident and apparently resilient, raised in a loving home. The same terrible crime, two radically different outcomes.

Andrea went on, "I've told my husband, but my kids?" She shook her head. "The whole situation is overwhelming. I'll need to pray on it."

"Pray fast," Frank said, "because we won't be able to keep the lid on the news much longer. I bet Oprah will be wanting you both to come on her show." It was clear from Andrea's expression that the possibility made her queasy with dread.

Another tap at the door. Miss Sorrel stepped into the room. Cradled in her arms was a blanket-wrapped bundle. She came over to Lis and kissed her on the forehead, then stood back and appraised her. "You're looking better." She looked across at Frank. "She is, isn't she?"

Then she turned to Andrea Pines. "You must be Abby."

"I guess I was," Andrea said. "And you are?"

Lis said, "She's my mother. Sorrel Woodham. Everyone calls her Miss Sorrel."

"I haven't seen you since you were three years old," Miss Sorrel said. Andrea looked surprised. "Your parents asked me to make a special doll for you and you sat for a portrait at my house. But you disappeared before I could give it to you. You know what they say, it's never too late." She transferred the bundle into Andrea's arms.

Andrea opened the blanket and looked at the doll. Then back at Miss Sorrel. "My girls will fight over this. Thank you."

"I so hoped one day I'd be able to give it to you." To Lis, Miss Sorrel added, "Jenny's been helping me put the dolls back together. I think she could probably make dolls herself, if she put her mind to it."

Lis got the message: Jenny was talented in a way that Lis would never be. Lis felt actual jealousy, the kind that would have made her want to kick Jenny under the table if they'd been sitting at one. Instead, she laughed out loud, welcoming the emotion: sibling rivalry, in the flesh.

Lis's phone pinged from her tray table with a text message. Jenny handed her the phone. "It's from Vanessa."

Lis read the message. "She's at the airport. Her plane leaves in thirty minutes."

"I know she needed to get back, but right now I wish she were here," Miss Sorrel said.

Lis handed her cell phone to Frank and gestured to Jenny and Andrea to pose with her and Miss Sorrel.

"Wait," Miss Sorrel said. She got a brush from her purse and ran it through Lis's hair. Pinched her cheeks. She perched on the bed beside Lis and Andrea Pines stood beside her, holding the doll. Jenny sat on the other side of the bed, leaning in, her arm around Lis. Frank snapped their picture.

Lis texted the photo to Vanessa.

48

Vanessa sat at the departure gate at the Savannah Airport, waiting for her plane to board and working on her grant proposal. At least she wasn't going to fail to get it in by the deadline, and with the additional research she'd done and Jenny's solid data, it felt like a respectable body of work, worthy of the committee's consideration. Her thoughts kept straying to her mother in the hospital, looking pale and wan but summoning the strength to order Vanessa to go home. She'd just texted her mother, well aware of the irony of the shift in who was worrying about whom. Aware, too, that when she returned to Bonsecours, the home she'd grown up in would be forever transformed. More than a kiln had exploded.

She was sliding her computer into her carry-on bag when a reply to her text came. A picture. She opened it. There was Lis, sitting up in her hospital bed, surrounded by Grandma Sorrel, Jenny, and a woman Vanessa didn't recognize. Vanessa guessed she was Abby Verner, Jenny's half sister. If clothing was any indication—Jenny, in skinny jeans and an oversize tee, looked like she was about to climb onto a bar stool at a roadhouse, while Abby dressed prim and proper resembled a person-size Little

House on the Prairie doll, minus the bonnet—they were polar opposites. How Vanessa would love to have been a fly on the wall, watching those two get to know each other.

But what caught her attention, too, was the blanket-wrapped bundle in Abby Verner's arms. Vanessa enlarged the picture. It looked like a doll. A porcelain doll. Vanessa enlarged it even more. A Miss Sorrel doll.

Flooding back came the dream Vanessa had had before she left Providence. She could still see the towering wave, Grandma Sorrel emerging from a wall of water and offering Vanessa a blanket-wrapped bundle. It hadn't been a baby *or* a doll. It had been both.

ACKNOWLEDGMENTS

Authors hear it all the time: "I have a terrific idea for your next book." And, maybe once in a lifetime, it is. I got lucky when a friend told me about her doll-maker mother and her mother's best friend, also a doll maker. When my friend helped her mother clear out the house she'd grown up in, under every bed she found boxes of doll parts. Legs. Arms. Bodies. Eyeballs. So creepy/sinister and sweet/innocent at the same time. Thanks, Mary Alice Gallagher, for that.

Thanks also to Michael A. Grandner, Ph.D., who answered all my questions about nightmares and behavioral sleep disorders. I made up everything about Vanessa's sleep research (there are no dream catchers), and any errors in the book on the science of sleep are strictly my own.

Anyone who's been to lovely Beaufort, South Carolina, will recognize it as the inspiration for this novel's Bonsecours. Thanks to the generous souls who helped me when I traveled to Beaufort to research the setting: Marilyn Harcharik, president of the Friends of the Beaufort Library; Beaufort reference librarian Ann Cox; and Grace Cordial, who oversees the Beaufort District Collection at the Beaufort County Library. And most especially Connie Haskell, a true pal whose love for the area inspired me, and Gale Touger and her husband, Steven Kerchner, who trawls for shrimp off the South Carolina coast.

Thanks to doll collector and book maven Sheryl Hagan-Booth and Janice McIntyre of Jenny Baby's Doll Hospital. To D. P. (Doug) Lyle, M.D., the author's go-to guy on all things medical. To my pals Hank Phillippi Ryan and Roberta Isleib for helping me worm my way through plot holes, and to my dear husband, Jerry Touger, for reading and enthusing.

Thanks to the real Elisabeth Strenger for her generous contribution to Mission K9 Rescue.

Last but far from least, I owe a huge debt of gratitude to Katherine Nintzel, whom I am so fortunate to have as my editor, and to my agent, Gail Hochman, who over and over save me from myself.